# CROSSING WYOMING

# CROSSING WYOMING

## DAVID ROMTVEDT

WHITE PINE PRESS

Acknowledgements

*The Casper Star-Tribune*: "Play It Again in the Equality State"

*Pushcart Prize*: "1989, Gillette, Our Navy"

*The Sun*: "1828, Middle Fork of the Powder River," "1866, Fort Phil
Kearny, Cutting Wood," "1989, Gillette, Our Navy"

Thank you to the staff of the Johnson County Library, Buffalo, Wyoming,
and to Lyn Dalebout of Moose, Wyoming.

Publication of this book was made possible, in part,
by grants from the National Endowment for the Arts
and the New York State Council on the Arts.

Book design by Watershed Design.

Printed in the United States of America.

ISBN 1-877727-23-7


White Pine Press
76 Center Street
Fredonia, New York 14063

F 79, 403
R9. 90

*for*
*Caitlin and Maggie*
*the near twin girls*

# CONTENTS

## PART ONE

1940: Uruguay: Latin American Historian Eduardo Galeano / 15
1493: Near the Boundary of Haiti and
    the Dominican Republic: The Horse / 17
1989: Buffalo: Winter, The Cold / 19
1965: Dubois: Seven Half-Miles From Home / 21
1871: Greasy Grass Creek: In the House of Song / 27
1650: Dayton: Someone / 30
1866: Fort Phil Kearny: Cutting Wood / 32
1869: Cheyenne: After Tea in South Pass City / 36
1942: Heart Mountain: Building a Home / 39
1969: Laramie: Black Armbands / 42
1989: Cheyenne: Play it Again in the Equality State / 46
1942: Bomber Mountain: Magnetism / 51
1979; Green River: Spanish Music / 54
1875: Rock Springs: The Miners Strike / 57
1923: Barber: A Rowboat / 60
1890: Mato Tipila: Releasing Souls / 65
1947: Near Manderson, South Dakota: Haunted / 68
1828: Middle Fork of the Powder River: A Thief / 71
1880: Union Pacific Line: A Friendly Contest / 74
1846: Sublette Cutoff: Little Left But Graves / 78
1989: Gillette: Our Navy / 81
1989: Buffalo: The Anxiety Now / 83
1950: Highway 395: A Bleeding Trailer / 86

PART TWO

1839: Indian Country: Free Trade / 93
1889: Bothwell: A Hanging / 97
1899: Cheyenne: To the Memory of Those Pioneers / 101
1890: Wind River: Picture Painting,
        Dancing and the Closing of the Frontier / 104
1875: Bristol, England: General Carrington Addresses the
        British Association for the Advancement of Science / 109
1892: Buffalo: Another Gruesome Farce / 112
1866: Lower Powder River: A Visitor / 116
1868: Powder River: The Thieves' Road / 118
1836: South Pass: Double Honeymoon / 122
1928: Hollywood: Ed Trafton's Bad Luck / 124
1878: Brickwall, Northiam, Sussex:
        Mortal Ruin's Western Adventures / 127
1946: Thermopolis: In the Beginning / 132
1929: Cheyenne: Another Day / 134
1935: Lander: Three Lives / 138
1879: Carbon: Compassion in Wyoming Territory / 141
1909: Campbell County: Voices / 143
1920: Buffalo: Amatchi, Grandmother, the Dignity of Work / 147
1912: Sussex: Moreton Frewen's Loss / 149
1989: Buffalo: Atatchi, Grandfather, a Weed / 154
1920: Jackson: The First All-Woman
        Town Government in America / 157
1927: Jackson Hole: The Name of a Summer / 159
1928: National Elk Refuge: Why are the Elk Dying? / 161
1943: Jackson Hole National Monument:
        The Shadow of the Old West / 163
1945: Whetstone Creek: The Return / 166

# Part Three

1989: Sheridan: Beauty and the Sacred / 173
1853: Fort Laramie: Innumerable Treaties / 176
1971: Bighorn Mountains: Another Circle / 180
1856: Belgium: In Perfect Submission to
       the Orders of His Superiors / 184
1985: Ethete: The Paint Ceremony / 189
1959: Past Farson: The Emptiness / 193
1985: Guatemala: Behind the Mirror / 196
1845: Red Creek: Renaming the Nameless / 200
1890: Absaroka: Home of the Hunt / 203
1836: Wind Rivers: A Beautiful New Species of Mockingbird / 205
1986: Washington, D.C.: Tantos Vigores Dispersos / 210
1941: Cheyenne: from the *Wyoming Labor Journal* / 216
1876: Cheyenne: "A Pardonable Mistake" / 218
1942: Casper: Aloha / 223
1776: Hole in the Wall: A Scavenger Hunt / 227
1945: Albany County: War Business / 231
1890: Rawlins: Money Sings / 233
1890: Cheyenne: For Statehood / 236
1914: Chihuahua, Mexico: A Long Way to Go / 238
1988: Yellowstone Park: Fire / 241
1963: Jackson: Again / 244
1990: Cora: These Names / 246
1965: Lander: A Little Speech / 248
1958: Mountain View: The Biology Lesson / 251
1927: Lower Wild Horse Creek: A Photograph of Education / 255
2075: Shell: Sunset Man / 258
1870: Bridger Basin: Fifty Million Year Old Eohippus / 261

CROSSING WYOMING

PART I

# 1940
## URUGUAY
### LATIN AMERICAN HISTORIAN EDUARDO GALEANO

The author of *Memory of Fire,* is born in Montevideo, though from that city of dark fumes and flowers he has many times wandered, and not always because he was in the mood for a holiday. No, the gentlemen who rule his homeland have often suggested that don Eduardo might profitably take a rest from his task as spokesperson for the voiceless. And so the good señor has found himself clambering into the back of a truck as it speeds toward the border, or waiting discreetly in an airport lounge, his fingers restlessly caressing his passport.

Don Eduardo has passed through all of the Americas—both in this body and in the bodies of others. He has walked sniffing at the air, inhaling deeply whatever sweet rot was there to be found. Sometimes he has bent to taste the earth itself—to take a chunk of this dark, rich soil and crumble it into his mouth.

The animals know don Eduardo speaks for them, too, and so, though they are not friendly, they show him respect. Great flocks of birds rise above the Central American hills. Their wingbeats scatter light so that when don Eduardo lifts his face to the sky, it is not birdshit that greets him, but diamonds—light and dark, transmuted and precious.

The birds take flight, winging their way from Salvador and Nicaragua and Guatemala all the way to us here in Wyoming, the northernmost province of Latin America. For the birds do come to us you know. Their home is both here and there. When they arrive again this summer, you will see—they carry the Americas with them. Don Eduardo's voiceless souls. The sounds and smells. It is one more reason why we love the birds, why we love don Eduardo—for his implacable spirit, for his words, for his great laugh bellowing forth, and for his hope. That is the most important thing, the hope.

Don Eduardo, chronicler of time and tears, the years pile up one upon another like garbage at the dump, until those years are centuries and the litany of crimes one man has committed against another is as endless as the sky. And you think if you read one more story, one more word of human cruelty, one more, if you read it you will explode. But then here is don Eduardo like a barking dog, waving his arms, and there in the distance some woman or man is standing up saying no to cruelty and violence, and yes to faith and possibility.

Don Eduardo cups his frail hand to his ear and shouts "What?" And the answer comes, "Yes." In Bogotá, in Caracas, in Zacatecas, in Sao Paolo, in Paris, Madrid, Nairobi, New York, in Rock Springs, Casper, Sheridan, Lander, yes, to history. Even in all the distant corners of our cold, blue Wyoming, "Yes." For that, don Eduardo, thank you.

## 1493
### Near the Boundary of Haiti and the Dominican Republic
### The Horse

Son caballos y yeguas de Córdoba y Sevilla—Arabians, both stallions and mares, descended from desert horses the Moslems brought to Spain in the time of their conquest. After more than three months at sea, rocking in putrid stalls built on the decks of putrid ships, the horses are ready to land. Almost half were so anxious for their delivery into freedom that they died during the voyage, their bodies scraped up and heaved into the water.

Slapped gently on the rump by deckhand Eduardo Galeano, the first stallion careens down the plank onto land. When he touches earth, he stops and batters the spot, scraping and smashing. He tears at the grasses, pounding his hooves down again and again. He turns in a circle and flings himself to earth, twisting and turning, rolling from side to side, his tail and head flipping violently from back to belly.

Deep frozen world thousands of miles away, a man leans dizzy against a tree—not banana, cinnamon, magnolia or palm; some kind of juniper, some kind of pine. The tree's roots go down and south to warm tunnels, rock passages, hidden flowing water. Standing with his ear against the tree, the man can hear the passage of deer or pronghorn or elk. Completely still, he receives the vibration of the sound. Rocked, he quickly pulls his ear from the bark. He turns and looks at the tree then makes a complete circle around it. He is the moon circling a secretive earth. The moon swings across the gray sky and down to the gray below that can't be seen. He leans and places his ear again against the tree. And again the vibration—it's an animal but not one he's ever met.

Seaman Galeano slaps again, and the first mare steps forward, down the swaying plank to the ground. Her left ear snaps forward, her right ear backward. Then they switch, they flicker, they turn as if to listen in every direction at once. She flares her nostrils and smells the new—chile, chocolate, tomate, aguacate, maíz, café. Galeano and every other sailor can smell it too—chile, chocolate, tomate, aguacate, maíz, café—and the perfume of it almost makes them faint.

The mare leans down and sniffs the grass. She takes one bite and chews, snapping her head back up and looking. Her eyes cross rivers and mountains, far deep deserts and plains. She picks her way around elephant cactus and cardón, saguaro, organ pipe, her eyes both here where she stands and there in the north, years and miles away.

The man leaning against the tree feels the rocking subside, relaxes for a moment then tenses as the hair on his neck rises. He is being watched. He drops to the bare, cold ground and waits, eyes looking back.

That hoofbeat. Those eyes. The mare and the stallion with Cristóbal Colón. Twenty-six years later Hernán Cortés lands at Vera Cruz with eight mares and eight stallions. Twenty years after that Francisco Vázquez de Coronado rides north with one thousand stallions and two mares.

The beat of the horse grows inexorably louder. Galeano smiles. In the north a man rises from the ground and walks away from a tree unsure quite who it is he's about to meet.

# 1989
## BUFFALO
### WINTER, THE COLD

Of course it is cold. As they say, winter is long and life is short. You must step out, even if it is night, even if that dog, the cold, bites off your nose. But this is different. This is the year the cold is coming home for good. The first postcards arrive from Alaska—from Anchorage where the usually mild sea is a sea of ice and from Fairbanks wrapped in the white shroud of its own deepest wintery image.

Sled dogs walk in circles and hiss ice through their teeth. Taxi drivers drop to their knees and cover their heads as automobile tires explode into frozen, black shrapnel. Bush pilots nudge their planes toward the sky only to find their propellors unable to cut through such frozen air, and so the planes fall back to earth.

By February, King Cold has tired of undisputed victory and is ponderously walking south to Wyoming. The sun rises on a mild winter day. Children bicycle to school in windbreakers and light gloves. Babies, sickened by constraint, tear their arms out from under blankets and wave naked fingers in the cool air. By the creek, a stand of willow has begun to bud.

But the fall, as they say, the fall. At noon the temperature drops to twenty. Each passing quarter hour sends two more degrees farther south. At midnight it is fifteen below, and next morning under a bright unrepentant sun, it is thirty-five below. The days follow, and the nights—forty below, forty-five below, sixty below.

The King flies on, farther south still. In Mexico City there is no word for sixty below. But it has rained, and the night has grown cold enough that the oily puddles are smothered by an opaque skin. The shoeshine boys and newspaper vendors stand shivering in wet tatters, their teeth clacking like those in the cadaverous skulls of wind-up toys on the Day of the Dead. At the train station everything has stopped. Don Eduardo sits in a borrowed apartment drinking cup after cup of tepid black coffee and vowing never to take a step farther north.

In that north, on Main Street in Buffalo, the pick-ups idle, waiting tensely for their owners. White clouds of exhaust fill the street, white clouds of breath, white clouds of ice. Buildings topple into one another, held aloft only by the frozen air. The women of our town hold a meeting and promise not to mention the weather. As the temperature drops and drops, the men gather at stoves and talk on and on as if somehow the steam of their breath could heat us all, could burn its way south and join us again.

# 1965

## DUBOIS
## SEVEN HALF-MILES FROM HOME

Suffering from circulation problems bad enough to kill her and on the advice of her doctor, artist Mary Back has for two years been walking a mile every day before breakfast. From her house she has laid out seven half-mile-long courses, one for each day of the week. Each walk brings her home through another world—the world of the living river, the boggy meadows and swamps, the fence rows, the thickets, the forests, her human neighbors' yards and gardens, and the desert. All these worlds form a great circle—the circle rotates around Mary and she around it.

Mary Back calls the circle of worlds her study area. But she is no scientist. She is too much the lover for that. She would not tear the feathers from a bird to find out how many of them it takes to cover the soul's nakedness.

Hanging out laundry one morning, the toothy west wind tearing the pins from her hands, Mary saw the return of the blackbirds, a great ball of them, the limits of the flying globe unmarked but secure. Two hundred blackbirds came rolling up the river. They leapt and turned, squawking and screaming. The laundry flew from Mary's hands, and she ran to meet the birds, to jump up and down, to join the circle as it passed. Now they poured up the river, clattering on the cobbles, pecking at the ground, climbing back into the air, and always rolling upriver.

On another day, Mary stood witness to destruction. A neighboring rancher had ripped apart a beaver dam and house, and on that day Mary's walk was hard and bitter, the air biting at her skin. She stepped into the cold river wishing to do penance, allowing the frozen stones to scrape her ankles to the bone. But the river refused to hold a grudge—the water-worn stones slipped smoothly past her hardened feet.

In seven days Mary Back has created seven worlds and in these is a goddess seven ways. She is a goddess without a church, without holy law, without retribution. She is a goddess the way the sky is goddess to the sun and moon, the way the earth is goddess to the grasses, the way the eye is goddess to the mind.

Don Eduardo is surprised to find himself standing at Mary Back's bridge over the Wind River. Behind him he can see the Red Rock Motel and in front of him the New Red Cliffs. So much is happening in the world. How did he come to be here where all the so much adds up to nothing?

Seeing the stranger, Mary calls out, "Hello. Are you staying at the Red Rock? If you're out for a walk, there are some nice paths on this side of the river. Come on over if you like. The bridge may look a little rickety but it's solid. Some years during spring flood, the water comes right up over the top."

Don Eduardo hesitates. In Santo Domingo, Juan Bosch sits imprisoned, slapping himself on the head with the flat of his hand. Somehow it's all got to be explained—how the Trujillos ran the Dominican Republic like a private country club of which they were the sole members until Rafael Leónidas Trujillo was assassinated and, after a period of military control, Bosch was elected in 1963 only to be deposed by a military coup eight months later and then in 1965 the people rose demanding that Bosch be returned as president, which he was, and that's when the U.S. Marines invaded and Juan Bosch was imprisoned in Puerto Rico.

"Thieves!" don Eduardo shouts to Mary, but his voice is carried downstream with the river.

Juan Bosch was not only the people's choice as President; he was a writer of stories about the campesinos of his country. And he read North American literature. A journalist asked him, "Are you an enemy of the United States?"

And Bosch replied, "No, I am an enemy only of United States imperialism. No one who has read Mark Twain could be an enemy of the United States."

Having seen don Eduardo open his mouth, and thinking the man was trying to smile, Mary smiles in return. "Come on over," she says. "I'm Mary Back. My husband Joe and I live right over there. I'd be happy to show you around what I call my study area."

"I am Eduardo Galeano," don Eduardo says, but still he hesitates on the bridge.

In Santo Domingo the uprising is bloody, and it will get worse. The U.S. Embassy has called the Dominican people fighting for their country a gang of thugs and communist scum. The generals of the military government have flown into action. What shimmers in the sky like numberless crystal raindrops is in reality a cloudburst of bullets and bombs.

"The whole goddam city is on fire, María." says don Eduardo, and he slumps, as if he might weep.

It's not just the city but everything that's on fire—shiny cars smashed by tanks, stacks of smoking black tires turned into barricades, students and their books, workers and their tools, flowers and trees, the fish in the river and the stones along its banks, stacks of garbage spewn from overturned barrels, money flying from office buildings whose doors have been ripped open. It is not so much that the city is on fire, but that it is an ode to fire. Even the fire is on fire.

President Johnson announces that he will not tolerate another Cuba and calls on America's allies to help preserve freedom. America's allies respond. The military dictatorships of Brazil, Paraguay, Honduras and Nicaragua all send troops to save democracy as that fragile flower threatens to bloom before the horrified eyes of the comandantes.

If you can't uproot the flower, the next best thing is to kill the gardener. And landing with the Latin Americans are 42,000 U.S. Marines, prepared to kill every gardener on this island if that's what it takes. The gardeners gone, the flowers will be gone.

"And when the flowers are gone," don Eduardo shouts, "it will be that much easier to pave the earth and build American-style democracy—shopping malls and K-Mart stores and McDonalds fast-food restaurants, as if democracy were simply the right to consume as much as possible."

Mary stands still for a moment watching don Eduardo, then quietly says, "I know it's bad, Edward, but there's no need to exaggerate. There isn't a K-Mart for hundreds of miles. Do I look like the queen of consumption? If you come over we can sit and watch the river. It always makes me feel calmer."

Don Eduardo is both repulsed and drawn in by Mary's mild chiding. "Already an American soldier is dead." he cries, then he pauses and goes on quietly. "A young man who'd never seen such romantic streets, who'd never touched tropical flowers, their sensuous reds and blues, who'd never imagined chaos and beauty as one and the same, who'd never breathed air so perfumed it made him dizzy. Now he lies in one of those romantic narrow streets, his skull split and the blood oozing out of his ears.

"And a five-year-old Dominican child is tumbling in this very minute from the rooftop of the building where he hid watching the Americans advance. He peeked over the edge of the roof and a Marine, mistaking a five-year-old for a sniper, fired, the bullet entering the child's brain flush between the eyes.

"The Dominicans are a magical and powerful people, María, and children everywhere are filled with light, but this five-year-old cannot fly, and, as he falls, a crimson thread of blood spins off the spool of his body."

At this, don Eduardo faints and his body collapses on the bridge. "He certainly gets excited," Mary thinks as she runs to where he's fallen. She picks him up and carries him to land in the center of her study area. He is light as a child, she realizes, as if his bones were hollow like those of a bird.

She is stunned, realizing he really has been flying over all the countries of these Americas, flying from one end of the continent to the other, driven to tell the truth of history, to reveal both the degradation and grandeur of the human spirit. And she is stunned also when she realizes that, mostly, all he's found is blood and more blood, lakes of blood, rivers of blood emptying into oceans of blood, clouds darkening and bursting forth storms of purpling blood.

Mary notices that when don Eduardo fell, he hit his head on something, and his cheek is dripping blood. She holds his head in her lap. As the warm blood seeps through her dress, she strokes the man's face and smoothes his matted hair.

"Maybe you're right, Edward," she says aloud to the sleeping historian, "You've certainly pointed out some horrible events that we should try to stop. Living way out here, maybe it's too easy to ignore the problems of the world. I don't know—even here, it's hard to be blind to cruelty. One day my husband Joe and I watched a flock of mallard ducks fly past our window. We jumped up to get a better look. In the very moment when we stood up, an eagle flew into the flock, stretched out its talons and grabbed one of the ducks. The duck was heavy and dragged the eagle down, but the eagle flapped furiously and managed to stay in the air. It crossed two barbed wire fences and settled in a field where it began to tear the duck to pieces, ripping through feathers and pulling flesh out in large, wet bites. The duck was still alive and kept flapping its wings as it was being devoured."

Mary looks down and sighs. "I could tell you a thousand stories like that." She says. "Birds crippled by incompetent hunters. Deer running for hours as their steaming intestines unwind behind them over the snow, the trout that escaped but was paralyzed by a kingfisher beak that sliced through its body, the elk dropping dead of hunger as winter goes on and on. I'm not oblivious to suffering, you know. Oh, Edward, maybe you're right, maybe I've made my world too small and too safe."

When don Eduardo opens his eyes, there's a ringing in his ears as if a grenade had exploded nearby. The sky swims above him. He notices it is blue. He notices the river is still flowing, the water clear and cold. As he sits up, five big Canada geese pass, and their deep call makes the hair on don Eduardo's neck stand on end. The low sun outlines the birds in silver. They hold their heads high and stare down on the man and woman sitting near the bridge. The geese are somehow both comforting and unsettling. They appear and disappear in a great wedge, rising and circling, first north, then south.

Don Eduardo notices that. "First north, then south," he whispers to himself, "then, of course, north again."

"What's that?" Mary asks.

"Oh, nothing. Just that the geese fly back and forth north and south, as if bringing the two together to remind me that there are no countries, and no boundaries, and no animosities in the kingdom of flight. I'm sure I noticed this before but I must have forgotten . . ."

"Yes," Mary says, "forgotten . . ." then stops.

Before she recomposes herself, don Eduardo speaks, "What I mean is, perhaps, it could be I should stay here a little, not to stay forever, of course, because so many things are happening, but if I stay a week or two I may see more clearly what is ahead of me. In this study area of yours, there are seven worlds. If we walk together, María, will I be stepping into one of those seven worlds, or will we be creating an eighth that is our own?"

Mary didn't answer, but in that moment again they could hear the voice of a bird calling out—not in speech but in song.

## 1871
### GREASY GRASS CREEK
### IN THE HOUSE OF SONG

Nine winters have come and gone. Black Elk is a boy walking with other boys and with men and women and girls. Each walk on two legs. In the world of the four-legged, each person is only half an animal. They walk into the Rocky Mountains, into those towering spires the explorers likened to a cathedral. Cathedral upon cathedral, and all of them an inconsequential room inside the house of song. Black Elk hums and spins as he walks, spins as the sun, spins in the direction of a clock. Flowering trees rise in the direction Black Elk faced. The bushes are in blossom. Catkins and buds pop and spread. All the animals—the shaggy, annoyed buffalo, the pale, mild deer, the nervous, skittering mouse—furiously copulate and give birth. The fish pour out of the rivers, flopping forward across the prairie, gasping and squirming toward the boy who hums and spins.

Only nine years old, Black Elk faces the field of old age, the gnawing at the edges of worn leather with the blunt stubby ends of ancient teeth. The old mouths open and close as if to speak to the boy, to call him forward or backward, or up or down, or around and around as he turns.

He faces the steep cliff of white horses, lightning falling and rising from their tails and manes like crystalline flames of ice. White geese whirl and honk above the cliffs. From their wings fall white feathers, flakes of snow, frozen rain. White hair frames faceless faces, wispy strands of human longing waving from where left behind in winters past.

Black Elk ends at the room of light and understanding. Only nine, he enters his second childhood. He throws himself into the sun's hot arms, spinning and spinning. The more he thinks about it, the more his nine winters become nine hundred and the more his flesh is the flesh of the earth, his mother.

The spinning boy crashes into the back of one of his grandfathers, and the old man, plodding forward, carrying the weight of ninety winters and nine thousand songs, turns.

"Careful there, grandson, you knock down an old man, you'll have to carry him the rest of the way," and the old man hums a little tune.

"That Black Elk is maybe a little crazy," someone whispers.

"He lives with himself is all," is the answer. "He is learning the river course of the inside of his head."

And someone else agrees, "Both those things are maybe sure things. Who could live in this world and not be a little loony?"

That grandfather whom Black Elk keeps banging into lifts his head and speaks to no one, "Even the tiny gnat and seed is sacred and each step on the earth is a gesture, but I don't think of that every minute. I get tired and my feet come down with a thud, and the earth gives a little groan."

Not the boy. Watch him. Each step is a prayer. The trees bend toward him and brush his cheeks as he passes. He is not just spinning; he is dancing. And he is singing. The mountains, rivers and trees sing back. Like the old song says, "Glory to the birds, the little fishes and the eels." Yes, everything sang, and like the other old song says, "And it was singing for me."

Even the sky sang to him. There was a lot of singing in those days. Now it is only in church where one can sing. It is not really song, though. It's more like the memory of song, or a large group of people moaning together and holding their hands as if in pain. And the songs have only a few notes. Too many notes are gone. They have fallen to the floor, been shoved under the pews, been swept up by a janitor, been shaken out in a rug or tied up tightly in a bag and thrown on a heap of other discarded things.

Black Elk has nine winters. Too few to have learned to worry life to death. He still believes that every song shaken out of the church rug will find its way back into the sky, which will continue to sing, and he is confident that every dawn is a holy moment of laughter in honor of which he will dance.

Black Elk has nine winters. In his collision with the world, he has already remembered many things. But life is long, and there are many more things he will be forced to remember before he is through.

# 1650

## Dayton

## Someone

An unknown Spaniard has left his rapier to be found later on the banks of the Tongue River. Or ten unknown Spaniards, or a hundred. Along with the blade are left a bit of worn leather, a knot of rope around a splintered piece of wood, and a circular iron medallion about the size of the palm of a woman's hand.

And the Spaniard's tongue, or the ten tongues or one hundred on the banks of the Tongue River. Tongues without teeth or lips. No mouths. No eyes or faces, no arms, legs, hands or feet.

It could be the Spaniard was an Indian, and the rapier borrowed, begged, bought or stolen. Or traded. White Man's Dog passed the double edged blade to Screech Owl who passed it to Tricks Buffalo who passed it to Seated Elk who passed it to He-Of-Blue-Water and so on until it came into the hands of Black Tongue who, with it, cut out his own tongue, dropped the imported sword and walked swiftly to the river where he rinsed the blood from his mouth, bled some more and died.

Black Tongue may have been the liar his name made him out to be, a man whose hands couldn't trust their arms. Or it could have been that another, fouler and cleverer, maligned Black Tongue as a rapist and plunderer, a man not to be trusted among women, children and dogs. In either case, Black Tongue was alone and in exile from himself.

Still the blade is not explained. The unknown Spaniard opened his mouth and shaped the beginning of a name—the "Y" in Wyoming. Only the Spaniard spoke no English and in Spanish the letter "Y" doesn't mean "what for?" It means "and."

As alone as Black Tongue, the Spaniard walked, slowly shedding his gear, feeling it rot off his body as the seasons passed. He was invisible but for his pale skin, mark of some ghastly disease from which he would surely die, sooner or later.

The big, dumb, mute trees watched wordlessly as the body fell. The blade slipped away and drove itself into the speechless earth which, as silently as the trees, began to digest this bitter dinner. Three-hundred and sixty-one years later some of the meal was still on the plate when don Eduardo, lost and walking and not yet able to sing, bent down on the riverbank and pulled out the blade, recognizing it as his own.

"I have been here before?" Galeano asked, and waited. "If so, why is there no other trace of me?" No answer.

Who will speak? Only the Tongue River, which continues to flow, indecently babbling, unable to shut up, passing information like gas, which everyone pretends not to hear.

# 1866

## Fort Phil Kearny
## Cutting Wood

How often it seems that what was the center of something so quickly becomes its margin.

At dawn the wood train set out, the teams of mules hauling empty wagons, the armed guard heavy with loaded guns. A little firewood, poles for construction, larger trees for planks and boards. A mission of no ill will and all to make more bearable these days and nights of stunning cold when, at each hour, the temperature is called out until the mercury reaches bottom, settles in the bulb, and in solidarity with every other artifact of the season, freezes solid.

How like a holiday these little remissions, days when the sun fires its weakened arrows into the heart of winter and enough flame is made to bring a smile to the face of every man, woman and child, red or white. Today even the obligatory Indian raid on the wood train reeks of empty formality, a desultory commitment to a circus act whose banners are worn and faded and whose audience is yawning while dabbing its sweaty forehead with a huge, greasy handkerchief.

Sweeping down off a ridge, the painted men on painted ponies cry out, but their cries seem more yip than howl. And almost before the picket can set off for the fort, it is all over, the bright December day's silence broken only by the sound of ax and saw.

It is enough, that yipping feint, and Captain Fetterman sets off, mad for revenge, his mouth wide as he rides, the wind drying the saliva as it hardens on his chin. Fetterman leads himself and eighty men straight ahead, no hesitating now boys, no matter that the sun is shining in warning, and no matter that the Sioux fire their horses away in abandoned flight. It is the favorite act of invitation for these people desperate to relieve this land of the burden of the white man.

They think the land is sacred—the blades of grass and the fallen leaves, the lice and the worm-infested dead dog lying out in a winter so cold flesh won't disintegrate. It won't disappear. It's going to be there forever as if degradation, like loss, can go on endlessly, can go on until every animal—dog, Indian, or white man—is frozen dead, and snapped like a twig in half by a God ready to start a fire and warm his hands.

But that's for later, that loss and sorrow. Today Captain Fetterman careens happily and blindly up Lodge Trail Ridge and beyond. For weeks he's been telling everyone that he has to get one Indian scalp before he returns to Fort Laramie. This may be his only chance.

He and his eighty men are out of sight, but when the gunfire starts, it is clear they are not out of hearing. First a few shots, then shots uncounted, shots as many as the new leaves of spring. And then silence.

Adolph Metzlers, bugler, Company C, 2nd cavalry, was standing up a moment ago. Now he lies on his back staring at the distant blue sky. The bugle remains in his hand, and he ponders whether or not to put it to his lips, does, then ponders what to play. There are so many beautiful songs, even in the limited canon of the U.S. Army manual of bugle calls. The day becomes night, and the sky is a theatre of shooting stars, brilliant and bright. On every star, Bugler Metzlers makes a wish.

Those are not stars, Metzlers shrieks, sitting up like a knife. They're arrows, and he begins to count—40,000 arrows spinning through the sky as a river otter spins through water. The feathery guides barely make a wave. When the shaft enters flesh, its grooved edge will allow the blood to keep running, to stream down the arrow and out onto the ground, the way winter snowpack will melt and run into all the creeks and finally to the sea.

Those aren't stars, and they aren't arrows either, Metzlers thinks, opening his eyes again, but this time he does not sit up. No, they're not arrows but owls, 20,000 Long Eared Owls. The owls fly, singing their hoots, whistles and shrieks. More beautiful songs arriving as gifts to Adolph Metzlers.

Everything about it is wrong. Long Eared Owls are silent except when near their nests. And they are nocturnal. And they do not fly in groups. And even if they did, there are not 20,000 Long Eared Owls in all of Wyoming.

All the same the owls continue to fly, and they continue to sing. Bugler Metzlers knows the best thing to do would be to play, but he can't. He can't find his hand, and he can't find his lips. The owls plummet, their eyes fixed so that when one turns to look around its entire head moves. Their flight is silent song to match the shrieking. They are awash in a field of rodents, and so they hunt.

Of some of these rodents, the eyes are furiously ripped out and laid on flat rocks. Noses are bitten off, ears sliced away from heads. The owls batter their bodies against their prey, cracking off chins and bashing in teeth. Tiny fingers are broken at each joint. With sturdy beaks the owls split open skulls and wrench out brains. Entrails are threaded out into long chains and left to dry.

Twenty-thousand Long Eared Owls fall from the sky like stones and crash against Fetterman's eighty fellow mammals, small and weak. Frozen or not, now everything is disappearing. Bugler Metzlers' hands are gone, and his feet. His arms are ripped from their sockets. His penis is cut off. His ribs are snapped in half. The muscles of his thighs, his calves, his breast, his back are sliced out of his body.

Painted ponies and painted men, the flags from a wood train fluttering on a warm winter day, over a ridge and down a draw. Come on, come on, come on, come on, come on, calls the wind. And Fetterman responds. He comes on.

Twenty-thousand Long Eared Owls, Metzlers thinks. Why would they help these red Indians? Metzlers remembers his childhood, the ries about the savage, and about nature. Oh, that's it, he smiles, that business of nature. And he looks up again at the sky from which the owls fall. But there are no owls; there are no arrows; there are no stars. There are Indians on a ridgeline. And like the ridgeline, they are silent and still.

# 1869

## CHEYENNE
## AFTER TEA IN SOUTH PASS CITY

The train makes its deadly iron halt, wheels grinding against tracks, both committed to the destruction of the other. The wheels scrape away, rounding the angular tracks, while the tracks do the same, flattening the circular wheels. When the two give up, both defeated again, steam hisses up from the cracks in the platform floor.

Suffragist Anna Dickinson steps from the coach for a breath of fresh, high-plains air. Immediately surrounded by a crowd of puffing spectators, Anna flees back inside the train. When she slams the door behind her, the man who shares her compartment jerks upright holding his arm across his eyes as if to protect his face or blot out what he doesn't wish to see.

Don Eduardo mounted the southbound train from Santiago de

Chile bound for Chillán. He followed the migratory birds and sodden, winter rain deeper south from village to village where the destitute citizens sat by the tracks selling fermented milky sweets and trinkets made of gray sticks. Now he shakes sleep from his head and looks around, dazed. He rubs the dusty window with the sleeve of his coat and presses his face to the glass. He recoils from scores of faces pressed up to his own, only the windowpane keeping their skin from touching.

The people on the platform are pushing and leaning. Galeano can see they stare past him, unaware of his presence. He turns and faces the woman they stare at, the woman to whom he has not yet spoken.

Someone gasps and cries out that, "Anna is good looking." A cloud of hot breath fogs the window and Anna disappears.

Don Eduardo is quick enough to notice he is no longer passing through Araucania, the rebel lands of the Mapuches. No, it is not Araucania, but America. He turns to the woman and boldly but politely asks, "Forgive me my impertinence, but who are these people flattening their faces against the window, and why are they shocked to find you are a beautiful woman?"

"These people are simply curiosity seekers. I am a suffragist, an agitator for the vote for women. Somehow to many people it is important what a suffragist looks like. Our looks are taken to be the reason for our acts."

"Forgive me then my comment on your beauty."

Anna Dickinson sighs and sits down. Yes, it is important what a suffragist looks like. Elizabeth Cady Stanton and Susan B. Anthony lecture in Cheyenne. *The Cheyenne Leader* reports of the speech that neither woman is good looking and Susan is less so.

Esther Morris of South Pass City is the least good looking of all. Six feet tall, 180 pounds, her craggy, granite-like face can happily be likened to a rapidly eroding rock. Her chopping block of a head presses down on a neck thick as a sausage. She is a lump, it is true, and this seems to be important in these days of emphasis on beauty, delicacy and helplessness.

But Esther Morris has eyes that are deep and penetrating. She invites community leaders and legislators to her house for tea. Later one of the guests, Mr. Bill Bright, introduces a bill granting suffrage to the women of Wyoming Territory.

The senators laugh and pass the bill, thinking it a good joke to play on the House. The representatives laugh and pass the bill, thinking it a good joke to play on the governor. The governor signs the bill and, for the first time in the home of the brave and the land of the free, women have the right to vote, and Wyoming becomes the land of Equality.

Folly and madness have escaped into the newest of civilized man's dominions. "How can this be?" lawyer Ben Sheeks asks. He'd tried to help, introducing an amendment to the bill guaranteeing the right to vote to "colored women and squaws." That should have reminded everyone what this could lead to, but they voted the amendment down and passed the bill all the same.

The bill's original sponsor, Mr. Bright, explained to his colleague, Mr. Sheeks, his feeling that if Negro men had the right to vote then his white mother and wife ought to have that right, too. Mr. Sheeks maintained that Mr. Bright only said this because his wife was twenty years younger than he was, because she was an ardent suffragist, and because she was very good looking.

With the vote came the right to serve on juries. Men declared that they would abandon their wives if those wives sat in judgment of other men. Some feared what women would vote for and against. The legislators reassured everyone—there are 6000 men of voting age in Wyoming and only 1000 women. What can they do? In the eastern part of the United States, it was noted that Wyoming's women were all prostitutes anyway, and so their vote would reflect little of general interest. Remarks best left unmade shot from mouths like vomit from the gullets of a horde of frightened vultures.

Having checked his timetable and his watch, don Eduardo has again dozed off, confident it will be a long time before he reaches Chillán. Anna Dickinson sits, back straight and eyes ahead, studiously awaiting her train's departure. The crowd on the platform continues to shove, faces flattened like water against the window.

All this furor because 1000 white women, all of whom are more or less good looking, have been granted the right to cast a ballot in favor of this or that white man wearing a dark suit. And what about "colored women?" Are they more good looking? Or less so? And what about "squaws."

# 1942
## HEART MOUNTAIN
### BUILDING A HOME

"If you can drive a nail, you can qualify as a carpenter." said the newspaper ads, and so the workers came swarming like a flock of bees, enraged by the defiling of their hive.

This summer 2500 of them hammered up homes for Japanese Americans soon to arrive from the West Coast. Almost a city—456 tar paper huts, community latrines and laundries, and block mess halls. Really, it might have been mistaken for another hurriedly constructed army camp but for the barbed wire fences and the guard towers.

The Heart Mountain Camp took all summer to build at a cost of $5,095,000. During the war 14,054 Japanese Americans passed through the gates. That's about $362.53 per person of Japanese ancestry.

And how is a city made from scraps of wood and the silent conspiratorial sky? No sidewalks, no trees, no grass growing, in the barracks neither running water nor heaters. Each model home comes furnished—one U.S. Army cot, one mattress, and one blanket per person. The two person model is ten by twenty feet. The family model, designed for five to nine people, is twenty-four by twenty feet.

But somehow, against all odds, the city grows. Never has Wyoming been so popular with immigrants. Why now? Why would people leave their homes in Seattle, in Berkeley, on Bainbridge Island? Why leave the dense luscious greeny growth of those moist lands to come here where it rains six inches per year? And why leave the polished smooth mildness of days during which the high and low temperatures are almost the same to come here where the thermometer is endlessly bragging about its abilities—careening down to 40 below and leaping to over 100?

Much is inexplicable in the heart of man. And the little town of Heart Mountain for Japanese Evacuees by order of the War Relocation Authority grows and grows until it is the third largest city in Wyoming, home to 10,872 souls.

It is true that the vegetation is sparse, the rainfall low, the weather harsh, but still there is something here that is magnetic. Ah, but the land is beautiful. Heart Mountain itself rises beyond the fence, Heart Mountain, looking almost like a hat cocked jauntily on the head of a man about to embark on a grand adventure. "Yes, I'm off," the man says, "Who knows where I may land, who knows what I will make of this world when the train finally stops."

So much to do when one is starting from scratch. The camp newspaper has called for a campaign against flies and the people respond. In only one month 104,300 dead flies are delivered to the newspaper office. All one fall the high school boys give up many hours of their lives to practice American football and at Christmas reign as champions of the Big Horn Basin League. The war effort itself requires increased production, so the newly-arrived Japanese farmers grow green beans, peas, carrots, napra, spinach, beets, popcorn, sweet corn, tomatoes, cabbage, winter squash, Chinese cabbage, potatoes, garlic, daikon, lettuce, takana, misuna, barley, wheat, Swiss chard, watermelon, canteloupe, eggplant, peppers, onions. So many mouths to feed.

For a prison it is not so bad. Wyoming's U.S. senator Robertson is even willing to state that the government is pampering these people. Robertson's friend Senator Reynolds of North Carolina agrees— "Why, the Japs are getting everything, and our people aren't getting anything. I've even heard the Japs are having tractor races in the fields."

And it's true; it's not so bad for a prison. It's just that you can't leave—you see, it's a prison. The old life is gone—houses, jobs, savings. Families are separated—some members to one camp, some to another.

Yes, it's not so bad for a prison. And in fact, if the truth be known, it is possible to leave. There are work passes to the fields, and the young men are drafted into the Army and encouraged to go traveling to Italy, or Germany, or France.

Sandstorms, blizzards, hail, wind that will strip the clothes off man, woman, and child, then sun that will scorch skin until it peels back. Once the skin is removed, the sun can broil muscles, bake ligaments, fry cartilage until little remains but bones that rattle and collide, crumpling in a pile. And the bones of a person are as romantic and as unrecognizable as the bones of a pronghorn antelope, of a white-tailed deer, of a coyote.

Ghost towns exist in the United States only west of the 100th meridian. Gold is discovered, or coal, or uranium and, boom, overnight new people appear. For a few years the citizens of Park County, Wyoming discovered the profit to be made in the bonsai cultivation of Japanese souls. But even stunted flowers will not live for long growing in dust and ice. And every war, eventually and thankfully, comes to an end, at which time the survivers do their best to find their way home.

# 1969
## LARAMIE
### BLACK ARMBANDS

On Friday morning, October 17, when fourteen Black football players walked into the office of University of Wyoming football coach Lloyd Eaton, don Eduardo sat quietly in the corner of the room. He wouldn't miss this talk for anything and made himself so silent as to be invisible. Not a sneeze, a cough, or a fart would don Eduardo release. And he certainly wouldn't allow himself to jump up and interrupt no matter how strong his opinions. He sat there invisible, a sturdy though thin, balding Uruguayan who knows next to nothing about North American football.

But don Eduardo knows buckets about the conversation ready to take place. When he isn't sitting in this centrally-heated office, scootching around in his chair to get comfortable, leaning forward to hear, don Eduardo is busy walking through the rest of the Americas. Many things are happening in this busy world, and he works day and night, almost without sleep, trying to keep abreast of events. Of course it's impossible. Don Eduardo listens and scribbles, asks questions and records answers, runs everywhere and still he falls further behind. The world fills up like a water balloon. It stretches and sags. Its contours grow slippery and obscene. Soon it will explode.

In Lima, José Maria Arguedas has put a bullet through his head. Born white, raised by Indians, José was Quechua, in language and person. But he wrote in Spanish of his people. His people? Which people, the white or the Indian? Both. Neither the bankers nor the peasants of Peru, and least of all José, could put up with this. Like the old song says, "How can you be in two places at once when you're nowhere at all?"

Don Eduardo wasn't there when José died. He was in the middle of a sweaty crowd pushing itself up to the display window of an appliance store where a console model TV showed commanders Aldrin and Armstrong landing on the moon. When Neil Armstrong put his foot down and likened his first small step to one large step for mankind, don Eduardo felt that he was there, too, shuffling ponderously across the airless surface of the moon. The Uruguayan astronaut looked down and, seeing José, smiled sadly. In the moon's lowered gravity, the smile spread until it covered the distance back to earth.

In Bogotá, don Eduardo squats in the dirt on his haunches. He wobbles, faint from hunger. Arturo Dueñas, seven-year-old orphan and thief, has stolen a chicken. Hidden under the dirt, Arturo shares the chicken with his dog Broncas. He looks at the wobbling man, but says nothing. When he goes to sleep, the man is still there.

Though his ankles are killing him, and though his doctor has told him not to sleep on the streets, don Eduardo wobbles there through the night and all the next day. Arturo and Broncas come and go. Finally, Arturo offers the stupid, dirty old man a piece of rotten mango. Don Eduardo politely declines and, after days of waiting, stands up, his knees crackling like burning branches, and happily walks away.

In Rio de Janeiro, don Eduardo tries out his Portuguese. He hasn't got a job; he doesn't appear to be a cop or a pimp. To the inhabitants of the Praia do Pinto slum, don Eduardo can only be a Martian anthropologist on holiday. There he is in a smoky bistro taking notes with a stub of raw pencil, jerking his head up and down, stuffing papers into one pocket and ripping them out of another. The poorest of the poor stare at him and conclude that, surely, he is a madman. This being the best of the possibilities, they ask him to sing.

There is so much happening in 1969. On a cliff above a polluted beach, Gabriel dos Santos is making sculptures out of garbage—scrap metal, cast-off car parts, injection-molded plastic, broken bottles, bits of wood and bent nails. The director of the National Museum calls dos Santos an important folk artist.

While dos Santos works, the president of Bolivia dies when his helicopter explodes above Arque Pass. Out of the ball of flame falls money—scorched pesos, soles, francs and dollars—fluttering down like blackened leaves.

As don Eduardo sits here, the heat pump whirring, in Laramie, Wyoming, he thinks of the soccer war between El Salvador and Honduras. The dead and wounded are hauled from the stadium. The fans scream through the streets. Soon from sticks and bottles and stones, the war graduates to portable rocket launchers and machine guns. Except for shooting at each other, the two countries cut off relations. How crucial is sport, don Eduardo thinks. Somebody won the match. Somebody ought to send telegrams to the four thousand dead and thus reveal the final score.

Yesterday morning Willie S. Black, the chancellor of the Black Student Alliance, hand-delivered identical letters to Coach Eaton and to the president of the University of Wyoming asking that the university schedule no games with Brigham Young University so long as the Mormon Church continues its racist policy of excluding Blacks from the church priesthood.

That afternoon Coach Eaton whispered a reminder to Joe Williams, one of his team tri-captains, that no protest would be allowed. "And besides," coach grins, "What self-respecting Black would want to be a priest of the Mormon Church?"

This morning when the fourteen Black athletes stand in street clothes wearing black armbands, the coach decides to give them a helping hand. "I can save you fellows a lot of words," he says before they speak, "You've made your bid, you're all off the team, your football scholarships are canceled. You agreed not to take part in any demonstrations and, by wearing black armbands into my office, you've broken the agreement. So long. You want to go to school, you can go somewhere besides Wyoming."

If don Eduardo steamed, the room would be a cloud. He can't

sit silent and leaps up, pulling a smudged notebook out of his brief-case. He reminds Coach Eaton that the U.S. Supreme Court has ruled that school children in Des Moines, Iowa can wear black armbands to school to protest the Vietnam War, that the wearing of a black arm-band is a constitutionally protected and legal exercise of freedom of expression.

"Don't give me that shit, you little South American prick," the coach says, displaying no emotion.

One of the Black students jumps at this. "Coach, what're you doing? This is Eduardo Galeano, one of the world's great writers and historians and a fighter for freedom. You can't call him a little South American spic."

"For Christ sake, I didn't call him a spic, I called him a prick. And who told the little prick he could shove his skinny ass into my office and sit in one of my chairs. Great writer, my ass. He's a com-munist. Get the hell out of my office, you commie bastard. And you," the coach says pointing at his player, "You admire this guy so much you can get out with him. You think you're so smart with your big head. Yeah, that big head won't fit in a football helmet ever again—too big, head's getting bigger and bigger, oh, yeah, bigger."

Another player leaps forward now. "You can't call him nigger, coach, what's the matter with you?"

"Oh, shit, I didn't call anybody nigger, you dumb fuck. I said big-ger. Bigger! His head's bigger than his helmet. Looks like your head's getting smaller. It's getting so small I can't see it anymore. Don't mat-ter if you're white or black; you broke the rule. Just so happens you're all Black."

The conversation going along like this, it seemed futile to don Eduardo to read any more from his notebook, and he got ready to leave. He did jot down one more thing, a little fact from Laramie that he might want to pull out and read to someone in Casper or Caracas or Buenos Aires. In 1969, Coach Lloyd Eaton dismissed fourteen Black scholarship students from his football team because they'd come to him asking if they could wear black armbands in the university's game with Brigham Young University. Shortly after the dismissal, Coach Ea-ton was named by United Press International as Wyoming's Man of the Year for 1969.

## 1989
### CHEYENNE
### PLAY IT AGAIN IN THE EQUALITY STATE

By a committee vote in the House of Representatives, the State, and by the power vested in the state, the People of Wyoming declare that Martin Luther King Day will not be a legal holiday in these collected counties whose population is ninety-seven percent white.

For those who wish to honor Dr. King and the vision by which he lived, it is tiring, this battering against the gates. And for those opposed to the now defunct holiday, it is tiring, too, the never-ending effort to remind people that the world is not going to change easily, that nothing has anything to do with anything else, and that those in power are in power.

Everyone is tired. Tired enough, exhausted enough, worn out enough to forget there are some things a person is not supposed to do. That's what made forty-three year old Mrs. Rosa Parks take the load off her swollen ankles and collapse in the closest seat on the bus home—Montgomery, Alabama, 1955. Not that Mrs. Parks hadn't thought about sitting down like this many times before, but today she did it. Happened to be the White Only section of the bus, and the driver had to get up out of his seat, walk back to Mrs. Parks and demand, as was his obligation, that she move.

The tired lady didn't move. A seamstress, she had worked hard all that day sewing clothes that white people would wear. She'd run her hands along the material, pleased by its feel, pleased by the work she'd done. She had no desire to be intimate with white people, and it never occurred to her that the material she carressed at work would soon be bending gently across the skin of its white owner.

Plopped down in the seat on the bus, Mrs. Parks' thoughts were more general than this. A simple matter of wondering, as she had idly wondered so many times before, when and how people like her would ever determine their rights as human beings. Speculating on such, or maybe just daydreaming, she didn't respond when the driver told her to move.

It is possible she doesn't hear me, the harried driver may have thought, and he told her again, "Get up." This time, when she made no move, he called a cop who arrested the recalcitrant seamstress.

Well, everybody seeming to grow increasingly more tired as the century wears on, this was all it took. The Negro people of Montgomery organized a boycott of the city bus system. Car pools were set up to take people to work—though most simply walked. Mrs. Parks must have been smiling now—all those folks walking to work cause of her and her sitting in that cell, the weight off her feet for the first time in years, and her swollen ankles shrinking back to their normal size.

Against all that walking, the city struck back, arresting one hundred leaders of the bus boycott. White segregationists, inflamed by the empty sections of the usually jammed buses, planted bombs in black churches. Martin Luther King, a leader of the boycott, was walking through his living room when a shotgun blast splintered his front door. As he sat thinking about his options, a bomb came whistling into the house. The integrity of the public transit system is paramount in a busy urban center.

When King spoke in a church that had not yet been bombed,

2000 Negro people were there. They filled that church from the basement to the balcony. They spilled out into the street. They chanted and sang, shouted and prayed. In the magnified heat of the steamy building, some collapsed in the aisles. They took a pledge of passive resistance.

Martin Luther King told his brothers and sisters that "If we are arrested every day, if we are exploited every day, if we are trampled over every day, don't ever let anyone pull you so low as to hate them. We must use the weapon of love."

People want to love—not just their own kind but all other people, and all the creatures of this world. People are born to love and King knew this. The willow's branches sweep the ground. On a distant slope the coyotes howl, their weird music a harmony that everyone feels. The raindrops bounce from the grass, and their shiny surfaces reflect the clouds from which they fall, the partially obscured sun, the pale rising moon, the bottoms of the shoes of the child skipping through puddles along the edge of a street.

Martin Luther King knows that love is the most triumphant force in the universe and he reminds everyone.

Love or not, there are a few problems left. In Detroit four men—three white and one black—kill three black teenagers. Though the defense attorneys admit the four shot two of the teenagers, a jury finds the murderers not guilty. In Jackson, Mississippi, the police decide a barrage is the suitable response, and for twenty-eight seconds, using shotguns, automatic rifles and a submachine gun, the air is shimmering with flying metal. Four hundred bullets or pieces of buckshot are later pried from the walls of the girls' dormitory at a black college situated in front of the police. Two black students are dead. Judge Harold Cox reminds all that students who engage in civil disorder must expect to be injured or killed. In Boston City hospital, a black patient armed with a towel snaps said towel at a policeman who shoots and kills his assailant. A municipal judge finds the murder justified.

The air over America is reeling from the flight of bullets. The smell of fire and gunpowder overpowers that of roses and cherry trees. Clubs and sticks spin like murderous candy from a poison piñata, and bottles and cans, as soon as emptied, are put to more sinister uses.

While Martin Luther King said, "I have a dream . . .", his co-worker in social change, Malcolm X, called for black people to physically defend themselves against beatings, rape and murder, and said, "This is a revolution, the black revolution."

Malcolm X was murdered while speaking on a public platform. Martin Luther King, still committed to the power of love, granted that this love must be massive and organized. It must be love on such a scale that no one can stop it. So much love that we drown in it and are reborn without memory or hate.

We are one. The poor in Alabama are the poor in Wyoming are the poor in Vietnam. A rapist Nigger is a drunk Indian is a skinny gook. King persisted in his trust that whites too could be niggers, Indians and gooks, and he spoke out loud the words of connection.

"We are spending all this money for death and destruction and not nearly enough money for life and constructive development . . . Somehow this madness must cease. We must stop now. I speak as a child of God and brother to the suffering poor of Vietnam. I speak for those whose land is being laid waste, whose homes are being destroyed, whose culture is being subverted. I speak for the poor of America who are paying the double price of smashed hopes at home and death and corruption in Vietnam. I speak as a citizen of the world . . ."

When King linked the poor in America with the poor in Vietnam, Negroes in Birmingham with Asians in Saigon, the man's days were numbered. Standing on the balcony of his hotel room in Memphis, where he'd come to support the garbage workers' strike, Martin Luther King was shot and killed by another human being.

In Albany, Georgia, one thousand Negroes were arrested for protesting segregation and discrimination. There were so many arrests that the Chief of Police himself came out of his office to help take down the names of those who were being held. Busily writing, he looked up to see a nine-year-old boy before him.

"What is your name?" the police chief asked.

And the boy answered, "Freedom, Freedom."

As Martin Luther King had, the boy stood up and gave his name. He did not weep for himself, nor for his brothers and sisters. He felt neither pity nor shame. "Freedom, Freedom," is what he said.

Exactly as it was in that time, it is in ours. Exactly as it has been in every country of the world it is in our tiny, backward and isolated country of Wyoming, the state known in this union as the "Equality State."

The state does not represent the people. The people neither honor

nor attend the state. Love is as big as it always was. Here in Wyoming, there's a stand of cottonwoods whose leaves shimmer and turn in the breeze. The summer air is sweet and warm. The mountains tower, calling us to look to the sky.

This is Dr. Martin Luther King's state. He brings his ghostly beauty here. He sits under a cottonwood tree and watches the light dapple his skin through the leaves.

Some of the people who live nearby go and sit with Dr. King. For one day, they don't go in to work. They have a picnic. They call it a holiday.

# 1942
## BOMBER MOUNTAIN
## MAGNETISM

Smack. The magnetism of the mountain, inviting all who dress in metal toward it. The first to arrive is a shiny steel bomber, a quiet evening at home that will last for years. It being World War II and in the interests of national security, the army doesn't report the missing plane. Reported missing or not, it's gone and so are the crew members, strapped into their seats as late fall turns to winter, as the wind turns to snow, snow swirling in through smashed plexiglass and rent fiber, burying the men in purity, in cold.

In the spring of 1943, Simon Iberlin, Basque rancher, looks up from where he stands amidst a band of sheep, and wonders about the shine on the mountain. But by the time he thinks to go climbing, he's in the service himself, pursuing the national security.

In 1944, someone in an office remembers the missing plane and types up a report. When the rescuers arrive, the crew is still resting, waiting for the melt that will unburden their wings and allow them to lift off once again, to climb deep into the open sky.

But even if the snow had released them, they wouldn't rise. And they couldn't have known how long they'd been grounded. Every man's watch was gone, and the pale lines of the watchbands had faded from their wrists. Their rings were gone, too, gifts to the mountain, or to some friend of the mountain who could use some new jewelry.

Tired, don Eduardo rubs his red eyes. The pressure feels good. He pulls his palms around to the side of his head and rubs his temples. When he drops his hands and looks ahead, he can't see. The window in his room is fogged over. He rubs furiously at the glass.

"I better watch it or I'll get my shirtsleeves all wet and cold," he thinks. Then notices four gold stripes on his almost black cuff. And a nametag over his breast pocket—Captain Galeano. He swings around, suddenly aware that his room is the cockpit of a Boeing stretch jetliner. Lights and dials buzz in his face. Next to him a man with three stripes on his sleeves dozes, a thin smile on his face, a little moisture on his upper lip.

"Captain Galeano—oh, Jesus." He rubs again at the window glass, runs back into the main cabin and leans out the emergency exit over the wing. Staring backward, he can see painted on the plane's tail the letters P.L.U.N.A.—the Uruguayan National Airline serving Buenos Aires, Porto Alegre, Sao Paulo, Rio de Janeiro and Asunción.

"PLUNA?" Don Eduardo slaps his forehead with the butt of his hand. Where has he seen that word? "Es como la pluma, the bright feather with which we fly." But what does it mean? He can't remember. He blinks and shakes his head, and when he looks again PLUNA reads United. United with whom?

Captain Galeano hurries back to the cockpit to set his ship down on its scheduled flight to Sheridan, Wyoming. But drawn by the shine, the Boeing jetliner lands thirty-six miles to the south at Buffalo. The doors open and the ground crew stands grinning in disbelief. It's a small town. And the airstrip is too short for jetliners. No matter, it's a perfect landing. The dazed passengers step out into the blinding light, the silver sheen of the bomber flashing into their eyes.

"Would you like to take a hike into the mountains?" the locals ask. "Some of you may even want to live here."

The bulk of the passengers, though, line up to climb aboard buses and make the long, grounded ride to somewhere else. And Captain Galeano sends his fatbodied big plane screaming up and down the single runway of Buffalo. He can ride up and down forever and still be in Buffalo.

"This runway is just too damn short. How did I manage to land here? How did I manage to land anywhere? And if this window is really fogged over, why aren't the stripes on my sleeves wet?"

He lets his head sink into his hands as the jetliner rests on a mesa a few miles below the crew of the waiting bomber.

Thirteen years of flying this Piper Cub up and down every draw and wash in Johnson County. Thirteen years skimming eerily over the treetops, letting the wings rock, coming screaming down as a god on top of some coyote on the run. The gunner leans out the right side and fires. The coyote darts left then right, into the trees, back out in the open. The Piper Cub is slammed into a stall, drops, the engines cut, then back on and full throttle. Forward and back. The two men are upside down. They rock and roll.

"There he is," the men shout and are slammed into their seats as the little plane balances on the edge of coming apart, every rivet remembering the days of freedom, the days alone jumbled together in a box. And every rivet, too, thinking of magnetism, of the pull toward its mate on the mountain.

Coming over a rise, pilot and gunner both leaning far to the right, their eyes intent on the coyote they've almost cornered, the ground makes its grab, a lunging leap high into the air, and wraps its hand around the plane, fingernails deep into fuselage.

Pieces of metal scatter in every direction. The rescuers will try to pick it all up, but there will be shards that escape—sharpened slivers of steel and aluminum that peel themselves away from the whole and slip unnoticed into a hole in the ground, under a piece of rotten fallen tree trunk, into a pile of leaves, behind a rock.

Two more men await the day they will again take to the air. And Bomber Mountain rests, worn out from the labors of magnetism.

1979

GREEN RIVER

SPANISH MUSIC


The singer wants to give the song a little bit of soul, wants to, as they say, sing it from the heart. It is possible to come to tears giving the song the emotion it deserves.

Manuel Lucero is dead. Manuel Lucero, Jr. writes a sad ballad for his father, wanting to tell his father how his father's son feels. "Dearest father," he sings, "I want to give you back your verses that cause my heart to burn, your verses within which lives my loss." Now it is too easy to come to tears singing a song.

More often Manuel Jr. sings happy songs—cumbias, polkas, rancheras, two-steps—for dancing. And even if the happy beat is accompanied by sorrowful lyrics, mostly no one here knows since only a few people speak Spanish. "Soy un Borracho" is a good one, and "Encantadores Ojos." The crowds love "Dos Palomas al Volar" about the two shining doves that fly. They ignore the fact that the birds are love and that the love doesn't simply fly, it flies away.

The Luceros are a family. After Manuel Sr.'s death, the family has gone on. The little children and the adults step up onto the bandstand together, and together they smile through their tears to make other people happy. The music drops and pulls, drops and pulls.

In one song, El Chino, the Chinese street vender, rambles through the town calling out his wares. He is selling needles and thread, bone candies and tiny, delicate pastries in the shapes of hearts and flowers, tin cups and blue enameled bowls, ground chile—chile verde, chile rojo, chile amarillo, chile jalapeño, chile piquín, chile chino—votive candles and candles for home use scented of oleander and chamomile and vanilla.

El Chino goes walking, shouting out what he sells. In front of a pretty Mexican woman, he stops and runs through it all.

The woman can't understand the Chinese accented Spanish and asks him what he has to sell. "¿Pero, El Chino," she asks, "Qué vendes tu?"

El Chino calls out his list again, this time more slowly, and somehow all the words are slightly changed. The needles and thread become jasmine and pillows, the candles are moonlit nights, the tin cups are filled with wine and the blue enameled bowls with luscious fruits. Only the chiles remain chiles and El Chino smiles.

He is courting the pretty woman. He calls out, "You are a good Mexican woman; I am a good Chinese man, let's get married. From your bed to mine is only one short step, come close. . ."

And the Mexican woman smiles back, asking, "¿Pero, El Chino, Qué vendes tu?"

In another song from the same faraway land, don Eduardo is drinking alone in a bar. He's not a regular in the cantinas, but today he's had too much. No one asks him what misery he attempts to hide or magnify. He begins to sing and keeps at it through all the long afternoon. A stranger, unfamiliar with the bar, the music, the drunken man, or life in this town, grows impatient and throws the man into the street.

Don Eduardo lies face down in the dusty deaf street singing. "Life of my life," he cries out, and gasps. The mariachis are chasing him. They are on his heels, sturdy in their razor sharp pants, their jet black gleaming boots, their trimmed vests, shining with silver threads. They play twenty thousand songs, finally remembering the one about this man in the street—he has fallen from the clouds. It is impossible to tell if he is an angel or a meteorite, burnt to death as he comes screaming through the heavy gaseous atmosphere.

"I am neither angel nor meteorite," don Eduardo cries. "I am Uruguayan, in Wyoming."

And in Wyoming, the mariachis are like gods—men who after twenty, thirty or forty drinks still stand rigidly at attention, men whose lips are made of steel, whose eyes have closed forever on the ordinary, whose fingers are never-tiring termites or red ants who will work to the end. You may pull off a leg, pull off another leg, pull off all their legs and still the ants struggle forward, pushing some boulder of a crumb up an incline a bird couldn't ascend.

Los Luceros are proud to play the old time Hispanic music, proud to reveal their feelings through that music. A woman's voice calls, "Of the birds beating against the wind, I like best the crow because my love dresses only in black."

There is a chord change, and a man's voice begins, "Dearest Father." Manuel Jr. cries. Don Eduardo, working part time as percussionist in the Lucero family band, trying to save enough money to get home, and understanding the language, cries along with Manuel. The walls of the room ache and want to fall. But like the mariachis, the walls stand and the song goes on, the words flooding the dance floor, "Dearest Father."

1875

ROCK SPRINGS

THE MINERS STRIKE

It is difficult to get lost in this empty, open land, but somehow easy to get misplaced. And so everyone has misplaced himself—British and Scandinavian coal miners, Union Pacific bosses and managers, the Knights of Labor and 150 Chinese men hired as strikebreakers.

Even objects begin to wonder where they are. On New Year's Day, the Chinese Dragon, blue skin over yellow skin, parades through town, turning its head left and right, seeking bearings in the unfamiliar streets.

The houses, shabby and clumsy, imagine themselves parading with the dragon buoyantly and easily down some Shanghai lane a hundred years in the future. But this parade of houses is only the long-ing for motion of the permanently immobile, and the word "house" grants this construction too much grace. These new dwellings for the Chinese visitors are no more substantial than a scrap of fur left in a trap after a coyote has escaped. Houses that are leaking windbreaks, fashioned from rotten boards, discarded packing crates, flattened tin cans, and dirt.

First the pay rate for coal was cut from five cents a bushel to four. Then the Union Pacific forgot it had promised to lower prices to miners at the company store. Then the company demanded an increase in production of twenty-five percent. The miners called for changes, but as the old song says, "I can't get no satisfaction," and that's when the UP brought in the Chinese.

The years went by, the Asian and European workers alone together in their separate rooms underground until one day in 1885 a group of white men had had enough of living in a world that isn't white and decided to deflate the dragon. Hidden in corners and holes, along the banks of Bitter Creek, between the walls on crowded streets, the Chinese found themselves in a curtain of fire. Some stayed inside expecting friendly White Boss Man to appear. Some leapt into the air, rolling, then tumbling down the embankment, across the creek and into the sage and greasewood. Some ran from Rock Springs to Evanston.

The fires lifted and turned, spinning in the ever-present wind. Twenty-eight men were murdered, fifteen were wounded, hundreds were disappeared. Rescuers were paid $20 per Chinese body they dug from the charred ground. Now the ghost wolves feast on the spirit bodies of yellow men turned black by coal and time.

But the Chinese dragon returned the next year. Over one hundred feet long, it took forty men to carry it. Its long, new back and sides were deep blue silk stretched taut over steamed bows. Its curving face was that of a Texas Longhorn steer, and its eyes were those of an enraged bull, shot through with flame—red and green—and bulging, popping, exploding out of a burning brain. Its forked tongue snaked out toward bystanders while a brass band played the song of the ten thousand firecrackers, brass cannons in ash-filled streets.

The United States Army parades behind the dragon and protects it. When the miners go back to work, there are only a hundred Chinese prepared to enter the earth and a scant half dozen of white men. But the days pass and the miners return, both white and yellow. The coal comes smoking out of the dark caverns, the coal shining with its heart of fire. The Union Pacific trains grind forward. Yellow and white men die together of the same miners' diseases. The Army, now permanently at home in Rock Springs, engages in target practice near Bitter Creek until 1898 when the romantic song of the Spanish-American War is sung and lures the resting soldiers away from the now placid mines.

1923

BARBER

A ROWBOAT

In the night the sound of water taps at the inside of Dave Muir's head. It has rained six inches in three days, and Powder River has renounced its name. Clearly, even Nature periodically proceeds along paths of grievous error. Six inches in three thousand days, or in three hundred days, or even in thirty days could be absorbed, but not in three days.

Muir wakes and blinks into darkness and dampness. Lifting his arm, he can't see his hand in front of his face. He rises from his bed and steps toward the window, feeling the bedstead, the straight-backed chair, the wall. He touches the wall, sliding the palm of his hand along until the surface is smoother and colder. He presses his face to the glass. There are no stars in the sky. Straining to see the thousand points where yesterday's light now passes through the falling droplets, he surrenders to blindness. He feels his way back to the bed and lights a kerosene lamp, but the bright dry flame is swallowed up by the dripping blackness.

In a land as dry as this, rain you cannot see is worth being cautious about. Muir knows he should leave for higher ground, but he also knows he may be out for a good long while and so boils potatoes and beef and sits down to eat. In the middle of his meal, he hears the squawking and flapping of the chickens in their house, and when he steps off the porch to go to them, he steps into waist deep water.

"Maybe I'm not really hungry after all," Muir says out loud, "Maybe I'll just be on my way right now." But how, he thinks? And again, as if addressing a friend, speaks out loud, "I can't swim, and this water is too deep to wade through."

Nothing for it but to plunge forward. At the chicken house, Muir forces the door open only to feel the water rip it from his hand. One wall gives way. Stunned by the crash of his building being pulled into the river, Muir nearly fails to notice he can again see. There leaning out of a rowboat, oars hanging limply in their locks, is a man gathering chickens in his arms. He's tying their legs up with wire and strapping their wings to their bodies with sisal twine. Each one finished, he throws it in the bottom of the boat. In his teeth the man holds a chromed cigarette lighter from another time, the blue butane flame illuminating his acts.

Unaccustomed to the light, Muir shields his face then with eyes half closed and lids fluttering he looks again. "Stop, thief," he shouts and, forgetting the flood, turns as if to run to the house for his gun. But the water has now risen to his chest, and it's impossible to run. His head going faster than his body, he ends face down in the black water, gurgling, "Stlop, Stlop."

The man in the dinghy ties up the last chicken and rows hard across what's left of the room. Removing the flame from his mouth, he says to Muir, "Get in. I can't help you, but if you can get in on your own, I can let you stay." When Muir hesitates the man says only, "These must be your chickens. It's a lucky thing I came along."

Little does don Eduardo know. This is a river in flood, but it's the wrong river. Don Eduardo's ticket was punched for the Guayas River at the port of Guayaquil, Ecuador. There was a flood there, too, but it was a flood of workers. Desperate from eating only the bread of their own hunger, the workers had risen and taken over their city. The women were the worst of all—the washerwomen, the short order cooks, the midwives and wet nurses, the street peddlers—they defied the men who ran their lives.

Carlos Arroyo, President of the Chamber of Deputies, was grinning. "Today the rabble awoke laughing," he admitted. "But tonight when they return to bed, they'll go to sleep crying." The army opened fire, and the crowds hissed and popped like raindrops set ablaze. No one counted how many human souls were thrown into the river, their bellies slashed open by bayonets, their stomachs and hearts spilling bloody into the black churning water of the Guayas.

Now in the river float thousands of tiny white crosses, bright and beautiful as a field of wildflowers in the Bighorn Mountains in June. Each flower is a murdered worker reborn, each petal a memory of one moment of happiness.

In that moment of happiness, don Eduardo realizes the man next to him, three quarters submerged and nearly dead from shock, is speaking English.

"Where am I?" the man says.

And Galeano looks at him and repeats, "Dónde Estoy?"

Powder River rages forward, downstream and north.

"Chicken thief!" the man screams again and lunges toward the boat, almost upsetting it. Some of the chickens fall over the side and disappear into the current, their feet and wings tied, unable either to walk or fly, incapable of thinking they might swim.

What ship let down this dinghy here? What ship sailed these many miles upriver from the coast to land in splinters in another dark distant flood? Before either man can choose a language in which to answer these questions, Muir tumbles over the side and lies panting in the bottom of the boat, his weight full over don Eduardo. The waters continue to rise and, the oars knocked loose and drifting away, the boat can only go with the current, spinning downstream, careening north toward Montana and the Yellowstone.

The cigarette lighter, too, has been knocked overboard and again all is darkness with only the noise of the water as a guide. Neither man can make out the other's face, and neither says a word. From them both rises a smell. From Muir, the smell of wet wool and bentonite clay. From Galeano, something like rancid fruit and burning leaves. Even in all this water, there is the smell of dust and smoke.

Eduardo Galeano of Montevideo, Uruguay and Dave Muir of near Barber, Wyoming ride through the night in a borrowed boat. Powder River spreads across its entire valley. Sometimes the current surges left or right, sometimes back whence it came. The water carries away houses, haystacks, tractors and tools, fences and trees. Entire ranches—grass, soil, sheep, cows—disappear underwater. The only buildings that remain are those filled with sand, weighted like stones at the river bottom as the water rushes by. The pilings below the railroad bridge are washed away, but the rails and ties hold together and the unsupported track undulates overhead like a bull snake learning to fly.

The two men continue their ride north. Sometimes don Eduardo tries to row with his hands, to give direction to the journey, but mostly he makes no such pretense and waits patiently in the bottom of the boat, only now and then lifting his sodden face and peeking over the gunwales nearly even with the river's flow, each time expecting to see those crosses and workers floating face up toward the sea.

It is hopeless to pretend anything and the night stays as black as before, so all directions are equal.

Galeano and Muir are asleep when their boat slips sideways through the window of a half-submerged house. Muir reels awake and gasps.

"I know this house," he tells don Eduardo. "Help me." He leaps from the boat and begins running from one wet room to the next. Following as quickly as he can, Galeano is unable to stop when Muir does, and the traveler slams into the back of the citizen knocking him down and into a room that has been turned upside down. Crushed by her bed, her face underwater and her eyes closed, is a pregnant woman.

"Help me." Muir repeats, and don Eduardo tries to stand, the water making his shoes and socks into great clammy sponges, his hair matted in his face, and a chill running down his spine that snaps his entire body taut. The two men, strangers to one another, go to work and deliver of the dead woman a perfect, living six-pound girl.

Carrying the baby, they struggle back out the window and into the boat. Muir begins untying the remaining chickens' feet and wings. No room in the boat for all of us, no point in trying to hold onto these. Let them go. They can fly enough to get to shore. The two men settle back into the damp rowboat smelling of feathers and blood and baby.

They aim themselves south against the current.

The sky begins to gray. In the distance, the water has begun to recede, and along the shore the cottonwoods replant themselves in the soft ground. On the now bare branches, the bodies of cows are draped like ghastly ornaments on concrete Christmas trees.

Look again and each cow is the pendant body of Christ or of some defiant woman. Already they have begun to bloat, and their unnaturally fat bodies glisten and dry under the sun. Trying to keep their eyes on the water ahead, don Eduardo and Dave Muir in silence take turns rowing with their hands. The rain has let up so that now only a few drops fall, landing on the men's faces at discrete intervals where from a distance they could be mistaken for tears.

## 1890
### Mato Tipila
### Releasing Souls

In his dream, don Eduardo is dreaming that life is real. The governments seem real enough—the government of the United States, and walking in a clockwise motion, the governments of Mexico, of China, of Canada, and of England.

The Lakota Holy Man, Black Elk, is dancing at a reception in London for Queen Victoria. He shows her the steps of the Dance-Before-War, the Dance-in-Celebration-of-a-Successful-Hunt, the Dance-to-Purify-the-Lodge-of-One-Who-is-Ill, the Dance-With-No-Meaning. Black Elk is careful to turn counterclockwise at least once during each dance, to turn the dance from real to dream, to preserve the real dance and the people and land from which it comes.

The old man finishes, and the crowd of dignitaries applauds. Now stepping from the audience is a young officer in dark uniform and white gloves. He has the wistful eyes of an adult remembering a happy childhood. He begins to tango—to show the old gentleman from the northern plains another dance born of sorrow and tenacity. Even though the young white man is in full dress uniform, Black Elk can see the tango's birth in dusty, shit-filled corrals near the slaughterhouses, and in tenement courtyards whose paving stones daily soak up urine, whose sky is forever filled by rows of laundry. The soiled clothing is taken from its owners, pounded clean and pure, and left to flap whiplike in the blue until it again covers a body.

The tango is the dance of poor workers and petty criminals. The tango's dance floor is pounded earth. This is the dance of the hammer and of the knife. Men dance with women, men dance with men. The steps are broken and jagged, the embraces tight and blasphemous.

In don Eduardo's dream, Black Elk hands him a small buckskin bundle. In such a bundle should be the soul of a dead child, don Eduardo's daughter or son, or the soul of a great person. Don Eduardo takes the skin bundle.

"Be careful," Black Elk cautions, "Today is the day we release this soul, the soul of a young English officer who died in a drawing room spinning in a dance he could not stop. He died *wakan*, and today we release him to Wakan-Tanka."

Black Elk smiles and steps forward. Just before he reaches don Eduardo, the old man stumbles and falls forward, the bundle leaving his hands. At first it rises. Don Eduardo leans toward it and can feel its weight increasing as it descends toward him. The body leaves, but gravity remains. The bundle rests in don Eduardo's arms. And grows heavier.

"Be careful," Black Elk repeats, "I think there is something strange here. I think there may be two souls in there. Or maybe even more."

The bundle grows heavier and heavier. Don Eduardo sinks to the earth inside the round tipi. Someone scratches a circle on the ground in front of him. Someone begins to dig a small hole into which will be placed food for the soul. Outside the circle and around it walk several men. They are smoking, and at the same time they are chanting "Hee-ay-hay-ee-ee." Four times they sing this—Hee-ay-hay-ee-ee, Hee-ay-hay-ee-ee, Hee-ay-hay-ee-ee. Four young women enter and sit. They are women who have not yet known men. They will touch the soul before it leaves. They will eat.

A buffalo falls. The tallow is scraped from along its back. The sacred red and blue days pass, the days at the end of the world, the days at the end of a man's life.

Black Elk places a pinch of tobacco in a pipe and faces east. He speaks low, mumbling. Don Eduardo tries to hear, but too much is going on and he can barely hold the bundle, which continues to grow heavier. It has pushed him over, and he lies on his back looking up at the small circle of light above the tipi. He feels himself being pressed into the earth as if he were digging the hole for food in front of the soul, as if he were the purified food to be fed the soul before its release.

Now Black Elk is speaking toward the west.

When a soul is kept it is to purify it. When it is released, the pure soul can go home and need never wander the earth again. Take a lock of hair from the dead. Take a glowing ember. Take a bit of sweet grass and place it on the red hot coal. The smoke rises to God, the smoke drifts throughout the universe, and its fragrance is known to all things.

Wrap the hair in a skin bundle and keep it. We belong to the earth. Those who keep the soul must live in a sacred manner. The habits you make will stay with you through your life. No bad person will be allowed in this house. There will be no arguments, no dissension. Only harmony. In this house we live with the soul of one who is departed.

Black Elk has filled the pipe—all things and all space are held within the tiny bowl, the heart of the smoking universe. Don Eduardo smokes with the others then he places the pipe over another ember. He turns the pipe so the smoke enters the bowl and goes out the stem aimed toward the sky. The universe, too, smokes the purifying fire.

When don Eduardo rises, the bundle is as big as a mountain. He staggers forward toward the doorway of the tipi. Reaching the opening through which the bright sun shines, he is momentarily blinded. He feels the bundle rise away from him, but he can't see it go. The spirit is released. Black Elk turns over his shoulder and calls, "Remember us, look back now and again and see that we walk only on the sacred path."

Black Elk goes to don Eduardo and helps the exhausted man up. He takes him in his arms, holding him tight, holding him close. The hot breath of one man mingles with that of the other. The newly released soul is flying away and home.

"Look," Black Elk says, "Stand up straight. Now bend your knees like this. I want to show you how to tango."

# 1947
## Near Manderson, South Dakota
### Haunted

To bring to life the flowering tree of his people. That is what has been haunting Black Elk all his years, from his boyhood when he danced, when voices sang to him, when the hunt and freedom were one. It is an awful responsibility for a man to bear. That is the truth. And though Black Elk is clearly one of the great men of this world and of others, still he is a man. He must eat and sleep. He worries and frets. Sometimes it is too hot; sometimes too cold. He can become sick and old.

All his life he has been hearing what others say, and he has been telling what he can. Now in these latter days, it appears people no longer know how to listen, and when they talk, nothing comes from their mouths. That is why Black Elk has decided to call a white man to him, a man of writing and reading who can make a book. Reading a book is not the same as listening, but maybe the record a book can be will remain intact until the day when people will remember once again how to hear.

Shyly, don Eduardo appears as Joseph Epes Brown who appears in a potato field where Black Elk and his family have been working. Brown is a scholar, but also a man, as Black Elk and don Eduardo are men. Brown reads and writes in English and knows what must be done to make a book. He has dealt with the universities and their publishing offices. Brown also knows the Oglala Sioux, the Western Teton, the Lakota dialect of the Siouan language family. He does not know it perfectly, but he knows enough. And Black Elk's son, Benjamin Black Elk, is ready to help.

It is the story of the sacred pipe Brown is to record and preserve. Elk Head told the story of the pipe to three men. Two are dead and the third, Black Elk, is old. All the men of those days—both the men who were wise and the always ubiquitous fools—are even older than Black Elk, or they are dead.

Black Elk shows Joseph Brown a photograph of seven men, the seven Sioux alive who fought at the Battle of the Little Big Horn. The picture shows: Iron Hail, age 90; High Eagle, age 88; Iron Hawk, age 99; Little Warrior, age 80; Comes Again, age 86; Pemmican, age 85; John Sitting Bull, age 80. All are alive. All are dressed in deerskin and wear feathered headresses. Little Warrior holds a pipe. Iron Hail holds the primary feathers, almost the entire wing, of a bald eagle. The seven men look in many different directions, some into the camera, some off to one side or the other, some up into the invisible sky. Black Elk mentions to Brown that these men were all his friends and that the photo is from the files of the Illuminated Foto-Ad Service in Sioux Falls, South Dakota.

All that winter of 1947, Joseph Brown had been looking for Black Elk, following the thread of the old man's travels across many western states. When they first met, the two men sat side by side on a sheepskin and in silence smoked the red stone pipe Brown had brought. There was no talking, and, in that sense, there could be no listening.

Black Elk did not seem much of a great and powerful holy man. He wore greasy, tattered Salvation Army clothing. His hair was thin. He was so nearly blind that he had to be guided down the rows digging and harvesting potatoes. Still, in that first, strained meeting, what Brown noticed was the beauty in Black Elk's face and the reverent quality of his motion. Black Elk was a beautiful man, and his face shone because of that, no matter how old, how wrinkled, how filled with despair and the bitter soup of failure the old man might be.

Brown spent that first winter living with Black Elk and his family in a hand-hewn log house under pine-covered bluffs. It was very cold, and much time was spent cutting and hauling wood for the cast iron stove, cutting ice in the stream or hauling water from a handpump eight miles away, and hunting for wild game. In the time that remained, Joseph Brown was able to record many thoughts and words of Black Elk and of his family members. All these records Brown made into a book called *The Sacred Pipe, Black Elk's Account of the Seven Rites of the Oglala Sioux.*

In 1947, specialists in universities believed that not only was the hoop of Black Elk's nation and of all the Indian nations broken, but that very soon all Indians would be assimilated into a thing the specialists called "larger American Society."

It hasn't turned out like that, though. Even the rich and powerful wonder if what they've done is right. There's been a shattering of a world of false dreams, a world that for all but a very few people has been an eternal nightmare. All the lands are lands of dreamy dreams, and all the peoples are relearning how to make choices about which dreams they choose to live with. Soon people will know not only how to read and write, but how, as Black Elk remembered, to listen and speak.

## 1828
### Middle Fork of the Powder River
### A Thief

Private property is theft, we all know. It doesn't take a Communist to figure it out. But if you are a thief, you can dream up a million and two methods to defend your right to steal. Everything we take from the earth, every drop of rain and every blade of grass, every bit of flower and fruit, the sinew and muscle of the animals we kill, we borrow these things for a brief time, and we will pay them back. The records are kept from the beginning of time.

Now Antonio Mateo is ignoring what he knows. He is hacking down trees with a dull axe. The rough handle releases splinters into Antonio's hands. He thinks these will be his only punishment for appropriating the earth for himself—small price to pay—and he proceeds as if nothing left behind will ever catch up. He builds several rough cabins and calls them a trading post. The cabins are his property, the first property in Wyoming, and he will defend his right to hold them forever.

That is why it is no surprise that the first wheeled vehicle—a haphazardly built carriage—to cross the mountains carries a cannon. And no surprise that the cannon is hauled by a team of mules—animals made from the unnatural crossing of the horse and the ass.

There are more events in Antonio Mateo's life, and they all serve to increase his property. Now, long after Antonio is dead, men own more things in Wyoming. There are thirty-eight species of mammals here, and men own them. The State owns them. The State owns the elk, moose, black bear, grizzly bear, white tailed deer, mule deer, pronghorn antelope, Bighorn sheep. The State owns more animals than it can name. It owns the undiscovered insects and the fossils of animals dead before it was born. The United States Biological Survey owns the migratory birds—the ones that live part of the year in Arizona, in Sonora, in the southern states of México, in Guatemala, Honduras, Nicaragua, all the southern lands to the burning tip of frozen Tierra del Fuego. It owns the coyote, bobcat, mountain lion, bald eagle, golden eagle, all the hawks and owls. The Forest Service, the Game and Fish Commission and the officials of the various grazing laws share ownership of the ptarmigan, swan, seagull, and bittern.

In winter the snow falls from the unowned sky to the ground. In spring the snowpack melts into creeks and streams; the runoff pours downhill into rivers and reservoirs owned by the U.S. Bureau of Reclamation. The Reclamation and Fisheries helicopters thwunk-thwunk-thwunk their way into the air and over water release a silver cloud, a sheen, sparkling and dappling in the air—fingerling fish of many kinds, and the Bureaus own the fish. Bureau airplanes seed the clouds to see if perhaps the renegade sky might become property. The Department of Agriculture, and the Department of the Interior own the trees. They own the sage and the wild raspberries.

Somebody owns everything. Everything is private property. This way no one—no person, no other animal, no plant, no rock or clod of dirt—owns itself. Everything belongs to someone else and will be used by its owner.

A magpie spins across an opening, black and white flashing, long tail whipping tartly behind. It is not so simple as saying that, like the sky, no one owns the magpie. The bird is not arrogant, not laughing, not craftily eluding the owners. No, the magpie is out of breath, nervous and running for its life.

## 1880
### Union Pacific Line
### A Friendly Contest

Fifty million buffalo have disappeared. Some have died of the assorted diseases of old age, some of cold and hunger, some have found themselves running impossibly off the side of a cliff. They fly up and out for a moment then begin the drift downward into the waiting arms of their Indian friends.

These events account for many deaths, but there are others more numerous. The Union Pacific Railroad grinds inexorably westward across southern Wyoming. As the buffalo stray along the route, the workers shoot them—in anger, in desperation, in boredom. Along the shining track smelling of steel and oil is another smell—that of rotting flesh. It is piled up in mounds, a swath of death miles wide.

When the tracks are finished and the trains begin to roll, the custom continues. Whenever buffalo are sighted, the trains slow and the passengers get ready. The railroad offers the pleasure of shooting buffalo from the comfort of one's coach. The men (and a few ladies guided by these men's skilled fingers) lean out the car windows, and from breech loaders the bullets fly. Thousands of the animals fall and die. Others fall, rise, and stumble away from the tracks to die later in hidden ravines.

The train steams on, and with each sighting of buffalo the shooting is repeated until the thousands become hundreds of thousands become millions. The entire plains becomes a chain of putrefaction. The valleys and hills disappear under the carpet of disappearing buffalo.

In the interests of personal hygiene, Union Pacific rules forbid the dragging of the bodies on board, so they lie where they fall. Soon all runs must be made with the windows closed to spare the sensibilities of the passengers.

The famous hunter Buffalo Bill Cody got his start this way—not as a passenger but as a marksman for the Kansas Pacific Railroad. In one seventeen month period, he singlehandedly killed 4,280 of the large beasts. Of fifty million, that is not so many.

The buffalo is as endless as the plains. This is its doom. Rancher Granville Stuart says two animals sustain the Indian way of life—the horse and the buffalo. Get rid of these two and you will have gotten rid of the Indian, no matter how many red-skinned men continue to walk the earth.

But the Indians are oiling their bodies, a few horses have escaped into the hills, and there are still ten million buffalo. Buffalo Bill sends forth a challenge. "Let us have an afternoon contest to see which man can kill the most."

Another famous hunter—Mr. Comstock—responds, and the day is set. But on the appointed morning, Mr. Comstock suffers diarrhea and queasy stomach and cannot attend. He is still adjusting to the food and water of the West. In his place he sends a Mr. Galeano.

Buffalo Bill rides straight into the herd and splits it in two. He gets his group of buffalo circling, always crowding the animals. He shoots the leaders and keeps the others circling. In a few hours he has killed 69 buffalo. He steps down from his horse, sweaty and pleased.

Now it is don Eduardo's turn. Surprising everyone, he spurns the horse and appears driving a Jeep. He stands up in the back of the speeding vehicle and holds an American made M-16 automatic rifle above his head. He fires off a rapid burst, then another. He pumps out as many bullets by himself as an entire trainload of hunters. But instead of firing into the herd, Galeano fires into the sky. The clouds crumble, and the fragile blue is rent.

The weapon heats up, burning the hunter's hands. Galeano hurls the M-16 away then he jumps from the speeding jeep which, driverless, veers precariously left and right until it rolls and bursts into flame. Now Galeano rises, again himself, and brings his hand to his face. The skin on the right side is scraped off, and blood covers his nose and mouth. His left shoulder is dislocated, and his right knee is swollen and bruised. His pants are torn, and he's lost one shoe. He feels pretty bad, but he also feels momentarily at ease.

Seeing his opportunity, Mr. Comstock rises from his dysentery like torpor and grabs the automatic rifle. He charges into the herd driving it straight ahead in front of him. With the same zeal of Buffalo Bill, but without this latter's finesse, Comstock begins to fire, oblivious to his burning hands. The buffalo fall in a great mound. In a short time the entire herd lies still, a smoking pile.

Mr. Comstock walks back to the reviewing table with a smile on his face. Ever the gentleman, Buffalo Bill runs to congratulate the victorious hunter, slapping him on the back and shouting, "Good work."

Both Cody and Comstock look happy, but the buffalo do not look happy—they look dead. And Galeano doesn't look happy—he looks as if he's caught Comstock's illness and might soil his pants.

When whites began to kill the buffalo, they learned that if the lead buffalo is shot, the others will be unable to act. They mill about and paw the ground. They bellow and rumble. The contending males must negotiate for a new leader, and until that time the herd cannot act.

During this process, the hunters kill the young and the females. Frenzied by the deaths, the remaining animals sometimes go crazy. They attack one another, gore and trample the injured and dying. The local Indians say that a herd that has had this experience never recovers. Its members will be forever deranged, impossible to approach, impossible to hunt on horseback with bow and arrow.

"That's right," don Eduardo says, "An experience like that deranges you." He grabs the still-hot automatic rifle and aims it at both

Comstock and Buffalo Bill.

Cody smiles and says, "That's some rifle you got there." Then he turns away. When he turns back, he is holding two glasses of champagne. Buffalo Bill extends one glass to Mr. Comstock and another to Mr. Galeano, saying, "Here's to the winning hunter. It's a good day for champagne, champagne's a good drink for the prairie, and a buffalo hunter's a good man to do the drinking."

## 1846

### SUBLETTE CUTOFF
### LITTLE LEFT BUT GRAVES

In Mexico City another sixteen-year-old girl enters the convent
and dies to this world:

>Thou hast chosen the good road
>now no one can remove thee
>chosen one
>no one no one nothing
>can remove thee
>far from the battles of great Babylon
>corruption temptations dangers
>far
>never

María, Teresa, Juana, she waves goodbye, riding in a gilded carriage through streets of silver, waving goodbye to those she will never see again. She eats a last meal, listening carefully to the ring of precious cutlery on handpainted china, memorizing the scenes painted under the steaming food—the pointing dogs holding ducks in their mouths, the bucolic misty afternoons of country life and squires and dames, the mighty four-masted ships sailing across the bottomless seas.

She strokes her hair one last time and carefully removes her many adornments—the blazing feathers of formerly sacred birds, the priceless sapphires and pearls, the fabrics dyed with the intensity of indigo. When the last comes off, the light comes with it, and she is bathed in darkness.

Now her hair is shorn. She eats from a heavy clay bowl and in the center of her table is a skull for centerpiece and companion. She sleeps on a bed of stone and raw lumber. Her dress is a robe of harsh wool tearing at her fine skin. When the sun shines, she sweats and stinks and is thankful for her shame. Walking in rain, she becomes heavy, dank, unbearable. She is praying to not know herself, to suffer humbly for sins she has not committed, for acts she is unable to picture, for desires she has never grown to have.

Women's voices chant, then sing. Blackness spins around her face and black wings sprout from her shoulders. The black light of blackened candles smokes, filling the room.

Crossing Wyoming, a young girl is reborn. The handhewn wagons with wooden wheels as tall as a man bounce noisily over the rutted high plains. Each rut delivers a blow that can break the teeth in the jaws of the most determined soul. Up the North Platte River, they toil to Fort Laramie and on to the confluence. They follow the Sweetwater to the Continental Divide at South Pass then the trail splays out, collapses in myriad directions, becomes purposeless.

In late June along the Sweetwater, there are two feet of new snow. A thousand oxen are dead, and the causes are too many to name. Everyone has suffered violent racking fevers. Some say it is from saleratus picked up on alkali flats and used in cooking. Potash poisoning. One man has whirled in a wind and mistakenly shot another man. The rivers run high and strong, and, at every crossing, ferries must be built from green timber and lashed with rotten rope. At one crossing, as if in retribution, a whirling man is washed away and drowns. Even on the Sabbath, unremittingly, they push on to escape infected water, malarial mosquitos, blowing sand that penetrates half-inch canvas and closed eyes.

Each summer thousands stumble and burn across a sweltering desert, then freeze and fall ascending mountains never devoid of snow. The usual crossing of this yet-to-be-named purgatory is under thirty days. For most travelers, that is the plan—to cross as quickly as possible. It occurs to scarcely anyone to make this place a home. The men whip their oxen, whip their wives and children, whip themselves, and long to whip the red men who slow their passage. Thousands of lashes of the whip each summer for thousands of sometimes equivocal, sometimes confident adventurers. They are driven onward by lust, by fear, by dreams weighty with obscene mineral riches, or by the tentative hope of a place of their own.

So many travelers; so many passages. And how much they leave of themselves to mark their transit. There are the deepening ruts in the earth. There is the long list of unreadable names and dates etched haphazardly into eroding stones and trailside cliffs. There are pieces of oak planking and walnut chairs and bedsteads, wheezing organs the wind fills with melodyless song, fractured pianos with severed strings, leather trunks sprung open, and silk dresses and scarves strewn across the sage.

And there are graves. Two days past Devil's Gate, Matilda Crowley finally dies. Born July 16, 1830, she dies on July 7, 1846. Nine days short of her sixteenth birthday, she dies to this world. Sweet sixteen. Never been kissed. Her pale lips are parted by the heat. Her hand rests half closed in a parody of a wave. Her mother throws herself across the silent girl and smothers her with life. Her father slams his fist into the side of a wagon and screams. An ashen skull smiles from the center of a perfectly set table. The wagons roll on, and behind distant gilded carriages, beautiful blue flowers spring up and blossom together.

# 1989
## GILLETTE
## OUR NAVY

The U.S. Navy recruiter in Gillette answers the phone "Ahoy there, shipmate," and concludes his conversation by wishing to all "Fair seas and fresh winds." Or else "Fair winds and fresh seas."

But the seas departed Wyoming millenia ago, and in this land of almost 100,000 square miles, only 366 are water. Of the Platte they say a mile wide and one inch deep. And the Powder isn't named such for capricious reasons. Mostly, there isn't enough water here to float a duck, and a battleship would make a nice windbreak for sheep. So eight recruiters sit in offices and polish their shoes until they reflect the sky a watery blue.

Far away in Puget Sound, the Navy attempts to train bottlenosed dolphins. Never mind that these bottlenose are Atlantic dolphins unable to live in the North Pacific's cold water. The blood vessels in their skin contract to retain heat, the skin disintegrates and sloughs off and the dolphins are vulnerable to infection. And never mind the family and social life of the dolphin. Here, each animal is placed in a twenty-five square foot tank fourteen feet deep.

Dolphins can protect the Navy's submarines from Russian frogmen; dolphins can learn to fire poison pellets, or $CO_2$ cartridges, or bullets; dolphins can learn to kill.

But so far the dolphins have learned to kill only themselves. Some bash themselves against the walls of their pens until they pass out and, unconscious, drown. Some die of stomach ulcers. Some refuse to eat, starving themselves to death.

Those who do not kill themselves are "destroyed." The Navy says they destroy only those dolphins who "go insane." One dolphin is blind—her trainer has beaten her across the face with a bucket. Another dies of open wounds—he has been kicked in the head until he bleeds, and the bleeding will not stop.

No one knows how many dolphins the Navy has. No one knows how many dolphins have died, have been murdered, have committed suicide, have "gone insane."

"Ahoy there, shipmates," Ron says with a smile. And on the billboard above scrub desert, the U.S. Navy jets scream sweetly toward the sea, toward the dolphins.

The U.S. Navy in Wyoming has eight sailors and an officer, all recruiting. When they snap to attention, dust flowers around their heads, obscuring their eyes. When they speak, dust billows around their mouths, and mixed with their saliva, muddies all their words. When they walk, dust rises from their feet and mixes with the snow to form a gray wall reminiscent of a fog bank settling on a dock.

In Wyoming, the U.S. Navy is silly and superfluous, but the world is small and one. Though the cottonwoods, the aspen, the willow, all the trees of this quiet dry land, are rooted, though they would be terrified by the sea, though they have never felt the touch of a dolphin on their bark, though everything that a person could say of them about ignorance and distance is true, still, they know. The trees of Wyoming know the lives of the slave dolphins of Puget Sound. The trees refuse to fight so they weep. And in this driest of lands, we too commit that ultimate act of excess, we weep.

## 1989
### BUFFALO
### THE ANXIETY NOW

Lt. Col. Bill Cappella announces that a test of the MX missile rail launch system has been successful. A 200,000 pound slug of concrete and steel has been shot one hundred feet into the air from a rail car, and the rail car did not collapse.

Now it will be possible to give freedom to the fifty MX missiles locked underground near Cheyenne, Wyoming, to lift all fifty up into the sunlight, load them on rail cars and send them touring throughout the state. They will ascend the steep grades of the mountains, run through the shimmering heat waves rising from the basins, circle the sites of Yellowstone Park and cruise dreamlessly along the artificial-looking ramparts of the Tetons. These missiles will not be made solely of concrete and steel.

Wyoming potter Margo Brown sits down at the wheel before a lump of clay and begins to spin. She has thrown thousands of pots, but today she feels unable to work, as if something were throwing her and she hasn't the strength to throw it in return. While she works, her husband scrawls on page after page of paper, then crumples each and lets it fall to the floor. He will sweep up later.

The couple's eleven month old daughter, Caitlin Belem, smiles at both her parents. Then she cries, screams, wails, gurgles, smiles again and falls silent. Living with their child, the couple learns both joy and despair. It is no longer possible to watch life as if one were in a train station in winter watching the bundled up passengers ascend and descend the 5:30 Express.

Caitlin Belem is an old soul, one who for many generations has lived in the world of spirit. Now she enters a new world, a world threatened by poisons of many kinds, poisons made and distributed by her human brethren. She is trying out the body one last time.

Sometimes in the most difficult of situations people will attempt to smile and tell one another a small joke. A woman will screw her face up into silly parodies of other faces. A man will hold his hands up before the light and make shapes that throw shadows on a wall—a rabbit, a barking dog, a butterfly in delicious flight. A child will join in—grabbing a broom and demonstrating a dance recently learned at school, the dance in which there is one extra person and when all the couples sway together, that extra person is left alone dancing perfectly with the broom.

Now everyone is dancing the adult version of this dance. Each dancer is alone, swaying with the bomb.

The missiles ride among us making their threats. As they ride, the days grow hotter and hotter. It is really summer. The temperature is rising, and the U.S. Environmental Protection Agency tells us that because of human actions in the past this rising cannot be stopped. Wyoming's weather tomorrow will be what Colorado's is today, then Arizona's, Sonora's, hotter and hotter. Uncovered skin will bubble and peel. The seas will rise and cover the shores. The amount of carbon dioxide in the atmosphere will double. Human beings are sending themselves on a long trip to another world. They plan to leave nothing behind.

Since the beginning of time, the inhabitants of Wyoming have awaited summer. It is so brief! From its first moment, its ardor is cooled by the knowledge that winter will soon return.

Sometimes the buds begin to pop in March only to be coated in ice—frozen and blackened. Every year the trees take this risk—pushing to burst into leaf long before a thoughtful or reasonable creature would make the attempt. And the birds return from the south only to find themselves huddled under the ubiquitous April and May blizzards. They throw their feathers out blowing their bodies up to twice their size. The people shake themselves out of parkas and boots then curse the cold as it slices through their frail skin.

We dream of summer, but, soon, we may die of our dream. The Environmental Protection Agency lists several ways people must adapt so that "summer mortality rates may be substantially reduced."

It is the summer of madness and fear—the earth is being poisoned, the air is being poisoned, the water is being poisoned. The bombmakers announce further successes. The businessmen of war invest some billions of dollars to build an airplane whose only passengers will be shining urns filled with radioactive flowers.

Potter Margo Brown and her husband sit down with their daughter. "Tree," they say, "This is a tree, a weeping birch." And the leaves tremble in the wind and the sky is the blue it has been for longer than can be named.

"The wind," Margo says to her daughter Caitlin Belem. "This is the wind," and blows in the child's face and the child laughs and sighs. They sit through the long, summer afternoon. At night Margo says, "Moonlight, my dear. Almost bright enough to read by. Soon you'll know how to read."

Tree and wind and moonlight in the sky. And rain. And the porcupine lumbering across an open field. And six elk on a hillside. And clouds. And the most beautiful word in any language is "and." And this, Caitlin Belem, and that. And. Because it tells us there will be some more. Because it reminds us of something we love but forgot. Because it is hope.

And we do have hope. So what, we laugh, when reminded of the missiles.

When don Eduardo appears, waving his arms and calling, Margo Brown nods and says, "Poor don Eduardo, regaling us with his bitter tales. Not that we don't agree with him, you understand. We do. And not that we don't know what the world is like. We do."

Still, Margo and her husband and their daughter sit together. Here is the world—trees, and wind, and clouds, and sky, and moonlight on the face of an old soul. And and, and and, and and.

# 1950
## Highway 395
### A Bleeding Trailer

Having had it with the tumult and slime of Wyoming's inelegant past, don Eduardo hotwires a black Ford pickup in Evanston and heads out across Utah for Nevada, whence he hops south through Arizona and Sonora to steaming Chiapas and the familiar reaches of Guatemala.

He drives through the first hot day and into the night. Sometime in that night on Nevada Highway 395, black rain begins to fall. Brightened by the yellow glow of the headlights, the black drops turn crimson and land. Under the incessant beating of the windshield wipers, the drops don't clear away like water but soften and spread like a delicious syrup. Soaking up the sweet paste, the glass begins to bloat.

Don Eduardo cranes his neck left to right trying to see through the thickening layer. He rolls down the window and leans far out to his left and forward, wrapping his arm around the radio antenna and scrubbing at the glass with his palm. When he brings it back inside the pickup, the smell almost makes him faint—blood. And only then does he notice it is not falling from above but flying back at him from a truck he has followed for miles, a truck that, it now appears, is leaking blood.

Forgetting the far reaches of anywhere, Eduardo Galeano makes every turn the truck in front of him makes, careening through the night. Galeano can't see through the blood-smeared windscreen and so follows blindly, by feel, and by smell. For part of the night he closes his eyes and sleeps, fitfully, following all the while the bleeding trailer.

Before dawn, the truck stops and the driver clambers down. Don Eduardo pulls up behind him and stops, steps out, and looks around, pulling a flashlight from his pants and shining it ahead of himself. In the narrow beams of light, he can see bits and pieces of animals shoved thickly into the trailer. They're horses, and the fleeing Latin makes a quintessentially Latin joke—"Oh, thank God, it's only a truck-load of bloody horses. I was worried your truck was bleeding to death."

The nighttime teamster looks at don Eduardo and begins walking around his steaming truck, a hammer in his right hand, striking each tire.

The horses are packed in tight, so tight that a colt who has slipped has been unable to rise and been trampled into a pulp of muscle and skin and assorted fluids. The stallion in the band is blind, his eyes shot out. The mares are pocked with buckshot holes. Several of the horses' lips hang loose and torn where they have been shot off. All the horses stand on bloody stumps, their hooves worn off from their ragged flight across rocks and ravines.

"Where did these horses come from?" don Eduardo asks. "Why are they in such bad shape?"

And the man with the hammer says, "Oh, they was run in by plane."

They was run in by plane. Over the Red Desert, over the Pryor Mountains, over the many-sided emptiness of the Great Basin, they was run in, the plane coming in low with sirens screaming, the horses screaming too as they back up into a corner. Men lean out and fire buckshot into the herd. The plane banks and turns, circling, buzzing the stricken horses who finally run.

Watch how the lead mare leaps, threading the countless needles through which she must pass to find escape. In the fall she was captured by men who tied her down and sewed her nostrils shut then released her. She can breathe enough to walk but not to run, and now she will slow down her band. But no, now she will run until her heart explodes, until the blood leaks into her lungs sealed from air and on blood alone she will keep running.

They stampede away and down, across the pocked land, onto the plains where they are shadowed by trucks that keep them running. The mare drops of exhaustion, and as she falls, a last burst of air comes from her, tearing the coarse thread from her nostrils which, again free, quiver and flare.

Watch how the second mare becomes the lead mare. In November she was captured and a horseshoe bent around her leg. She can walk, but when she runs, the cuff of metal bashes at her, bruises her, tears the hair and skin off. It slows down the band. But no, she runs—twenty, thirty, forty miles an hour—looping through the myriad eyes of the hidden needles. She runs until she can't. Her hindquarters go down and she keeps running, another quarter mile on a leg that's turned to spaghetti, a leg with pieces of bone protruding every which way, until she falls.

The stallion keeps on, bringing up the rear, turning periodically to threaten whatever it is that chases the band. For a moment he stops, facing what follows, and in that moment the plane banks and buckshot flies. Blind, the stallion turns and runs.

The other horses understand what's happening and try to turn but can't. The men in their plane understand, too. The airplane spins and reels. Now the trucks come on and, as a third mare slows, a man leans out and tosses a rope around the animal's neck. At the end of the rope is a hundred pound tire. If the whiplash doesn't snap the horse's neck, the weight will wear her down till she drops.

Deranged and dehydrated, the horses begin to fight with themselves. They rear up. They trample each other. Finally the mutilated remnants are roped and dragged on their sides up wooden planks into the waiting trailer, the trailer that stands, motor idling, bleeding in the night.

One more hammer blow and the driver is ready to move on.

"Where are you taking these horses?" Galeano ventures. "When do you feed and water them?"

"California, rendering factory. No feed, they're going Killer Rate."

"Rendering factory? Killer Rate?"

"Yeah, where you from? You don't work with stock. These are wild horses, brother, no good for nothing but dog food. Transportation Department reg—any animal that's being shipped to slaughter no need to feed and water, just a waste of money. They're dead anyway. The regs call it 'condemned cargo.' Just drive."

"Just drive."

"Yeah." And the man climbs back up in the cab. He leans down and says goodbye, "Adiós, amigo."

"Sure. Adiós." And, after wiping the windshield as clean as he can with his shirt, don Eduardo climbs into the pickup and turns back toward Wyoming, back to that land of wild horses and wild horse hunters. He parks the pickup where he found it, leaving the keys under the seat and taping a note of thanks onto the steering wheel.

Walking away, straight out into the Red Desert toward the horses, he thinks about that word render. "Render what?" he says out loud. Render oneself.

# PART II

# 1839
## INDIAN COUNTRY
## FREE TRADE

For some years Father Pierre-Jean De Smet, called Black Robe by the plains people who know and trust him, has written letter after letter denouncing the liquor trade with the red Indians. But his letters have disappeared like the leaves on the trees in fall. His Jesuit superiors have cut his letters to pieces and glued them together again so they make no sense or so they are only comments on the beauty of the scenery and the grandeur of God's work on this earth.

"Liquor will be the ruin of all the Indian people," De Smet warns. "It brings in its wake war, famine and pestilence. The country here is overrun with vagabond Americans trafficking with the perpetually drunken tribesmen."

Father De Smet cannot adequately express his outrage. He holds his head in his hands, looking up now and again at the scene around him. The government has decided to pay one tribe $50,000 a year, which the tribe turns over to the traders for liquor alone. These Indians are drunk from January 1 to December 31. They grovel and fight, falling reeling face down on the earth. They lap up the vermin infested dirt as if it were a sumptuous banquet. Their bodies are furnaces filled with flame. They are sickness. Liquor is a tarantula to them—once bitten, their bodies burst into flame. They burn and cry out only for more whiskey. More, more, more. Consumed by the flames, they collapse, a pile of rotten, stinking carcasses. As the alcohol haze and fumes evaporate, these same red souls rise ready to drink anew.

Father De Smet again takes his pen in hand. "I have walked by the trading houses where whiskey is sold, and the scene is of misery alone. The road is strewn with the forms of men, women and children in the last stages of burning intoxication. Naked, starving children lie in their own excrement and vomit, shaking, their bones rattling in the cages of their bodies.

"I saw a drunk man take his own child by the legs and swing it like a stick at one of the posts of his lodge. The child snapped and was crushed, its insides falling out onto the earth, its mother drunkenly watching."

Exhausted, Father De Smet throws the pen away and lifts his face to stare heavenward. It's spring and the trees begin to bud and the sky softens to blue. And the white traders arrive ready for another round in a prolonged war of extermination. They bring fifty barrels, each holding thirty gallons of whiskey, brandy or rum.

The traders distribute their gifts, and again the red recipients reel in confusion—screaming, singing, crying, roaring. Quarrel follows quarrel. Blow falls upon blow. Club, tomahawk, spear, knife, all fly soundlessly through the wailing air.

"Between May and September of this year," Father De Smet reports, "I witnessed seventy-four violent deaths due to alcohol. In winter, with no preparations made, the people were reduced to subsisting on acorns and roots. Some years ago, the American government, mindful of its responsibilities, passed a law forbidding the setting up of a still anywhere in Indian Country. But no one distills whiskey here, they just bring it in. It is whiskey that is killing these people, not stills."

"Ce n'est pas la verité," a voice says.

And Father De Smet whirls, "Who speaks to me in French, and what do you mean that what I say is not true?"

Don Eduardo beckons from nearby, from slightly farther west, from the great plains, from the mountains, from the beginnings of distance.

Father De Smet rises and the two men walk. They cross a prairie three miles wide and completely filled with wild onions. The air swings full of the pungent scent. They cross another field in which grows wild asparagus, hundreds of thousands of green spears shooting up from the earth. Everywhere there are strawberries, blackberries, gooseberries, plums, cherries, grapes. And nuts of all kinds.

"How far does this go on?" Father De Smet asks.

They walk for days across the same bluffs and bottoms and mountains. It is verdant and empty. A man is made dizzy by the unending sameness and wealth. God has diverted himself by repeating over and over the forms that first entertained him.

Now they walk through the trees—oak and walnut and cottonwood and willow and sassafras and the acacia whose flower loads the air with sweet perfume.

Father De Smet stops. "This land seems as pure and clean as the day God made it. People have not yet despoiled it. It is not yet afflicted by people's diseases and defeats. In this land I could do God's work bringing the true message of redemption and salvation."

Don Eduardo stops, too. To the good father he says, "Yes, this land is clean, but people have been here for millennia—red people."

Up the Missouri the St. Peter steams, bringing an assorted cargo. When the boat stops, the curious red Indians swarm over it, peering in every corner, touching every piece of metal and wood, every smooth enameled fitting. Everything these people touch is filled with disease, the one the whites call smallpox.

The St. Peter steams on and, daily, red men die. The survivors throw the bodies of the dead over cliffs and into gullies. Entire villages are filled with the stench of these dead. Tents stand empty, and tent flaps whip in the wind. This and the throaty call of the raven are the only sounds. There is no smoke from fires. No one is home. The river people are dead.

The two men keep walking. North and west, always in the distance, there are people living in the ever smaller clean land. The bright

Sioux lodges are painted with beautiful wavy lines—red, yellow and white. The bright lined Sioux lodges are covered with paintings of horses, deer, buffalo, moons, suns, stars.

His spirit lifting again, Father De Smet says, "It is truly a garden."

"Yes," don Eduardo agrees.

"How many buffalo do you think there are?" Father De Smet asks.

Looking up, don Eduardo answers, "How many stars?"

"You mean the buffalo are as endless as the stars."

"Yes, that's what I mean."

Yes, as endless as the stars, but the stars aren't endless. It's just that we can't see them all. If we start today, finally we will count them all. And if we fire a gun at each star one at a time, eventually we can knock every star from the sky.

"It's not whiskey, Pierre-Jean," Galeano says sharply, "Not whiskey that is killing your savage little brothers. It is the loss of all this—the wild plants, the trees, the water, the buffalo, the stars in the sky, the sky itself, the loss of everything."

"The loss of everything," Father De Smet whispers.

"Yes, the loss of everything," don Eduardo repeats.

"The loss of everything," God says from his Heaven.

Perhaps drink is the answer. Among some of the savages, one who returns from war having killed an enemy paints a red hand across his mouth to show he has drunk the blood of the slain one.

"I saw them lying in a stupor along the road—men, women and children, their hair matted, dried feces caked along their scabrous legs, the eyes blind in their emptied heads. Now and again one would rise from his drunken revery and angrily argue with a neighbor. The shouting would grow louder and louder until a fight would start, and often one man would bite off the nose of another. The nose spat out and lying on the ground, the two men would collapse, blood running down each one's face, blood pouring over them, splashing from their lips to their feet in puddles."

Yes, it's true, Father. Everything that happens is true. Look to the east, there coming toward the bloody, noseless drunks are the white men, red hands painted across their mouths.

1889

BOTHWELL

HAPPINESS

The Wyoming Stock Growers' Association decides who will live and who will die in the same manner that it decides the fate of a cow. Mr. A. J. Bothwell has incorporated himself on the banks of Horse Creek. He and $300,000 are now the Sweetwater Land and Improvement Company. His town, Bothwell, includes a store, blacksmith shop, post office, saloon and his newspaper, the *Sweetwater Chief*. Mr. Bothwell had planned to be happy, but so far he is not.

He is not happy because Jim Averell is running a road ranch—a store and saloon—three miles east of Independence Rock, within sniffing distance of Bothwell. And Averell has homesteaded along the Sweetwater a piece of public domain that Bothwell considers his own. And Averell writes letters to the editor of the *Casper Weekly Mail* condemning Bothwell and other "range hogs" who are preventing settlers from locating along the Sweetwater. In 1887 Bothwell told Averell to get out of the country while he still had his health. Averell's face makes Mr. Bothwell unhappy.

Ella Watson, another girl gone wrong, comes up to work for Jim and files on a homestead a mile from his. Now Mr. Bothwell is twice as unhappy. Jim and Ella are selling whiskey, beef stew and biscuits. Jim is selling Ella to local cowboys. The cowboys are selling cows to Ella. And there is some evidence that, in their spare time, with no thought of sales, Jim and Ella are making love.

The Wyoming Stock Growers' Association has had enough. When Ella and Jim file to register their brands, the Carbon County brand committee rejects both applications. Mr. Bothwell, along with fellow stock growers Tom Sun, John Durbin, Rob Conners, Ernest McLain and R. M. Galbreath kidnap Ella and Jim. They tell Ella they're taking her on a trip to Rawlins. When she turns to go into her house and change clothes, they throw her into a wagon. They tell Jim they have a warrant for his arrest. When he asks to see the warrant, they stroke their rifles.

At Spring Creek Canyon the men have thrown ropes over the limbs of a scrub pine. Mr. McLain is trying to place a rope around Ella's neck, but she keeps dodging her head around. When McLain finally succeeds, Ella and Jim are asked politely to jump off the limestone ledge on which they stand.

What matters in a hanging is who gets hung. No, what matters in a hanging is the act itself. When people decide they need to hang someone, that someone can always be found.

Don Eduardo wakes from a dream of enclosure in a nap of space. He's lying on a mat of scratchy brush, and the dust powdering his face makes him sneeze. He wipes the little moisture onto his dirty pants, wipes his face with his now damp hand, then rubs his neck, the back of which is burnt raw from a week of walking around hatless in the sun.

Last month don Eduardo was in London for Queen Victoria's birthday, the city lit up like a harlot. Then he was in Montevideo for a football match between Argentina and Uruguay. There was the clink of crystal glasses and the sharp report of silver knives on bone china plates. Legs of steel flashed, and mouths turned in parodies of pain. Blue blazers and mock coats of arms, overwrought silk ties and high black shoes of thirty eyelets to guarantee interminable lacing. History was spun with commerce and banking, sport with colonialism and blood.

Don Eduardo had reached an impasse. He'd reached a river impossible to bridge. He had his notebooks, but he no longer knew what to record and what to ignore. That's when he booked passage to the Sweetwater along which he's been wandering, his neck burning, his fingers scratching in the dust, calligraphing the questions that might illuminate the relations between his beloved history and that stranger nature.

Daydreaming as he walks, don Eduardo stumbles over a log. As he falls, he turns and sees the log is a leg. The man whose leg it is rolls away and aims his pistol toward the falling man. Don Eduardo, striking his head, returns to the world of sleep. When the shot explodes in the furnace that is his mind, don Eduardo stays low. The leg he'd fallen over is carrying its owner as fast as it can away. Other legs, both human and horse, churn past. For a few moments it is like everywhere in the world, the air full of bullets and wind, the good historian hugging the earth, which he is unable to love.

With the returning stillness, don Eduardo stands. He writes down the name of the man he'd tripped over—Frank Buchanan. In front of him swaying in the air are two bodies—a man and a woman. He writes down their names. He steps forward to act, then stops.

Yes, Don Eduardo has taken a vow of non-interference. As an historian, he has pledged to chronicle the suffering of all souls impartially and objectively. But even modern science knows the observer interacts with the observed. A man can ascertain where he is or how fast he's going, but not both at once. There is no truth that is not condemned and clarified by an equal and opposite truth.

Some days later, a sheriff's party returns to find three bodies swaying in the morning breeze. It's cool now, but it's been summer Wyoming hot, and Jim Averell, Ella Watson, and Eduardo Galeano swing rank and bloated. Their blue-black puffy faces resemble nothing so much as exploded prunes. Jim and Ella hang side by side, arms touching. All three leer, tongues protruding. Having fallen only two feet off the ledge, they died not by broken necks but by strangulation. The mocassins Ella wore, purchased at the river from a band of Indians on that long ago sunny morning, have fallen from her feet and lie on the ground. A local rancher's wife picks them up as souvenirs. Four witnesses name the men who murdered Ella and Jim. No one recognizes don Eduardo nor the foreign rope cinched around his neck. And when the living turn, the third member in the party of the dead disappears.

The murderers are indicted. But the Wyoming Stock Growers' Association has been carefully at work. The telegraph wires hum reporting Jim and Ella as notorious cattle thieves who have terrorized the honest citizens of the Sweetwater Valley for years and who are guilty of murders too numerous to name. Newspapers establish Jim as King of the Cattle Thieves and Ella as Cattle Kate Maxwell, Bandit Queen. There is no mention of a third body.

The indicted men's hearing is held privately in a local hotel room. No witnesses are called, and though first degree murder is not a charge subject to bail, the six men sign bonds as character references for each other and are released.

Later, none of the four witnesses to the murders can be found— Frank Buchanan and the second witness have disappeared, the third is shot dead and his body burned to ash, and the last, a fourteen-year-old boy, dies before the case is heard. The murderers are found not guilty.

Mr. A. J. Bothwell has Ella's cabin lifted up on skids, dragged cross country to his ranch and set up as an icehouse. Jim's ranch buildings are torn down. The pines in Spring Creek Gulch are dead from lack of rain while Jim and Ella's shallow graves quickly fill with water seeping from the river. There the two float forever, their bodies not at rest but seeming more to hover at the surface of the world, as if dancing. And, insofar as a cripple can dance, Bothwell is dancing along with the dead couple, luxuriating in the shadow of the strangled woman.

His stomach grumbling and his neck still burnt and raw, don Eduardo sits atop a peak in the Wind River range. From there he looks back and forth from the Andes to the soggy graves. He follows cattle and drinks from the creeks in which they have defecated. He cuts his own flesh inviting mosquitos to drink his blood. He jams hard steaming coyote scat into his bloody wounds. He happily awaits typhus, cholera, malaria, smallpox.

Eduardo Galeano will not break his vows. Because he will not, he is left with only the possibility of breaking himself. As the various hard parts of his body begin to crack, it is clear he is subject to the same pain offered every person, and as he accepts the pain, in that odd triumph, he becomes one with those he cannot help.

## 1899
### CHEYENNE
## TO THE MEMORY OF THOSE PIONEERS

Dr. Charles Giffin Coutant, dressed in heavy wool suitcoat and wide silk tie, his white hair trimmed neat and tight while his equally white beard grows cluttered and untamed, has published the first volume of his proposed three volume work: *The History of Wyoming and (The Far West) Embracing an Account of the Spanish, Canadian and American Explorations; the Experiences and Adventures of Trappers and Traders in the Early Days; Including Events of the Oregon Emigration, the Mormon Movement and Settlements, the Indian Tribes, their Manners and Customs, and their Wars and Depradations on the Overland Trail, etc., etc. Interspersed With Personal Reminiscences of Pioneers With Numerous Engravings.*

Coutant has grouped together the conditions of the wilderness at the time when white men first attempted to bring civilization into these solitudes. In those days ". . .the savage hordes lurked in the dark defiles of our mountains." This was before ". . .our pioneers had freed the land from dangers seen and unseen. It was before our cities, churches and school houses were built. Before our civil institutions were founded and law and order had come to rule the State! Before the great battle of civilization had been fought and won!"

Many are the stories of those first white men who came to name the unnamed, and tame the wild. They plucked the flowers and fruit. They shot the birds and beasts. They hunted the red men.

Now Coutant can report that "Savage men and savage beasts no longer lurk at will in our mountains or roam through our valleys. That great law of nature, 'the survival of the fittest,' has been applied and has done its perfect work. It will be found that what comes after is even more wonderful."

What comes after is even more wonderful. That makes don Eduardo smile his rueful, sad smile. He is sort of a white man himself, but he looks up at the black sky and the Seven Bright People and all the people of the above, and again he dreams. In his dream, every egg ever laid is broken and the shells scattered into the sky. The yolks and whites are endlessly sticky and alive. They take pity on don Eduardo. They forgive him his skin, his breath, his hair and eyes, his thoughts. They forgive everything and light the way. Don Eduardo is sheltered and relieved.

So many worlds, and so many souls all jostling around rampant to be born. One world is white and another is black. One world reeks while another smells sweet. One world is timeless while another is a factory of clockmakers. On one world, the sun is made of water while on another it is made of dust. The thunderclap follows the lightning. Rain falls from darkening clouds.

Like the little girl in the region of the great northern lakes, don Eduardo wakes up to discover he is alive. It is the wonder of this one unfortunate world that opens his eyes. He takes off running, at first as if with a purpose, later more and more in a random fashion. He is unhappy and bitter, then, strangely, the more misery he uncovers, the more he knows about this world of defecation and deceit, the happier he becomes. He thinks of freshly baked bread and falling snow, and the sweet delight of closing one's eyes to sleep.

C. G. Coutant was a historian, and so is Eduardo Galeano. Coutant's was one world, and Galeano's is another. Coutant never asked for forgiveness; don Eduardo asks most every day. But no one needs to ask for forgiveness. It was granted to each of us before we were born.

## 1890

### WIND RIVER

### PICTURE PAINTING, DANCING AND THE CLOSING OF THE FRONTIER

This is the year the United States Census Bureau declares the American frontier officially closed. This is the year 300 Sioux men, women and children lie dead before the wall of bullets from four Hotchkiss artillery guns mounted on a hill above Wounded Knee. This is the year the northern Arapahoe are dancing to bring their dead brothers and sisters home. This is the year the Cheyenne are painting beautiful pictures on vests worn beneath their tunics. This is the year.

Green is from the grasses and trees, from dried algae and the copper-filled earth under our feet. Green is the color of living things and growth. Who could not love green and paint it on her face?

Yellow is from the clay resting in one's hand and pinched into a tiny ball, from the ground gallstones of the buffalo, from the sunrise and the sunset, from pine moss dried in the sun. Yellow is the color of ripeness and perfection, a baby growing in the belly of a woman, a man come finally to be at peace with the urgings within himself. Who could not love yellow and draw it in a great broad stripe across the side of a teepee?

Brown is in every bit of the earth, in all clay, in the branches of the trees when they lie on the ground in the Moon of the Falling Leaves, and in the falling leaves themselves. Brown is from the gum-covered cottonwood buds. Who could not love brown and lie luxuriating in it filled by dream?

Red is from boiled roots and the iron oxide-filled soil and clay. A woman is cooking over a fire—food, warmth, home. Children play nearby and daub bright red on their noses, smear red over their entire bodies in make-believe as if they had been dipped in the blood of a butchered animal and have become that animal and will know it always. Who could not love red and burn in the heat of it wrapped around the body?

Black covers the sky. Gritty charcoal is mixed with yellow earth and with tallow and with the roasted inner bark of a tree. The light from the fire is out, and the flame's warmth is gone. The plants do not grow, and their leaves grow dull and brittle. Still it is only a slowing down, and sometimes slowing down brings ease and the end of struggle between men. Who could not love this black and wipe it in great dark circles around his eyes and mouth?

White is from the chalky earth and a powder found in only one place, a nameless powder that, if eaten, makes one sick. An antelope running moves faster and faster and becomes a blur of motion, a white blur. All the animals become a white blur, the clouds move overhead in a white blur, the earth itself rolls into a blurred ball incapable of being seen. We are alive and in motion. There is no sadness like that of the man in motion. Who could not love this sadness and its white soul? Who could not run long white lines from her shoulder down her arms across the backs of her hands and along each finger, ten fingers pointing away to another world?

Blue is from the excrement of ducks, serene as the open blue sky, and from blue mud and bentonite clay. The blue sky above and below. It doesn't matter where blue comes from. Its beauty and peace carry us away. What man, woman or child could not roll entirely in blue, become blue and fly upward, for all of time through the sky and to Heaven?

The messiah has returned and calls himself Wovoka. He is a fisheater from Nevada. From him comes the word that all Indians must dance. Dance everywhere, dance always, keep dancing and the Great Spirit will return, the game will return, all the Indians' dead brothers and sisters will return, the little children and the old people.

Wovoka displays the nail wounds on his wrists and on his face. "Go with peace in all directions and only dance," he says, "Those who do not will be made short, maybe only a foot tall, and they will become bits of wood to be burned in the fire."

Kicking Bear has been to the end of the line of the Iron Horse. From there he has gone farther and returned. He has passed through the land of the northern Arapahoe and watched them dancing. The men fall in great heaps, filled by visions of the return of the world.

"I swear to you," Kicking Bear tells Sitting Bull, "the world will return." He shows Sitting Bull the sacred clothing of the Messiah, the ghost shirts painted in all colors that stop bullets from penetrating the body or else send bullets flying off in new directions. "The prairie is vast, and the bullets will turn to fly in another direction and away from the wearer of the shirt. We have another chance. It is not too late. The whites can be driven off this land, and it will be as it once was."

Wovoka has had visions and been made promises. Next spring the earth will be covered by new soil that will bury all white people. From the bodies will sprout new sweet grass. In their deaths, the whites will replenish the earth they have depleted. What they have ripped open and left slashed and scarred will be healed. New rivers will run and new trees grow. The wild horse will run again.

"All the Indians are dancing everywhere," Kicking Bear goes on. "This dance will save the world and save us."

Now there is dancing around Sitting Bull, too. The Sioux cease eating and sleeping. They do not till their fields nor put their minds to their betterment. They dance. Only the dancing.

For allowing his people to dance, Sitting Bull is arrested and somehow in the arrest shot in the head and killed. The Sioux run in every direction continuing the dance in hidden caves and gullies. The breath of the white soldiers' horses comes near. The government cuts the meat ration in half on the reservations. One moon becomes another, and the days and nights grow colder.

The Chief Big Foot lies bleeding from his nose and mouth. He lifts himself up to speak with the army major sent to arrest him. He moves his people where he is told, to a place called Wounded Knee.

There is no more running, no more fighting. The Cheyenne do not paint, nor the Arapahoe dance. Yellow Bird goes blowing an eagle bone whistle among the surrounded Sioux.

"Remember your shirts," Yellow Bird sings in Sioux as the soldiers tear apart teepee after teepee. "The bullets cannot pierce your skin; you cannot help but be saved. The Lord God has come to resurrect the earth."

The soldiers do not know what Yellow Bird says. They go on as if he did not exist, as if the speech of this Indian truly were as meaningless as they believe the song of any Yellow Bird to be. They keep to their duty, throwing women and children against tent poles, piling up everything the Indians have in a growing mound.

Yellow Bird is still blowing on that eagle bone whistle. Black Coyote waves a rifle overhead. He refuses to give it up to the soldiers.

"I paid good money for this rifle," Black Coyote screams, "It is mine."

He waves the rifle in the air and a shot sounds. From his rifle? From another? Soon it is hard to tell as shots sound from every direction. One gun and another, and more. What sweet delusion is the desire to murder, and the Indians fall, stopped in mid-step. The soldiers, maddened by the pursuit of death, fire from all directions and kill each other along with their Indian enemies.

"Where am I now?" don Eduardo screams as the bullets fly around him. The bodies fall, and only he is left standing as if he were the ghost of the ghost dance, as if he were the only evidence of the new earth come to be. The whites will all die, and the Indians will be gone, too. The rivers will no longer flow; the clouds will fall from the sky and blanket the earth in a white shroud.

"Is this Wyoming? Is Wovoka alive in Nevada? Is Nevada Wyoming? Why am I naming names?"

Don Eduardo slaps his hands across his mouth and begins to dance. He lifts one foot high and brings it down so the thump goes through all the earth to the other side of the world. He lifts the other foot and does the same. He will dance until he dies. If only he could die, but since he cannot, he will dance forever. He will be the only living creature on an earth scorched by bitterness and memory.

Big Foot lies dead, his body twisted by the frozen winter air into a grotesque parody of a dancer. Yellow Bird gives himself a new name—Frozen Fingers. With frozen fingers he cannot blow a whistle, he cannot mix paints. Neither whistles nor paints can be made from an empty world.

Is Wounded Knee in Wyoming? No, it's in South Dakota. South Dakota? No, it's in Montana. Montana? No, it's in Nebraska, Nevada, Idaho, Colorado. Are we in Wyoming? Wyoming. Wy-om-ing. At Wounded Knee, soldiers run down the ravines and draws after fleeing women and children.

"Come out," the soldiers cry to the bushes and trees. "Any Sioux who comes out now will be protected and escorted to the reservation agency."

A few young boys come forth and the soldiers fall on them, hacking their bodies up, sending them finally to heaven in many small pieces.

Eduardo Galeano, returned again as Fools Self, Sioux Scout, bends over, sickened and throws up silently into his hands. All the colors of the rainbow unfold before him there, steaming hot in the frozen air, every hue of the earth. Who could not love the green and yellow and brown and red and black and white and blue? The sweet, sweet blue that is the color of the sky.

# 1875

"But, as with your fathers, so now, the Anglo-Saxon, in his westward march, still meets the red man. It is the old story of an issue of races, in the expansion of the stronger. The inferior must perish. . .all passions are stimulated to annihilate the savage, as a beast, because he tears and tortures in the throes of his death struggle. . . Fast as the mountain streams declare to the avaricious gold-hunter that gold is there, so fast comes fresh to the red man, the warning that, worse than the contracting iron chamber of romance, an inevitable doom is surrounding heart and home. . .I once said, in an extreme hour, when all I held dear on earth was in danger of self-immolation, or slow death at the hands of the red man, that if I had been a red man as I was a white man, I should have fought as bitterly, if not as brutally, as the Indian fought. . .The red men supposed that they were defending their native soil. . .The old chief Black Horse said truly: 'White man wants all. He will have it all; but the red man will die where his father died.'. . .When judgment shall be weighed out and history shall record the balance-sheet, the sad lament of the red man will stand to his credit and to the reproach of the Christian. . .The present generation is in the iron grip of the advancing empire and will be hurled aside in its progress. . .thousands of trappers and waifs, speculators, and fortune-hunters, engirdle the coveted region, killing buffalo for sport, that their carcasses may rot on the prairie, and then clamor for the right to travel the public domain; their success is assured, for the game will depart, and the Indian will barter his last right away. . .The tidal wave must sweep on. . .I watched the departing Cheyennes, led by old White Horse, with hair white as snow, Black Bear, Dull Knife, Big Wolf, and The Man That Strikes Hard. They started for the Wind River Mountains. Their lodge-poles, laden with all their effects, dragged behind the ponies in slow procession. The squaws bent under the weight of dried game, skins, arrow-wood and the supplies furnished from the post. Children were packed with all they could carry. The old men rode, or slowly trudged, along in the middle of the train, compelled to keep up or be abandoned. They were going to seek new hunting-grounds; leaving an Indian paradise, because the shadow of the advancing white man had fallen upon the trail. They were passing away. . .there was ever present that painful consciousness of their impending doom. . .I have seen all ages, and both sexes, half naked, and yet reckless of exposure, fording the Platte, while ice ran fast, and mercury was below the zero mark, for the single purpose of gathering from a post slaughter-house, to the last scrap, all offal, however nauseous, that they might use it in lieu of that precious game which our occupation was driving from its haunts. . .They, too, were passing away. In the wild rage of battle, in the torturing test of the sun-dance, in the hour of defeat and the howl of victory, in the spirited hunt, and in the solemn council—awake, asleep, in teepee, or on the prairie—I have found them the same fate-defying, strong-willed, and peculiar race—obdurate, steady, and self-possessed, in all their moods, yet passing away. . .On a generous gift of food, I have been startled by being the centre of a circle of old women, whose song of thanksgiving. . .with shrill screams and distorted faces they whirled and leaped, and swung their bodies, . . .and I have seen the same wrinkled hags grinding the knife, the hatchet, and arrowhead. . .Here, too, in the absence of all that should give glory to women, I read the ever-present premonition,—passing away. . .How shall I close this recital?"

## 1892
### BUFFALO
### ANOTHER GRUESOME FARCE

For some time now, the agents, spies and informers of the Wyoming Stock Growers' Association have been struggling to kill Nate Champion. The gentlemen of this kingdom of open country and cattle have made a pledge to exterminate all rustlers. By this they mean to shoot a bullet through the face or hang by the neck all those who homestead, who grow crops, who build fences, who own a few cows, who operate newspapers in opposition to them, who sell tools or food or clothing to their enemies, in short to all those who by dint of not being members of the Stock Growers' Association are rustlers.

There are so many old songs that people like to sing:

Git along, git along, git along, little doggies.

It's your misfortune and none of my own.
Your mammies was raised way down in Texas,
But now Wyoming will be your new home.

That's a pretty little tune, sung in twenty-two part harmony by the Texas gunfighters recruited to come north to Wyoming and help clear out the country. $5.00 per day wages and a bonus of $50.00 to each man for every rustler killed by any of them.

Major Wolcott comes riding north from Denver with his irregular troops in a sealed Pullman. In Cheyenne the steaming bawling train grinds to a halt in the Union Pacific yard. They're branding horses, taking inventory of tents, saddles, rifles, pistols, dynamite, fuses, camp chairs, cutlery, wagons, and names. Senator Carey's aide, Ed David, is cutting the telegraph wires into Johnson County. He drags each severed wire two or three miles out into the sage.

April is a lovely time in northern Wyoming but as fickle as a two-year-old mare. In the rain, the horses slip and slide through sheet gumbo. At a swollen river, the bridge collapses, and a team and wagon sink into the tumult. Then it begins to snow. "Dress for April," they'd told the Texans. April in Wyoming, they forgot to say, not April on the Pecos.

The secret invading army is so well-known that a vulture of the yellow press, Mr. Sam Clover, hears about it in Chicago and becomes the first journalist ever invited to report a lynching as an eyewitness. As the cattlemen stumble north, their journey is recorded by settlers, other cattlemen, roadranchers, coyotes and that ever present snoop, Eduardo Galeano.

One time the door burst open and four men stared down rifles at Nate Champion as he rubbed his eyes and yawned. "What'r yuh boys looking fer?" he asked and, stretching, pulled his gun off the bedstead and fired. The boys fired, too, and missed, the bullets winging by Nate's head as the visitors excused themselves for the day. "They fergot I was lefthanded," Nate grinned.

But that was yesterday. Today, the cattlemen and their Texan mercenaries have surrounded another cabin. Nick Ray is dead, shot in every visible part of his body. Nate Champion waits and writes in a pocket diary his last entry: "Boys, there is bullets coming in like hail. . .They are shooting from the stable and river and back of the house. . .Nick is dead. . .I see a smoke down at the stable. . .Boys,

I feel pretty lonesome just now. . . If I had a pair of glasses I believe I would know some of those men. . . It's not night yet. The house is all fired. Goodbye boys, if I never see you again."

When Nate leaps from the exploding door of the burning house, the bullets fall on him and stick, like petals of wet snow.

Always the man for a story, the *Chicago Herald* reporter Sam Clover, is firing away with the best of them, and when the running man falls, Clover quickly scrawls a note and pins it to the body—"Cattle thieves, beware." Then he files his story: ". . . the intrepid rustler met his fate without a groan and paid the penalty of his crimes with his life. A card bearing the significant legion [sic] 'Cattle thieves beware,' was pinned to his blood-soaked vest. . ."

Slowed by their day killing Nate Champion, the cattlemen turn to find themselves surrounded by four-hundred angry citizens, each one of them a rustler, as it were. The cattlemen surrender to the U.S. Army, called in by the President and the governor to keep the sheriff of Buffalo, Johnson County from arresting the invaders.

They'd murdered only two instead of the seventy intended. In Cheyenne, under protective custody though still at the head of his incarcerated troops, Major Wolcott paces up and down. "The bloodbath has just begun," he promises, spitting on the auditorium floor of Keefe Hall, the building 300 miles to the south rented by Johnson County to hold the prisoners until trial.

But there won't be a trial. Johnson County will go bankrupt paying the rent on that distant hall, buying the prisoners' food, paying the guards' salaries. The cattlemen have gone home to their beds and the Texans have been released on good faith bonds and have returned to Texas where the sun shines interminably and the birds sing a song ignorant of snow. As for the journalist Sam Clover, he goes home to Chicago a champagne hero.

Former Wyoming attorney general Hugo Donzelman, who had escorted Clover out of the state, now goes to work, along with every other lawyer in the state, defending the cattlemen, known locally as the millionaire murderers. Lining up behind these are President Harrison, Governor Barber, Senators Carey and Warren, the Wyoming legislature, the Republican Party, the Courts and the Army—the parties for the defense.

In Buffalo, the charred roasted trunk of Nick Ray is on public display. No arms, no legs, no head or face. Nate Champion's body, too, is offered up for public viewing. As the old saying has it, he was shot so many times you could see the clouds cross the sky through the holes.

No one's a rustler. No one's a cattleman. Each human being is naked and unnamed. When the invaders came down to the cabin, they could hear a fiddle playing. They do not know by whom. When the citizens of Johnson County arrived to stop further murder, the first thing they did was shoot the invaders' horses. Without a horse, a man is much less inclined to leave the scene.

And there is another truth. In the wars of the west, whichever side wins, the horses always lose. Both sides kill as many of the other's horses as possible. The animals stand, and when hit their eyes go wide and flat, their heads stretch toward the sky and they fall, legs flailing like malfunctioning wings.

The horses always lose. And so do the wagons cut up to set cabins afire, and the cabins ablaze, and the prairie grass blackened, and the sky filled with smoke, and the birds who cannot breathe.

In Buffalo, Wyoming, in Chiquimula, Guatemala, in Tacuarembo, Uruguay the land listens and speaks, and no man can keep a secret from his fellow. Every flower and tree knows who is honest and who a liar. Every reluctant drop of rain in a tractless desert knows who is the murderer and who the murdered.

All lives come to an end, and all endings are sad. Some endings are sadder than others, though, and each of us decides which.

## 1866
### LOWER POWDER RIVER
### A VISITOR

This empty land has found yet another chronicler to relieve its muteness and another defender to expose its shame. Margaret Irvin Carrington has come west with her husband, United States Army Colonel H. B. Carrington, and she will record her impressions in a journal of a summer's trip and a winter's experience.

All this land glitters and shines and is incomparable in its richness and grandeur. For example, gold color is found in nearly all the streams, and it only remains for the hard labor and good chance of the adventurer or for the skill and patience of the savant in order to secure rich returns.

It is not only gold that can be found, but lead and silver, too. Coal is exhaustless. There is so much it can never run out. And there is limestone and clay, which will make a firm, smooth plaster. Stucco houses can be built and fences to define fields. It is possible to stucco anything—clothing, wagons, horses, human faces, coffins, all covered in a cool, smooth plaster mask. The red buttes are filled with iron, and the tall pines provide lumber of any length or breadth, lumber perfect in its clarity without a knot or blemish to mar the surface.

It is a rich land, but Margaret Carrington reminds strangers that wealth does not come easy, that the bounty of this place will not fall from a tropical sky into the moist, warm laps of the lazy. The gold will not be stumbled upon by vacant treasure seekers. The coal fires will not light themselves at the feet of idlers.

It will take much hard work and true purpose. Such souls are invited forward to this land called Absaraka, Home of the Crows. Past home, for the Crows have retreated before the force of the Cheyenne and the Sioux, and the land, Mrs. Carrington emphasizes, is empty. But it is not empty for lack of utility. Up to now it has been left unoccupied only because of the hostility of Buffalo Tongue and certain other Indians who, Mrs. Carrington notes, continue to infest this empty land.

1868

POWDER RIVER

THE THIEVES' ROAD

When John Bozeman worked his way northwestward across the
Powder River country along the face of the Bighorns, he meant nothing. Bozeman had no interest in the sacred nor in the length of the
grass and the beauty of the moon. His was a quest across the mountains to the gold fields of Montana, a quest for cold cash. Bozeman
knew that if he could draw travelers off the Oregon Trail and guide
them directly to the Gallatin Valley where he owned land, then the
value of that land would go up and up until the mounds of dollars
reached the sky.

It is one land but, some say, many nations. In his peripatetic way,
don Eduardo has been studying up on the nations and knows there
are not so many—only two—the nation of those who remember noth-

ing and the nation of those who remember everything, who are doomed to be unable to forget.

In his spare time, the workaholic historian has been interviewing Indians he meets along the road. It is clear they belong to the nation of Those-Who-Remember.

"Sir," Galeano begins, addressing Sitting Bull, but before the interrogator can formulate his question Sitting Bull begins: "You remember that Federal Commissioner of Indian Affairs Francis Walker said, 'There is no question of national dignity involved in the treatment of savages by a civilized power.' And Commissioner Walker further explained that his task is to 'reduce the wild beasts to the condition of supplicants for charity.' By 'wild beasts' the commissioner means Indians generally and specifically Indians of the Northern Plains, Indians of the Powder River Country, that is to say, he means us."

Galeano goes to Commissioner Walker and asks him about this quote. "I said that?" the commissioner asks. "No, I don't believe so," and smiles, "I'm afraid I can't recall ever having made such a statement."

So don Eduardo returns to the Bozeman Trail and asks the assembled Indians about the 14th amendment to the United States Constitution, which expressly guarantees equal rights to all except the Indian.

In Galeano's absence Sitting Bull has fallen asleep, and Black Bear of the Arapahoe speaks. "You remember General Connor? You don't? Well, it doesn't matter. General Connor has said that we 'must be hunted like wolves.' When Connor headed out for his defeat at the Battle-Where-the-Girl-Saved-Her-Brother, the one he called the Rosebud, he gave his men their orders—'Attack and kill every male Indian over twelve years of age.' "

"Is that true?" don Eduardo asks General Connor, now retired and quietly sipping a brandy in front of a crackling fire.

"I really have no records of my exact words on that day," the General states and shows his guest to the door, "If you will excuse me."

Black Bear is still speaking. "Look, we're wolves—it's true. And we're bears and antelope and trees and running water and horses. We are the rosebuds along the Rosebud. Get it? How could the whites give equal rights to us? They'd have to give equal rights to everything, and that would be the end of them."

In these statements is the true birth of the science of psychology. Don Eduardo's Indian brothers begin the never-ending pleasurable pursuit of wondering aloud about the mental makeup of the white man. As in all scientific pursuits, the first chore is to begin the classification and naming of the species under discussion.

Begin with the "W" word—white man. We will call him Wasicu. It means maggot, He-Who-Takes-The-Fat—right out of the fire. He'll reach in and burn his arm to the shoulder in order to get the best piece of food for himself and keep it from someone else.

Risen from his nap Sitting Bull claims the root principle is a disease—"With the Wasicu, it is a disease called The-Love-of-Possessions."

Black Bear speaks again, "It is true what you say about The-Love-of-Possessions, but it is also true that the Wasicu will often give away with great generosity. Take General Connor who ordered each male over twelve killed. He went chasing all over the countryside looking for such males. He took men and horses, tents, bedrolls, cooks and doctors. There were wagons, rifles. All his men had to eat. Their clothes became worn and had to be mended. They kept needing new boots. All this costs money. Connor took all that money from the Great Father who had taken it from all the little whites and gave it away so he could kill us. In his campaign he spent one million dollars per Indian killed. He was a generous man."

Red Dog has another take on his paler brothers and says to don Eduardo, "It's not about the money or the deaths, not about who's a savage and who civilized. It's about roads, or better put, the idea of roads. The Thieves' Road—John Bozeman's Trail—wasn't what they wanted. It was this idea of roads. They want to carve the land up into roads east and west, north and south. They want to cut one animal off from its mate, another from its source of water, a third from its way in and out of the mountains. Roads are the real desire of the whites. They must be in motion as they do not know how to stay anywhere for long. Wherever we are, there we are. No matter where a white man is, he is nowhere. The real solution for the Wasicu would have been to put all us Indians on wheels. That way they could run us about wherever they wished."

"Don't be such a cynic," Gall chides, "Remember what you said—the whites are a people who live by ideals. When they build a road, some abstract principle is sure to be involved. They have a reverential attitude toward the idea of personal freedom for those who already have it."

When the smiles fade, Red-Calf-Road-Woman speaks seriously and bitterly. "The whites are the gods and goddesses of hatred. They hate everything, and most of all they hate nature—the living forests, the birds, the beasts, the grassy glades, the water, the soil, the air itself. They hate. Black Bear's joke about equal rights for all things was spoken truly."

"I hear you are talking," don Eduardo says, "but what will you do?"

"Spoken like an Indian," Red Cloud laughs. "Don't worry, the whites have taken everything. This is all we have left, this small bit of ground, and I tell you we mean to keep this land."

The days pass, and Red Cloud and his companions are everywhere along the highway, silently seated in the ditches, peering down from behind boulders, hidden in trees. For two years the Indians are busy conducting a guerilla war up and down the Thieves' Road until finally the distant government in Washington agrees to abandon the Bozeman Trail. On July 29, the troops leave Fort C. F. Smith, and Red Cloud's warriors enter the abandoned stockade. They set fire to every building. The departing troops can see the flames, and more than one poor soldier smiles watching his home go up in smoke. In August, the white men dressed in blue evacuate Fort Phil Kearny, Little Wolf and the Cheyenne people enter the log compound, and it too is burned back into the earth. A few days later, the scene is repeated at Fort Reno, and the land returns to itself—roadless and clear.

There is jubilation among the Indians and among their compatriots and allies—the plants and animals, the rivers and the sky. But the jubilation will be short lived. Don Eduardo knows but does not say for fear of disheartening the surrounding Indians. He need not fear for the Indians, too, already know. Sitting Bull knows, and so do Black Bear, Red Cloud, Little Wolf, all the Indians of these Plains, they know. Still, in order to protect don Eduardo's hopes, they don't speak.

"Why so down in the mouth, Little Brother?" Red-Calf-Road-Woman finally says. And all the Indians smile. They know but they do not feel sorrow. They remember.

121

1836

SOUTH PASS

DOUBLE HONEYMOON

The Mrs. Whitman and Spalding, recently wed wives of the Reverends Marcus Whitman and H. H. Spalding are diligently flipping the pages of magazines seeking the perfect spot for a honeymoon. Here are the steaming spas of the Tyrol, the delightful heights of the Materhorn, the Crystal Palace and the Albert Hall.

"What about the falls at Niagara, Narcissa?" Mrs. Spalding asks.

Mrs. Whitman licks her finger and turns another page. "Let's do something really new and grand," she smiles, "Let's be the first white women to cross Wyoming and the Rocky Mountains to reach the Pacific Coast."

"Oh, yes, let's do."

In the end and in complete accord with the suggestion of their sturdy brides, the two young missionary reverends set out on their cross country honeymoon. Mrs. Whitman, known for her sweet voice, sings as they go. The Reverend Spalding, a keen observer of both people and things, notices a soda lake and calls it crystallized Epsom Salts. Mrs. Spalding laughs and chides him for thinking only of his feet. As the days pass and the people come and go, the Reverend Whitman keeps to himself, mumbling, and recording in a journal which Indians seem ripe for conversion and which seem better left for another journey.

Camping at South Pass on the Fourth of July, the foursome is able to combine the pleasures of the body with patriotism and Christian devotion. The Reverend Whitman places a blanket on the ground and then on the blanket places a Bible. After a picnic and a pale blue nap, he takes in his hand the national flag and he calls to his wife and friends, "Let us Pray."

It is an odd celebration, but they have no fireworks, and there are as yet no cannons opening up the West. Praying seems as good a pursuit as any for this honeymoon of distance and motion. The four lift their heads to the Heavens and pray for the cause of Christ in these new territories. They officially take possession of Wyoming in the name of both God and the United States Government. Then Mrs. Whitman sings a sweet song.

The honeymoon continues at Green River where the two women find themselves among 200 trappers and several thousand Indians. Not to be outdone by the consideration shown these women by their white brethren, the Indians bring forth a banquet of mountain trout, venison and elk meat, then 600 red men mount their horses and ride a half mile into the distance. Wheeling, they charge the nuptial tents, flattening the grass and raising a curtain of dust that protects modesty and ensures privacy.

The two women's eyes widen, and they scream as best they can. But their screams are unheard amidst the thunder of 2400 hooves and the whoops and yips of 600 men. At the moment in which the newlyweds will be torn asunder, the horses and riders lean and, spinning off to left and right, pass around the tents and clatter off into the distance. Such horsemanship is rarely seen, but it is hard to say if the tired brides fully appreciate the act or welcome the trembling of the earth that comes to them.

That night the two women, profoundly worn out, sleep a sweet womanly sleep, bearing civilization in their hands.

## 1928
### Hollywood
### Ed Trafton's Bad Luck

In this life, things never seem to quite work out, or they work out just fine. In the end, both are about the same. Not that those were Ed's thoughts as his head flopped forward and he held out both hands to catch it, to gently lay it down on the counter of the soda fountain at which he'd ordered a cool drink on a warm day.

Like the old song says, "If it hadn' a been for bad luck, I wouldn' a had no luck at all."

"Ain't it the truth," Ed said out loud to the soda jerk. But the soda jerk was out front wiping down a table and heard neither Ed's garbled words nor his arhythmic cluttered breathing. "I'm Ed Trafton from Jackson Hole. Maybe you seen me in the movies." The soda jerk was working his way closer and might have heard but that a police car fled by outside, siren screeching. "Oh, well," fluttered feebly into the syrupy air of the soda shop. "I'll be damned if I ain't already paid a quarter for this drink," and Ed's hand slid out from under his head which fell the last half inch to the marble counter and slammed down. The free hand jerked forward for the glass and knocked it over. "Oh, well," fluttered again, "I'll be dead of heart failure in a couple of minutes."

Bad luck notwithstanding, a person keeps on going, a hand keeps reaching. The good luck began in Jackson Hole, but it went bad about as quickly as it could. To Ed, a poor man in a valley with a forty-day, frost-free season and a lot of horses, crime seemed a far better bet than agriculture.

The eternal ups and downs. Having escaped being shot for horse thieving (good luck), Ed tried robbing a store and ended up in jail (bad luck). But good luck soon reappeared in the form of a beautiful woman—the sweetheart of Ed's cellmate—who brought a gun, and the two men fled. At the Snake River, the couple went on, but Ed, never much of a swimmer, feared the rushing water and stood on the riverbank until he was in the middle of a crowd, all smiling and watching the water go rushing by.

Bad luck. When the door closed, it was twenty-five years. There's an old saying about how it's not over until it's over, and Ed's mother received a large insurance settlement after the death of a relative. The money went whatever way it had to, and in four years Ed was a free man.

In 1916, after years of work as a carrier of the U.S. Mail in the Teton Valley, a period in his life when Ed was unsure whether he was having good luck or bad, it was clear something had to happen. Ed set himself up at the bend of a road in Yellowstone Park. When a tourist coach came by, Ed stepped out, aimed a gun at the driver, and ordered everyone out of the coach.

"Form a line, one at a time walk by here and dump your valuables in this bag." Which everyone did. Then Ed ordered them back on the coach, then ordered the driver to go around the corner and stop there where another man was waiting.

It worked. Never occurred to Bad Luck Ed Trafton that maybe it worked too well, that some things could be just too easy and that a man with some sense might think about that, that carrying the mail in a place as beautiful as the Tetons might be grand luck indeed.

But the coach business felt right. There was no danger of getting shot as the Yellowstone Park Company didn't allow guns in the park. And the tourists thought the robbery was a stunt. They enjoyed the show, thinking that in a moment they'd be called back to pick up their watches, necklaces, earrings and cash. Yes, to Ed, the whole thing felt right.

So when the passengers ordered down off the fifteenth coach of the day smiled at him, Ed smiled back. An older woman dropped her entire purse into the waiting bag and Ed bent over, picked up the purse and handed it back, saying, "No, ma'am, you'd better keep this, you look like you need it more than I do."

Amidst the laughter of the victims, the woman asked if she could take Ed's picture. Assenting, Ed adjusted his hat, lowered his red bandana, and smiled. It made a lovely scene. The woman got her picture and Ed got five years in Leavenworth.

Bad luck or not, there's nothing but keeping on. Ed served his time and was released. The ideas poured forth including a plan to build a grand armored touring car with which to kidnap the President of the Mormon Church, holding him for ransom.

Then came the best of all. Ed left Wyoming for Hollywood where he would sell his life story to the movies—bigger than life hero of adventures and escapades in the Grand Tetons and Yellowstone!

But it didn't work out that way. Nobody wanted Ed Trafton's story. He got a few bit parts and lived alone in a furnished room. Then came a cool drink on a warm day and Ed's hand reaching out with that jerky explosive motion and the glass spilling over so that when they came to pick up his body, you couldn't tell if the old cowboy's pants were drenched in lemonade or piss.

## 1878

### BRICKWALL, NORTHIAM, SUSSEX
### MORTAL RUIN'S WESTERN ADVENTURES

Aged twenty-five, Moreton Frewen has left his ancestral home for the colonies—Wyoming—hoping to become the greatest cattle baron on the western range. To further his ends, this devotee of the drawing room and the hunt will make more than a hundred ocean voyages. He will speak with peers and ladies, capitalists and government ministers, sympathetic relatives and wealthy acquaintances. He will travel from Montreal to New York to London to Hyderabad. But no matter his peripatetic scramble, eventually he will be bankrupt and forced to return to England where he will end his days a member of Parliament in the House of Commons.

So many conspire to defeat this foreigner of privilege and leisure. "The great problem," Frewen notices, "is that I am a gentleman, and in Wyoming being a gentleman is much against one."

He has built three fortified ranches, one on Powder River, one on Crazy Woman Creek, and one on Dry Fork. Soon there will be a fourth ranch on Tongue River. Having considered the lions and elephants of Africa, the tigers and other brutes in the jungles of India, and the bounding kangaroo in the Australian bush, Frewen has settled on the land of the hostile Sioux and Bannock.

As both a gentleman and a rancher, Frewen dresses in decorated buckskins. There is floral piping on his pantlegs, an embroidered heart on each of his pockets. He is protected by fur wraps on his collar and cuffs and a fur ridge covering his buttonholes through which the cold winds might otherwise leak. A fringe lines and emboldens his shoulders, arms, and waist.

Well-dressed, well-fed, and well-housed (his headquarters ranch costs $900.00 a month to maintain), Moreton Frewen embarks on his adventure of becoming a resident, however misplaced, of his newly adopted homeland.

In these parts one is known by many names, some given and some earned. There is a white businessman called Two Winters—he has actually wintered over when his colleagues have left for milder climes. There is a cowboy called Cross Eyes for his inability to shoot a rifle straight. The Indians Frewen has met are named Afraid-of-his-Horses, Black Kettle, Child of the Deer, Star Woman, Long Walk.

Moreton Frewen begins to earn two other names—Mortal Ruin and Silver Tongue. The first has been given as an ironic comment on his business acumen, the second as witness to his success in convincing wealthy colleagues to fail along with him.

Mortal Ruin has gone to Leadville to buy a mine that holds no ore. He's ridden to Idaho to buy coal deposits—rich, easily-worked coal deposits, limited only by their inaccessibility.

"For $500,000, a forty-mile line can be built to the mainline of the Central Pacific, and this coal can be sold at high profit in San Francisco." Silver Tongue assures an investor.

Ranchers often are forced to sell their cattle at a loss in the fall. Mortal Ruin buys a hill between Laramie and Cheyenne and on its top builds a natural refrigeration plant—an uninsulated frame building. At over 8000 feet, ice forms on the puddles on even the warmest summer days, and the year round average temperature is comfortably below freezing.

"There is no need for expensive cooling machinery and lockers, no need to haul large blocks of ice from distant rivers. We'll slaughter the cows outside in winter then hang them in the buildings where we'll let them remain frozen until May then we'll ship them on refrigerated cars to Chicago at a tidy profit."

The profiteering mongrels of Peru are gouging honest agriculturalists by selling their stinking guano at inflated prices. They do nothing but watch birds fly through the air then clean up after these aerial citizens. Mortal Ruin buys the bat caves of Texas. Here there are thick deposits of bat guano. On an inspection tour, he finds 4000 tons lying visible.

"And the best remains hidden out of sight," the effusive Ruin glows. "From another cave millions of bats swarmed toward me. Untold wealth lies here in the form of free bat shit." But it turns out the bats' droppings are more water and less ammonia and so not as fertile as the droppings of those Peruvian birds.

What about those cows roaming around fortified ranches? It's been a hard winter, and they lie dead by the dozens along every thicket of the river. Undaunted, Mortal Ruin simply lists them in the books, and the business goes on. At the Spring sale, the paper cows bring $14,000 instead of the anticipated $48,000.

"This is a nuisance," Mortal Ruin complains, "I wanted to feel happy and vulgarly rich."

It is not such a problem. To his neighbors Frewen looks happy, remains rich and vulgar, and is a nuisance. If he returns home to England, he'll be pressured by his creditors, and so Frewen elects to stay on in Wyoming and get to know the land. But winter is so long! It's off to Pierre Lorillard's Rancocas farm in New Jersey to investigate breeding horses. Then there's an irrigation scheme—to sell small parcels of the ranch to English yeoman farmers who will till the land in a proper way. Mortal Ruin forgets that he doesn't own the land he runs cattle on. He doesn't own the water; he doesn't own the sky. Oh well, no one else seems to own it, may as well sell.

A lot of money could be made if cows could be imported directly to England through Canada, if the middlemen of Chicago could be avoided. Silver Tongue gets to work, and soon a bill is introduced in Parliament repealing the ban on the importation of live beef from the United States. And there's some iron ore in Duluth that could be developed if fuel could be obtained from nearby peat bogs, which could be purchased for only $75.00 per acre. And moving the ranches to Alberta might solve the cattle problem. Mortal Ruin is borrowing money on borrowed money. He is mortgaging mortgages.

"The real problem," he avows, "Is that Wyoming is getting too crowded with newcomers. Really, Montana would be better. But no matter, I have an idea."

Silver Tongue is in the offices of the Canadian Pacific Railroad, the Union Pacific, the Northern Pacific. He is marketing a lubricator that can be attached to railway cars to maintain permanent lubrication while the cars are rolling. Thick viscous oils oozing from his nostrils and from the creases at the corners of his upturned mouth, Silver Tongue assures the railroad executives they can prevent forever "hot boxes."

It's not too late for another solution entirely. Moreton Frewen investigates running for Parliament. He opposes suffrage for not only women but for certain men also. "The lower you carry a franchise," he promises, "The less it is worth to anyone." At the same time certain Indians are lobbying in Congress to give the franchise to Peruvian seagulls and Texan bats, to Thunderstorms and Lightning Bolts, to Squaws and Nigra Children, to Cottonwood Leaves and the carcasses of winterkilled Antelope and Deer.

"Let's carry the franchise as low as it can go," they suggest, "That way it will be worth nothing to each of us." They leave the polling booth smiling.

His views somewhat different from those of his constituents, Frewen turns from electoral to appointed positions. As assistant to Sir Salar Jung, Prime Minister to the Nizam of Hyderabad, one of India's Free Princely States, Frewen is assigned the task of keeping Sir Salar out of London during the Queen's Diamond Jubilee. The Jubilee ended, Frewen celebrates his success by ordering up a string of parties in London for the Nabob. Off to India again, he states that he is full of confidence.

But Wyoming awaits—receivership, reorganization, stock losses, paper shuffling. Frewen comes and goes like a grasshopper in a summer of drought. Selling this to pay for that. Closing up this house and this station. As his visit to the colonies comes closer to its end, he is forced to agree with his countryman and fellow rancher Horace Plunkett that Wyoming people "don't like us naturally and on the whole I don't like them."

Moreton Frewen, Mortal Ruin, Silver Tongue waves farewell and climbs onto the stage to the rail to the boat to England whence he writes a letter back to himself, examining his Wyoming sojourn and wondering if "I am as happy as I think I am."

1946

THERMOPOLIS

IN THE BEGINNING

Mr. Jones has only lived in this cauldron of boiling waters for five years, and perhaps that is why the truth of the creation is so clear to him. He goes preaching on the street—"none of us was made in this place. This is the true home of sulphur and clouds and emptiness, and everyone here is an immigrant—the migratory bird from Honduras, the Aspen tree cracking the earth from its spreading roots, the cowboy pushing cattle chained to his leg."

It is a good speech, but there is no one to hear it. The street is empty. The citizens of Thermopolis—City of Heat—are at home still celebrating the end of another long war. Only don Eduardo, reluctantly turning on his tape recorder, is in view. Against his will, from professional training and years of habit, he asks the speaker to go on.

And Mr. Jones does: "You have seen the first truth of this place—something about wet and dry. The second truth is that it wasn't without a fight that the first truth came to be. When there was only emptiness here, the creator began. It was with clay, thick red deposits of bentonite clay, that the first creatures were formed—the four-legged and two, the motionless, those we call plants. But when dry, bentonite clay is a mass of cracks and crevices. Struck by the pitiless northern sun, it becomes stiff as dead trees and then splinters in the wind. When the clouds burst into rain, the same clay is a slippery gumbo and every creature turns to a rubbery mass, a slimey, opaque wall of ooze. The first creatures could neither stand nor walk, just slumber deeply into themselves, and disappear.

"In Wyoming the maker of everything was in reality the maker of nothing," Mr. Jones goes on. "The options were two—drinking or driving. And the maker did both, ending in a ravine, wheels spinning, dead as a winterkill cow three seasons gone by.

"And so purity was retained for some long time. Only the white clouds flashed across the cerulean sky. And the rain neither fell from that sky nor rose up from the earth. Then the first people appeared—three Crow horse thieves, a drunken Anglo couple in a pick-up with Colorado plates, an Italian coal miner down on his luck, the second son in a Basque family. And with the people came their gear—leather leggings, lanterns and cast iron cookpots, spare tires, knives, forks and spoons, cotton cloth, pictures of the Old Country, drill bits, fiberglass insulation, broken umbrellas. The list is as endless as the spines of cactus littering the desert east of the Bighorn Mountains."

Mr. Jones closes his sermon by saying, "These were the first true people of Wyoming. And from them have sprung all of us now, with our moveable hands and feet, our eyes that open and close, our ideas about how to drill an oil well and get rich, how to kill a coyote and raise a sheep, how to cut down trees on even the steepest slope, how to find water, how to raise a child to be an honest, kind and godfearing adult."

Whether he began here or is an immigrant, it seems clear to don Eduardo, notwithstanding his limited experience of this land, that Mr. Jones is a true member of the Wyoming race. Only an iconoclast, only a preacher, only a fountain of bubbling thought, who goes on speaking even though no one comes out to hear.

1929

CHEYENNE

ANOTHER DAY

Mr. F. E. Warren is dead. He was territorial governor, first state governor, United States Senator, Chairman of the Senate Appropriations Committee, Head of the Republican Party in Wyoming. The history books teach that Mr. Warren is one of the three grand old men of this territory and state. They note that he was so well-regarded by his constituents that when he ran for office, he scarcely needed to campaign. They tell us that Mr. Warren worked for Wyoming and its people, that he brought us many benefits, that he was a leader, a man of sublime intelligence, a hard worker, an honorable citizen, a figure worthy of respect and acclaim. Shortly before his death, the *New York Times* wrote of him that "few Americans have led such useful lives..."

Even the greatest of men suffer some small shortcomings. Senator Warren, for example, experienced periodic short-term memory loss. When he served the people as Chairman of the Senate Military Affairs Committee, his son-in-law, Army Captain John Pershing, was promoted to Brigadier General. Eight-hundred and sixty-two officers were in line for this promotion before John, but he was the man promoted, flying over the ranks of major and colonel. When Senator Warren was asked about this promotion, he told listeners that at the time of the event in question he, Senator Warren, did not know of the existence of Captain John Pershing.

The world being filled with mysteries, and a United States Senator being a busy public servant, it surprised no one to learn that Mr. Warren had never heard of Captain Pershing. Still, it was odd that John Pershing was promoted in September of 1906 and had married Senator Warren's daughter Helen twenty months earlier, in January of 1905.

So what. It is easy to illuminate the failings of the mighty and dead. And forever and for more, those who sleep in the flowery field of politics find the ground is muddy and dank. One year when Mr. Warren was re-elected, he thanked out-of-state Republicans for helping, saying "There are large numbers of foreign voters in the coal mines where it was necessary to oil the wheels of progress in order to carry their vote."

Shouldering a pick in the dark, dripping earth, Eduardo Galeano remembers. He remembers school. A grand waxworks of the dead, it seemed to him. And he remembers his history lessons—lessons about the past that were given mostly to convince him that he could do nothing about the present.

Don Eduardo slams the pick into the coal-laced wall of the cavern where he stands. The coal is hard, and the vibration in the handle of the pick rattles his teeth. "Those teachers spoke to us as if we were caged animals." he says to the black coal. "They gave eulogies for men who had murdered our mothers and fathers, our uncles and aunts, our brothers and sisters. Those men—they were the pimps and whores of politics!"

And again Galeano attempts to drive the pick into the earth. This time, it feels as if the vibration in the handle will shake his arms out of their sockets. He sits down and wipes the sweat from his forehead. "Never thought it'd be this hot this far underground," he says, and then, "I don't know. Maybe that old woman at the river was right.

Maybe I am exaggerating."

Poor small historian who would bring the past to life, make it breathe, give yesterday back to those who lived it. Señor Galeano is committed to giving everything back—in Latin America, the gold, silver, nitrates, rubber, copper, oil; in Wyoming, the coal, oil, uranium, water, grass.

"Give it back!" Galeano screams.

And the chairman of the board of the Union Pacific Railroad laughs and mimics the cry, "Geef eet back, geef eet back." The pathetic little greaser. Galeano wipes a tear from his eye. "Oh, a tear," the chairman mocks, "Look at the little baby cry."

And Senator Warren mimics the mimicry, "Look at the little baby cry."

Though, at the moment, it is hard for don Eduardo to remember the fact, there are many who are with him. They feel his pain and do not mock it. Tugging a black sleeve across his eyes, don Eduardo reminds himself that if he wants history to live, then he must live. And if he is to live, he must feel, which means cry. This is as true in Wyoming as it was in Uruguay.

To tell the miners' story, don Eduardo stays deep in the bowels of the mine and works. He stands next to his fellow miner. When Senator Warren's man shows up with petty cash, he accepts his share. When he climbs up out of the mine, he gives the bribe to a dead miner's widow, or a dead miner's daughter or son, or to a living miner—anyone who needs the money. It travels from hand to hand until it ends where it can buy some bread or pay for coal to heat a house.

"Take the money," don Eduardo whispers, "And vote for whoever you damn well like. Warren won't know; he's dead."

When the Senator passes out the cash, no words leave his lips. Everything is understood.

"Maybe we don't understand." don Eduardo muses. "We are poor men—greasers, dagos, chinks. Most of us can't read or write, and we're not very smart. So we didn't get the message, and when we voted, we made a mistake. It's best to spend that money. I notice when I rub it between my palms, it burns my skin."

In another mood, don Eduardo throws the money back in the Senator's face. Angrily, he slams the pick into the black wall once again, finally hard enough to make the coal fall.

Those who live in this northernmost province of Latin America honor the makers of history—the clouds in the sky and the sunrise and sunset, the infrequent rain and the consuming sun. And these, begging the pardon of Señor Galeano, understand that Wyoming's great historian is neither Coutant nor Galeano. It's Mr. Coyote, the chronicler who pays no attention to ideas about truth.

Mr. F. E. Warren is dead. General John Pershing is dead. History is alive and continues to speak.

## 1935
### LANDER
### THREE LIVES

Albert Camus said, "In a world of victims and executioners, it is the job of thinking people not to be on the side of the executioners." And J. Krishnamurti said, "Life demands great seriousness—not casual, occasional attention, but constant alertness and watchfulness—because our problems are immense, so extraordinarily complex."

Take a man who lives three lives because there isn't enough time to find out all you need to know in only one life. Born Robert LeRoy Parker, raised a Mormon and initiated into earning his daily bread as a rancher known to have a gift with horses, in later life he was William Phillips, retired seaman, meditating on space as he walked daily the shores of Elliot Bay. From these two lives, he learned much of constancy, expectations and secrecy.

In a third place, sandwiched like a child between two interested parents, lived Butch Cassidy, the criminal outlaw described by the Pinkerton Detective Agency as a "cheerful and amiable" man with a "pleasant, almost gentle face." Though no mention was made of Butch's physical appearance—whether he was tall or short, dark or fair, taken to fancy clothes or scurrying about in rags, fat or thin, old or young, bearded or clean-shaven—this description of him as cheerful and amiable was thought in those days of sadistic murderers and high-waymen to be plenty of identification.

It was plenty, but because it was accurate, it did little to affect Butch's apprehension. Just as William Phillips had read Camus and Krishnamurti in his old age, and Robert LeRoy Parker had read *The Book of Mormon* in his youth, so in middle age Butch Cassidy had read the penny picture book versions of Robin Hood.

As Robin had, so did Butch take from the rich and give to the poor. With this difference—Butch was the poor to whom he was giving. He kept what he took, saving his money until the day when he could buy a great big ranch somewhere far away and once again, by merely touching their skin and talking as a compatriot, reveal to horses the truth that in any life, in any time, in any body, the world is a grand adventure dripping with terror and joy. And we, my dears, are called to live it as many times as we can.

So Butch avoided robbing those in need, avoided robbing the weak, avoided robbing those who without help from him faced plenty of adversity in their daily passage from sunrise to sunset. And Butch avoided murder. When he pointed his gun, he looked as serious as he was capable, but no one can recall ever seeing him buy any bullets.

Because of Butch's moral outlook, there were few resident souls in Wyoming worthy of being robbed. It required looking to transient souls, those who from the beginning recognized Wyoming as only pocket and passage, every day rolling through on iron wheels over iron tracks and encased in iron.

The Union Pacific railroad trains, the trains whose tracks were nailed firmly across all of Wyoming, whose stations were at the centers of towns given to the railroad executives and then sold at striking profits to immigrants and missionaries, whose engines puffed and growled, swallowing back the coal so shortly before ripped and torn from the belly of the earth.

When Butch blew up the tracks and waited for the train to stop, holding his showy gun smartly up, few grieved for the Union Pacific. And when finally a posse of Union Pacific detectives, Wyoming State militiamen, County sheriffs, and private for-hire sleuths chased Butch out of Wyoming across Montana and Washington to Seattle, from which port Butch departed for Los Angeles, Argentina and Bolivia, fewer still felt vindicated or relieved.

When William Phillips took his morning walk, he breathed deeply the moist sea air, turned up his collar, pulled down his wool hat and smiled. Every day for years this morning walk. He could name the various gulls and cormorants. He knew when the seals would be out near the shore. He knew the work schedule at Pier 54. If the morning ferry from Bainbridge Island was late, he knew it without consulting his watch. He knew the minutest changes in the wind and rain, in the season's turning. He knew the ground on which he walked as a friend.

William Phillips had learned much. Robert LeRoy Parker had learned much, too. Butch Cassidy, whether or not he had learned anything, had an appeal to young and old, and, in the end, it was to Butch that both LeRoy and William returned.

Someone walked down the main street of his old home town of Lander. Hats were tipped and greetings made. Smiles lit up all around. Someone made one last visit and then left for good, prepared now for a fourth life, a life lived without a name.

# 1879

## CARBON

### COMPASSION IN WYOMING TERRITORY

Last year, Big Nose George Parrot and Dutch Charley Burris tried to derail the westbound train by pulling out the spikes that held the rails. Too bad a section boss came rolling along in a hand car and, noticing the damage, rolled on to flag down the train. Big Nose and Dutch fled but were followed by a posse riding closer and closer. Hearing hoofbeats, the two railroad saboteurs leapt up from their hidden meal in a stand of willows and again fled. Members of the posse bent over to touch the still warm ashes of the cooking fire.

Now in a fit of stupidity, Dutch Charley has murdered coal mine boss and posse rider Bob Widdowfield. Dutch was not one of the great railroad hijackers and made a poorer murderer, having neither the heart nor the stomach for such a business.

Today when he was grabbed from the sheriff and handed into the keeping of an angry citizenry, Dutch decided his only hope was a complete confession and a sincere plea for mercy. In the clamor and jostle, Dutch screamed his guilt. For a moment there was a lull, and it seemed the crowd listened. Then a howling began.

Dutch was thrown up on top of a water barrel. One end of a rope was tied around his neck. The other end was thrown over a telegraph pole. Some gentle soul asked, "Do you have anything to say before you meet your maker?"

Dutch pondered the question but before an answer came to him, Mrs. Bob Widdowfield, who had remained silent and obscure while passion spilled around her, stepped forward and announced that "No, the son-of-a-bitch has nothing to say." Then she lifted a delicate leg and kicked the barrel out from under the man whose mild look indicated he wasn't in the least surprised.

Meanwhile Big Nose George too had been happily lynched after which a local doctor had cut the useless man down and deftly removed the pasty gray skin that covered flesh. From this human skin that so recently disguised a beating heart were made a pair of shoes, a gentleman's vest, and a new medical bag which, when sold, might aid some ignorant doctor in his work of easing human suffering and pain.

# 1909
## CAMPBELL COUNTY
## VOICES

Rain as rare as diamonds and dew as distant as a city. Born in eastern Iowa and come to this arid county through no act of her own, that's the first thing Elizabeth Herald noticed, "There is no dew."

When she spoke, the wind carried off the moisture of her breath, and her tongue blackened like a stump. Flaking bits of yellowed paper skimmed over the ground, preparing a bed of dust for Elizabeth's feet. Running as fast as she could, she lunged. In her hand splintered the brittle fragments of a promotional brochure from the last century promising that the simple act of turning the earth would bring rain; for as all men know, rain follows the furrow.

How many homesteaders had believed this fabrication, Elizabeth wondered to herself. This is the twentieth century; are we not too late to end up in this mythological joke? But again she kept her thoughts to herself.

Elizabeth could not speak. Her lips were dry and cracked. The skin at the corners of her fingernails had hardened and then it, too, had cracked. The capillaries in her nose, seared by the dry air, had broken and leaked blood down her upper lip. The damp was so gratifying that she almost didn't mind giving up yet another teaspoon of liquid to be carried off by the wind and turned into nothing.

In the beginning the silence, the closeness of the stars, the distance from all human companionship, was a solace. Later all three became one symptom of a disease she'd never name. When the first neighbors moved into her head, Elizabeth was pleased. She spoke with them for hours. She was a fine conversationalist, and soon more neighbors arrived. They too wanted to speak—all of them. None of them was willing to wait.

Without being able to say when it had happened, Elizabeth noticed all of the voices were speaking at once. She could hear every one of them and make out what each was saying. The particulars of the stories were different, but the point was always the same.

The voices were making threats. They threatened to kill Elizabeth, to rape her, to destroy her by speaking out loud in the presence of others, to never let her sleep or even close her eyes. They threatened everything, and when it seemed Elizabeth might be happy to see them carry out their threats, they threatened to leave, to blow away like the wind, to carry off the water she'd managed to store, to leave behind only the advertisements for insane irrigation theories printed on dusty sheets of paper.

On the day it occurred to her to make peace with the voices, to accept them forever into her world, the visions began. They were visions of people and, like the voices, might have been welcomed as undemanding unexpected friends dropped in for a night. They needed no guest room; they took no meals. But they were pushing Elizabeth out onto an even more arid plain than the one on which she'd begun to plow.

Elizabeth plugged her ears with wax and closed her eyes whenever she could. She began singing loudly to herself to drown out the voices. She turned away and walked in the other direction when a person appeared. She sang louder and louder. She sang in all her waking moments—at home, on the way to town, in town doing monthly shopping. At night she woke up singing. Still the voices remained, and the visitors.

She only knew one song—"The Yellow Rose of Texas"—and when she sang it, the words came out all wrong. They were the words to the poems of Emily Dickinson. It might have been funny, but it wasn't.

Because I could not stop for Death—
He kindly stopped for me—
The carriage held but just Ourselves—
and Immortality. . .

We passed the School, where Children strove
At Recess—in the Ring—
We passed the fields of gazing grain—
We passed the Setting Sun—. . .

I started Early—Took my Dog—
And visited the Sea—
The Mermaids in the Basement
Came out to look at me—. . .

And made as He would eat me up
As wholly as a Dew
Upon a Dandelion's Sleeve—
And then—I started—too—. . .

The Wind begun to knead the Grass—
As Women do a Dough—
He flung a Hand full at the Plain—
A Hand full at the Sky—
The Leaves unhooked themselves from Trees—
And started all abroad—
The Dust did scoop itself like Hands—
And throw away the Road—. . .

" 'And throw away the road,' " still another voice said to Elizabeth. It was a voice she had not yet heard, a man's voice, and it spoke with an accent she couldn't place.

The new voice went on, "Yes, throw away the road. It sounds

hard, but it can be done. Actually, I didn't so much throw it away as see it torn from my grasp. There is no road to follow or the road is all roads. It goes everywhere. I admit it's terrifying. Yet here I stand before you, alive, unrepentant, hopeful. We're all filled by voices. I tell them to line up and take a number. If I get around to them today, ok. If not, they'll wait. Do they ever sing to you?"

Don Eduardo usually doesn't talk so much and never so blithely. But Elizabeth is a person to whom he wants to respond. For once, he thinks, "Here is a person I may be able to help."

In her one room, it is as if Elizabeth Herald lives in a grand hotel. People sit, walk, turn everywhere before her. They are laughing, shouting, screaming, and all at her. Elizabeth paces furiously through a room full of people, and another and another and another, all the while singing the poems of Emily Dickinson to the tune of "The Yellow Rose of Texas." As she passes, the heads turn and the voices drop to listen, but just for a moment. Elizabeth, boring full speed ahead, disappears from the room, and the incessant jabbering starts up anew. Amidst the noise and gesticulation, don Eduardo sits unnoticed, thinking as hard as he can about what would be the best thing to say next.

# 1920

## BUFFALO

### AMATCHI, GRANDMOTHER, THE DIGNITY OF WORK

No top soil, no shuffle and leap to the shouts of the fandango. No Saturday jai-alai. No Sunday walks in the sweet sun, the music playing from the leaves on the trees. No rain, no rolling down deep, greeny, soft hillsides. No home, no friends, no family.

Sometimes for this woman, this human being who for fifty years will be known to all as Amatchi, it seems there is only nothing, plenty of nothing. But it's not true. As sure as the snow will fall again and bathe this empty land in brilliance and beauty, there is something. There is the dignity of work. She meditates on this and smiles secretly for herself. The man who thinks the worker doesn't meditate on the meaning of her acts is a fool or an owner.

A single woman among forty lonely sheepherders, she was married within months of arriving here. He was a shy man, quiet though not really dignified. How he caught this belle of the west is a mystery about which no one has a clue.

She walks twice a day from her house in town to a pasture a mile away. Twice a day she milks her cow. Letting her hands rise from her pockets, she warms them under her arms, blows across her fingertips. Gently, she squeezes and pulls, sliding the inside of her thumb and palm along the cow's pink, shining skin. She turns the cow's udder so the snow-white milk strikes the pail obliquely, the way rain strikes a windowpane and slides without splashing. The bucket full, she hefts it up and walks home. She follows the same route each day and each day sees how this town is more like the Basque homeland, more like the world than she would have thought, how all three are ever-changing and always the same.

Work gives a woman a sense of place, she thinks. "And it gets me tired," she laughs out loud, making over her husband's worn, wool shirts for her son Simon, sitting up for him when he is out late at night.

How little she needs to sleep, the woman awakened by her chores, by her task, by life. And some days it seems she will live forever. The work is always waiting. The chickens in the yard, the pig in its pen. Now it's time to kill the pig, make cured pork, make lard, make sausages, make ham. Now it's time to can vegetables—the beans, carrots, cabbage, tomatoes, all the wealth of the reluctant earth.

Not to mention sheep—moving sheep, doctoring sheep, shearing sheep, docking sheep, branding sheep. Five-thousand sheep, and on the day when the bank takes the three-thousand best youngest animals to pay the mortgage, it's almost a relief. Two-thousand old ewes to begin again. Either way it's a sea of work, the only sea lapping at life here on the plains. It is truly crazy, but it's worth it—life. "Hard, shmard," she says, "What did you expect from any place on this earth. The wind blows one way then the next. Some days the wind blows from every direction at once. Some days there is no wind at all. It's 100 degrees. I can dream of the rustling leaves, or I can reach up and shake the branch."

She reaches up and makes the leaves to rustle, and a bird sings, lifting and gliding in the air above Buffalo, Wyoming.

1912

SUSSEX

MORETON FREWEN'S LOSS

His castle is gone, and his town, named for the county of his
birth, has blown away.

Flitting noisy as a beast, Frewen flies from Powder River to Cheyenne, from New York to London and back. All the while he holds tight
to his simple colonialist's dream—to snatch all the money he can out
of this new country in the shortest possible time and take all that
money back home to spend.

Somehow it's all come out in reverse. One day in 1882, while
strolling around London, Frewen flicks a wrist, and when he looks
again at his hand, a million and a half dollars have been deposited
there with which he's to buy cows in dusty distant Wyoming. He blinks,
and in front of his eyes someone has shoved a piece of paper nam-

ing him director of the Powder River Cattle Co., Ltd. and resident manager of the 76 Ranch, with the Duke of Manchester as chairman of the board.

How many cows do the stockholders need? 40,000? 50,000? 90,000? Oh, well, the first thing is to build a house, a mighty grand house that will give the simple river folk something to gaze at and talk about when the owner is away.

A black and white log mansion rises from bare ground. The carters haul in logs, the delicate glass is set in place. The great hall is forty feet by forty feet with a man-sized fireplace at either end. The walls are covered with perfectly cured buffalo robes and the heads of elk and deer and pronghorn. The diners gaze languidly from these exotic artifacts to the unbroken blue sky. They rise and drift like clouds onto the piazza to watch the sun set over the Bighorns. A solid walnut staircase rises to the mezzanine from which music falls. Foreign succulents and trailing vines leap over the railing. The deep green plants and the individual musical notes strike the floor simultaneously. One flight up, secure in various guest rooms, wealthy travelers sleep the untroubled sleep of animals.

Summer and fall are one unbroken houseparty. Moreton Frewen has arranged relay points between Sussex and Rock Creek Station on the Union Pacific line 200 miles south. Visitors are pony-expressed north to this perfect garden.

And there is a telephone! The first in these parts. A twenty-four mile line connects the house to the store and post office downriver. A red Indian is placed at each end of the line and induced to speak into the device. Each Indian recognizes the other's voice and each looks around in the manner of a dog that cocks its head at a closed door behind which its master speaks. In a fit of scientific beatitude, Frewen explains the principle to these humble savages. And he further explains that rifles and pistols operate on the same principle. This is why a white man never misses his target. The bullet exits the end of the barrel and travels rapidly along an invisible wire until it reaches its destination and kills it.

Look at the guest book! A vulture for titles, Frewen flies again around the world and, returning, regurgitates what he's found—Lords This-and-That, and Ladies One-and-the-Other. But what is this? Sandwiched between Sir Samuel and Lady Baker and Lord Mayo and T. Porter Porter is an odd name—Eduardo Galeano, O.A. It's in a barely recognizable scrawl, as if the writer were suffering a massive heart attack, or as if the signature had been completed while a gun was held to the signer's head. And what is that title O.A.?

On the piazza, Frewen approaches the solitary gentleman who compliments his host on the quality of the cigars and the clarity of the port, the purity of the dark red color, its closeness to that of dried blood.

He must be Argentine, Frewen thinks, and asks about the cattle business on the Pampas.

"How is the cattle business on the pampas?" don Eduardo wonders. "I, you see, am Uruguayan, not Argentine, though there is an unfortunate historical relationship between the two, and you are clever to approach so closely my natal state. It would perhaps have been better had I been born Argentine and a cattleman but, sadly, I was not."

Frewen is reluctant to press his guest on a matter as delicate as the source of one's sustenance and so passes to titles, "O.A.—I don't believe we've been so fortunate as to have a bearer of the O.A. here in our humble Sussex, Wyoming before. We're honored."

"A fortuitous accident, a coincidental conjunction of unrepeatable events. I certainly don't merit listing as one of the Order of the Americas."

"You are too modest. Of course, you deserve it." Frewen smiles, wondering what is the Order of the Americas. "I haven't told you of our hunting. Of course, it can't compare to what you must be accustomed to on your vast plains but . . ." and Frewen waxes on. Fall arrives and, as the cottonwood leaves tumble, whispering their way to earth, Lord Manners kills ninety-five wild duck—shovellers, widgeon and teal—and all within a half mile of the house.

Another day as Frewen himself was dressing, a vision came to him. The aspens writhed burning gold against the green black of the pines. They remembered the red leaved wild plum, the crimson lips of a woman. They remembered the white clematis draping over the trees to brush a rider's face as he passed, the woman's white face touching his.

There had been a woman, the wife of a friend, who had longed for the head of a buffalo to take back to England with her. But, alas, the buffalo are nearly gone, and Moreton Frewen has put off again and again the futile, hot hunt.

Only half-listening as Frewen tells his after dinner story, don Eduardo watches the sunset. "What about a buffalo tongue?" the guest asks.

Frewen laughs, forced to assume it is a joke, if somewhat tasteless. "It's a tasteless request, wouldn't you say?" the O.A. goes on. "How about a wagon load of buffalo tongues, or a train load of them? Buffalo tongues swollen up and blacker than a hundred thunderheads. Stiff bloated tongues."

"I was standing there at the window," Frewen proceeds gamely, "When not more than a hundred yards away there it was—a lone buffalo bull, a shaggy stupid dull-eyed ancient bull. Well, old sport, half dressed, I ran into the hall and snatching a rifle from the rack, rushed outside and shot. I wounded the stinking Leviathon then followed him a quarter mile to get another shot." As Frewen turns back from where he's been pointing at the spot with his imaginary rifle, he sees his house guest is nowhere in sight.

"Must have stepped inside," Frewen hypothesizes, "Damned strange fellow that."

And Moreton Frewen, too, steps inside, and the other guests. The sun's fiery eye has sunk below the peaks, and the air grows cold. In the flick of a wrist, the blink of an eye, the slow squeeze of a trigger, the lords and ladies are gone, the speculators and colonialists, those who were invited for dinner and those who dropped by on their own. Now again the bluestem and the hot smell of sage.

It's not only the people who have gone but the objects—the china and silver, the saddles and boots, the telephone lines and running irons. And the house is gone, the black and white log castle that entertained the simple river folk. It's gone.

Some entrepreneur has cut up the entire castle and made the pieces into bookends and ashtrays to sell as souvenirs. Homesteaders and rustlers have stripped the wire off fenceposts, then wrenched the posts out of the ground. Trashmen and dealers in used hardware have unfastened each piece of glass and door latch and hinge and nail. The solid walnut staircase rises in a neighboring rancher's house. Whatever the land didn't want, someone else did. And the land remains, flat as the palm of an empty hand.

After the weeks of hot dusty roundup, winter returns. The relay station is closed. For those who stay the winter, it is a major social event when a neighbor comes lurching, nearly comatose, through the insupportable cold, red nose showing below layers of coats and blankets and robes. All those clothes make a man seem twice his natural size and give him courage against the season. The dry snow flies up from his boots like a shower of diamond knives.

Don Eduardo stops at the half-buried skeleton of a decapitated bull buffalo. He bends over and scrabbles in the snow, lifting bits of bone and scraping away ice. Picking up Moreton Frewen's Guest Book, he flips through the pages until he comes to Sir Samuel and Lady Baker and Lord Mayo and T. Porter Porter and that foreign name between them—Eduardo Galeano, O.A. Don Eduardo, greasy Arctic traveler, tears the page from the book, shoves it deep inside a warm inner pocket and stumbles on.

# 1989

## BUFFALO
### ATATCHI, GRANDFATHER, A WEED

Sitting at the Buffalo bar nursing beer after beer then getting up to leave. And it's a long haul back to somewhere. Just north of town, a pickup pulls onto the shoulder, and the driver gets out to take a leak. That's not so uncommon what with the distance between buildings and toilets here, and with the many ways a man's bladder can become pinched and full.

For the driver, there's no relief, and he stops again two miles up the road at the Rock Creek exit, parks the pickup right there in the lane, this time under the roof of the interstate. There's no place to pull off, and another pickup is coming down the road.

Sam Jensen is on his way home. He sees the pickup stopped on the road and notices a man between it and the retaining wall. The man is squatting as if he had been suddenly struck by the need to defecate, to "take a shit" Jensen thought. "Poor guy," and drove wide around him, looking away to allow the man a little privacy.

When Jensen comes back the man is gone, the pickup is gone, there's no shit on the road. But there is blood. What kind of an animal could have left that much blood on the road?

The night black clouds spin by over the red blood of Lucien Laurent Millox, who cannot see. Over his face the interstate makes a wall through which he cannot ascend, and the pickups churn by, one after another driven by men he does not know. Lucien is dead, and even if he were only almost dead and able to groan and turn and the interstate were to disappear, there would still be the fact of his face being smashed, his bloody, blackened eyes swollen shut.

Born in Bayonne, France, Lucien attended school there in a convent. During World War II, there were the eternal Pyrenees Mountains, reminding one that all things will pass, that only change will remain. After the war, there was the Foreign Legion and then the United States, Johnson County, Wyoming, where Lucien, a stoutly built man was known as a good worker.

Yesterday at age 63, Lucien stood firmly at the border dividing good worker from old age.

Lucien Laurent Millox is dead. Someone beat him with a blunt tool, a hammer maybe, a steel pipe, the flat of a shovel. Under the night sky filled with stars, the night sky that is a bowl and the stars needles of light that hurt your eyes when you look. And the stars are eyes, too, that look down on Lucien's nakedness.

It is no shame to be stripped of all that we have. Before birth, after birth, it isn't hard to be who you are.

Lucien Laurent Millox, Basque sheepherder, is dead. They pick up his body and carry it to the Church, and the priest tells the brief story of Lucien's life, how he worked on farms in the Basque homeland and on ranches in the Bighorn Mountains.

"He was as important as Gorbachev," the priest says. And more to the point, "He was as important as the Pope." That makes everyone think.

Sometimes Lucien drank too much then he'd offer to fight with you, or he'd pull out a wad of bills and suggest you pool your money with him and buy a ranch. He was as important as the Pope.

And each of us is as important as the Pope. What about the man who didn't need to take a shit? Shit is not a word to even think in the mother church, but the squatting man is as valuable a turd as we are.

After Mass, the battered body is carried away for burial. Domingo Martirena, Mike Iriberry, Charles Marton, Orturo Vasco, John Esponda, Mitch Esponda and Eduardo Galeano lift Lucien to their shoulders and begin to walk. With Galeano along, four men stand on one side of the coffin and three on the other. It makes the heavy box a little unbalanced, but even so the seven are able to carry Lucien away and home.

Galeano has hefted thousands of coffins and knows each one carries a brother or sister. And the pallbearers, whom he has never met, are brothers. And the murderers are not simply despised but are despised brothers.

After the funeral, three-year-old Matthew Iberlin Spotted Calf, half-Basque, half-Rosebud Sioux, returns to his home and struggles to help his uncle busy himself pulling dandelions from the lawn.

"Why you pull flowers?" Matthew asks.

"I don't want them here in the lawn," his uncle says, "They're weeds that will take over the lawn; they'll spread and soon there'll be no grass."

The uncle pulls the dandelions with a long, steel tool. Matthew asks to help and is handed the tool. The boy shoves the steel into the ground and struggles to pull up the plant. Mostly he only gets the flower, and the root remains deep in the earth. After two or three attempts, he speaks again, "How do you say weed in Basque?"

But this is Wyoming not Bayonne. So many possible words— how to say weed in English, how to say weed in Sioux, how to say weed in Basque. Would the squatting murderer know the word weed in any language? Would it be our word for the same plant?

The Uncle says, "I don't know how to say weed in Basque, Mateo. You'll have to go and ask your grandfather Atatchi. He'll know the word."

# 1920

## JACKSON
### THE FIRST ALL-WOMAN TOWN GOVERNMENT IN AMERICA

In a frail puff of poisoned breath, the Great War sighs to a close. Delicate clouds of noxious mustard gas drift silently away, and a soldier returns home missing a lung, wheezing as he leans out the window of his racing train.

"Hoxen! Approaching Hoxen! Next stop Hoxen, Wyoming!" the conductor shouts above the screech of the brakes.

The soldier blinks in the bright sun and holds one hand to his forehead to make a little shade. "Hoxen? I've never heard of Hoxen. Could the conductor mean Oxen? But I've never heard of Oxen, Wyoming either?" He feels mildly bemused as he looks out on what must be the wrong town.

And it's true town's different. In the last elections, it was all women elected to office:

> for mayor: Grace Miller
> for council: Rose Crabtree
> for council: Mae Deloney
> for council: Faustina Haight
> for council: Genevieve VanVleck
> for marshall: Pearl Hupp

Marshall Pearl Hupp? Yes. And in her race, Rose Crabtree defeated her husband Henry.

"Oxen?" the soldier asks as the conductor passes.

"Sí, Claro, Hoxen, Wyoming." don Eduardo answers as he ambles by.

"Approaching Oxen . . ."

"Oh, discúlpeme, señor," don Eduardo smiles, "Jackson. This is Jackson, Wyoming." A little down on his luck, broke, far from home, annoyed by the warped template of time, don Eduardo has traded in his notebook for a timetable, his black suit for dark blue, and as the steam billows around the train's steel wheels, he continues his cockeyed stroll through the aisles and passages, punching tickets on the northbound line.

He is no conductor. And really he has come only to breathe in the perfume of possible equality. "There is a flower here that will bloom one day," don Eduardo thinks. "I would like to at least be in the vicinity when the petals begin to open."

The newspaper reports that the election signaled the passing of the Old West. Explorers and settlers all done in, through building shanties and making clothes from the skins of dead animals, eating beaver and bear. Should we be happy or sad?

"You may step down now. The train will be stopped only a few moments."

"Huh? Oh, yeah, step down." The soldier does and stands in the light, still blinking and wheezing.

The passing of the Old West. The end of The Great War. The return home of one man missing one lung. The many dead and deformed. Everything changed.

The conductor continues his stroll through the cars. "Last call for Hoxen, all passengers, this is Hoxen, Wyoming."

The soldier smiles and laughs, but the sound that comes from his one good lung is a rattling cough unrecognizable as a marker for the joy that he feels.

# 1927
## JACKSON HOLE
## THE NAME OF A SUMMER

Biologist Olaus Murie tramps through the hills above town. With his wife Mardy and his children Martin and Joanne, Olaus will live in these woods all summer. The family pitches a tent, builds a shelf from the branch of a tree and makes a table and chairs from the dead trunk of another tree.

Olaus watches the elk, listens to them call, pokes about in their excrement looking for parasites and twigs, waits hour after hour learning all it is possible for a human being to learn about what an animal might do or be.

Martin and Joanne careen through the woods, tear off their little children's clothes, splash through streams and ponds, throw rocks high into the sky above them. And the rocks never fall again to earth.

Mardy watches the children. She smiles with them and she helps them. She scrubs out Joanne's diapers with water she's hauled from the creek. She hangs the diapers to dry on the bushes around camp. She pours the baby-shit-laden water out where it will sink into the earth far from the stream. By the time that water flows again above ground, it will be as sparkling pure and clear as the minds of both those little children. Mardy cooks mush for Martin every morning and mulligan for Olaus when he returns in the evening.

Everywhere the Muries turn there is more sky, more water, more trees, more birds and mice and deer and elk. And elk.

But the elk are not elk. "That is a misnomer," Olaus bellows like a bull clearing a territory and claiming a harem. It is not very scientific, but he's sure part of the problem he's noticed in the health of the elk herd can be attributed to the animals' name. Elk is a German word. It means deer. These are Wapiti, named by the Shawnee, the people who knew them. These are White Rump. Olaus knows that every time a thing is misnamed, every time words are allowed to be inaccurate, to make muddy the truth of a thing, every falsehood allowed to stand in the world, all of this, it means the world's sorrow and pain is increased by that much falsehood.

"Wapiti," Olaus shouts, but he's incapable of sustained anger. He throws his head back to the sky, smiles, laughs, dances around on his boot-covered toes, spins like a ballerina turned wood nymph, falls panting to the ground and buries his face in the soft earth, the rotting leaves and needles, the fragrant mulch spiraling down every moment of every day. "Wapiti, White Rump, Wapiti." Olaus is Norwegian, but he's been in Wyoming long enough to throw it off and smile like a devil.

And that devil of a sky smiles back. "Elk, Smelt. Wapiti, Hoppity. Wapiti, Graffitti," the sky rains. "What's in a name and a rose by any other name. . ." Who would have thought the sky would blabber such clichés. But it's true—the Elk does not know its name, and neither now does Olaus, still smiling, thinking of Martin and Joanne and Mardy and this life camping in the woods and how happiness itself is a boring cliché and how happy they all are as the rain continues to fall, and Olaus gets up to dance again in his heavy boots, soaked through so that with every step there's a noisy squooshing of water passing in and out of his leather soles.

# 1928
## NATIONAL ELK REFUGE
## WHY ARE THE ELK DYING?

It baffles everyone, though everyone has a theory about why the world's largest herd of elk is diminishing in size each year. They need more salt; they need less salt. They're starving; they eat too much. The ground is too hard; the ground is too soft. The sky is too low; the sky is too high. Theories abound and are capped by pronouncements like "We don't need some young college fella coming out here counting blades of grass so he can tell us what's the matter with the elk. We know what's the matter with 'em."

Still, it troubles even these cranky bastards that we know what's wrong with 'em, but we don't know why and we don't know when they're going to stop dying.

They don't die in the summer, and they don't die in the spring.

They don't even die much in the fall. After hunting season when the elk come down out of the mountains, when they leave the deep snow, which will spend the rest of winter alone with itself and silence, when they come down to the valley floor, that's when they're in trouble.

This winter 1175 are dead. Olaus Murie collects skin and blood, shines lights in their eyes, chips out their useless teeth, slices open their stomachs and intestines and empties the contents out on tables in warm rooms under hot lights.

Necrotic Stomatitis, another disease of which the world is full up to overflowing. When the elk eat sharp spiny food—foxtail grass or too much willow, say—they cut their mouths, throats, gums, tongues. Into these cuts climb the bacteria. After the elk gets too weak to stand or eat, it will die within twenty-four hours.

One revolution of the earth. One rising and setting and rising of the sun. And in that time how many things happen, how many children are born and die, how many trees are cut down, how many buildings go up. The great whirling blob we call the universe is unstoppable. The elk die. One thing turns into another. Somewhere a dictator is assasinated, and the assassin is captured and tortured by the dictator's friends. The rain refuses to fall over an entire country and millions weep, beg, condemn, cry. Sometimes it seems there is just too much for anything to matter, that everything is small and inconsequential, that nothing is worth the effort of laughter or tears.

One-thousand one-hundred and seventy-five elk dead in one winter. Useless, disease ridden, stupid animals. Each one a dull light in the center of a flame. But don't be fooled. For each elk that goes down on its knees, there is a roll of thunder that reverberates from that spot of ground to the far reaches of the universe, from the horn of a hoof to the watery softness of the mind. For each elk, and for each deer, and coyote and mouse, each water ouzel and blade of grass and for each person, too, there is the roll of thunder. No matter how many wads of cotton you stuff in your ears, no matter if you slice your ears off, or smash your head in with a hammer, it is impossible not to hear.

## 1943
## JACKSON HOLE NATIONAL MONUMENT
### THE SHADOW OF THE OLD WEST

After fifteen years of acrimonious wrangling among the people of Jackson, capitalist John D. Rockefeller, Jr. is finding it is perhaps too hard for a rich man to donate land to the National Parks of the United States. Dreaming of saving the Tetons for all time, Rockefeller has quietly and secretly bought the properties of small landowners all around these mountains and now wants to give these people's former homes away, saving only a small portion for himself such that he will have a good view of what he has saved.

To help, President Roosevelt declares 200,000 acres a national monument. The Congress blasts the proclamation as a usurpation of the authority to create national parks. Columnist Westbrook Pegler likens the President's proclamation to Hitler's takeover of Austria, and another critic calls the proclamation a Pearl Harbor-type attack. Western governors declare it a blow at the sovereign rights of states, and Wyoming's governor writes to Roosevelt saying that any federal officials who attempt to assume authority over the new monument will be stopped by Wyoming police. Wyoming's congressman introduces a bill abolishing the National Monument, and to another bill Wyoming's senator attaches a rider denying any funds to operate the National Monument.

Fearful they will lose their grazing and passage rights, local cattlemen plan to drive 650 head of yearling herefords across the monument. The cattlemen gather at the Elks Club in town to make speeches before the drive. They do not believe the U.S. Secretary of the Interior's promise that cattle will still be able to cross the monument and graze on its grasses. The men strap on their guns and saddle up their horses. They call for a showdown even if it means bloodshed.

Actor Wallace Beery, his sagging stomach camouflaging his belt buckle, joins the posse. Beery made a movie in Jackson once and has a summer home here. He wears the hat he wore in the movie and he carries a .30-.30 Winchester. Swinging gingerly up into the saddle, he calls out to his men, "Shoot to kill!"

But there are a few more speeches to be made.

As the talk drones forward, the cattlemen's wives gather and move cows to a ranch north of town near the new monument boundary. They get the cows in a bunch and hold them, the animals becoming more and more restless as the May morning sun rises, sending new spring blood coursing through every vein. The women decide to begin the drive. Before they know it, they reach the monument boundary and cross it. There are no federal officials to block the way.

At the marker itself, the only person visible is don Eduardo, who stands pointing out the peaks of the Tetons to a group of recently returned songbirds and a few squirrels dressed in their pocked and worn coats of late winter and early spring. Don Eduardo and the small animals flutter and wave as the cows pass driven only by women.

In town the men learn the drive has started without them and hurry to finish their business. Sure there will be a phalanx of federal guards awaiting them, they climb down from their horses and throw their guns and several cases of beer into their cars. They drive madly north out of town, the sun high enough in the sky and spring far enough along that a little cloud of dust announces their passage.

At the monument boundary—a creek dividing two bits of earth—the men find nothing. Their wives and cows are far upcountry. Don Eduardo has gone hiking with the squirrels while the songbirds have flown into the sky hoping to sew enough clouds together to make a little rain. There isn't a federal official anywhere to be found.

The men sit down on the creek bank and begin drinking beer. They throw the empty bottles across the water onto the new monument. Now and again someone fires a shot at a bit of glass and misses, the bullet striking a rock whence it ricochets off into space, spinning away perhaps to France or to North Africa or to the infinite islands of the Pacific or farther even into the deep reaches of the galaxy where it will circle, forever at home.

## 1945
## WHETSTONE CREEK
## THE RETURN

Because the animals fear and avoid human beings, these latter inhabit an earth of nearly unbearable loneliness. Those people who would sit with animals mostly hide themselves upwind, or high in trees or airplanes, or behind subtle, plastic blinds, or in the bottoms of small boats. Only a few people remain in the open, trusting in the animals they too are.

Of these few, two are Margaret and Olaus Murie. The Muries of the grand love affair. They have pressed the soles of their feet and the palms of their hands into the earth. They have compared these with the tracks of animals.

Olaus comes upon a confusing set of tracks beside a perfect example of coyote scat. Muddy fuzzy imprints of an animal's foot and drying mounds of animal shit are not revealed in the popular songs and sentimental poetry of the day as romantic, but Olaus Murie does not care. And neither does his sweetheart Mardy Murie. They walk, and the step is almost a waltz. They investigate whatever turns up before them.

Beside the man and woman, walk animals of all climes. Here is the opossum, the big toe of its hind foot slanted deeply inward, even backward. Here is the armadillo, the scuffed ground where it passed, sucking up insects and in so doing sucking up as much dirt and debris as food. Here is the deep impression of a bear, its wide hips and broad shoulders. The bear bites the trees, pulling off strips of bark, then lashing the wood with its teeth to make long vertical slashes, the syrupy sweetness followed by the taste of turpentine. Mardy sinks her teeth into the tree. It's bitter! But the bears like it. And Olaus, walking in the bear's tracks, has to half hop from one big print to the next.

Olaus takes a stick and pokes it into a piece of scat—the leavings of the sturdy Wapiti. He gently moves the stick around, then picks the scat up. What's in it? Grass, dirt, tiny parasitic creatures. There is always more to be known.

But not today. Today is for something else. Today Olaus and Mardy walk hand in hand, and now and again lean into one another and kiss. This woods was their home when they came to Jackson eighteen years ago. Their son Martin was two and their daughter Joanne nine months. Their son Donald was not yet born. Joanne, Martin, Mardy and Olaus slept together in a tent on the side of a mountain range in the sky. Unborn Donald watched his family breathe.

Now Olaus and Mardy return. Donald is a teenager. Joanne is nearly grown. Martin, injured in Italy, is home from war, struggling to understand a life he left to save. There is a sadness that wells in Martin. But he is home.

The war in Europe is over. And in Japan, in despair, the war has ended with a horrible scalding bang. Despair or no, it has ended. It is impossible not to be somehow, if only momentarily, happy. Mardy and Olaus are happy, and the grasses and leaves over which they lightly walk are happy, too.

In these mountains there is no season sweeter than fall. In the fall the days are warm and the nights sharp and cool. It may rain. The summer is, as Mardy points out, "one long glad song," but the fall is gladder still, gladder somehow for its touch of bitterness, for what is coming to an end.

When the children were small and the family was in the woods, Olaus would now and again declare himself on holiday. No work. They'd all take a hike, sit in the sun, stare at the blue sky as it came floating down toward the earth. And the kids and their friends became the Gang of the Mountains. And they gave themselves names. Caribou Foot. Eagle Claw. Fish Hawk. Winter Wren. Bluejay.

Mardy loved these children and their names. Nearly as innocent as they, she would laugh out loud. Then she'd cry, remembering the Indian children on the sidewalks of her native Seattle calling themselves Roy and Gwen and Howard and Ann. The joy she felt for her children was brindled in pain for those children of Seattle.

But how sweet the days were. No matter history and no matter the sadness of biography, each human being must have some small place of enchantment to turn to. Mardy knows that place. She gives it to all children, and she gives it to Olaus of the serious intent.

Just below the confluence of two forks of Whetstone Creek is a large meadow reaching back to a lodgepole pine and fir forest. There is a small beaver pond shining black. The stream comes down over mossy steps and jumps out into the meadow. There are mosquitos everywhere, but they only bite don Eduardo who is hiding in a stand of willow. His slaps can be plainly heard, slaps so hard they begin to hurt.

Olaus and Mardy sit together farther up the canyon. A water ouzel bobs and spins on the steely water. It drops, then rises and floats. It leads whomever will follow, traveling faster and faster until it leaps into the air dropping the notes of its song like blossoms or the scent of distant rain. The Muries follow the ouzel until it tumbles into a waterfall, into the spray and cold draft. On the wet cliff, one ouzel among others presses moss together to make a nest. The perpetual spray keeps the moss alive, and the ouzel enters the black hole of its house. The ouzel, the moss and the rock—one living house.

Olaus leans back on Mardy's shoulder, and she kisses the top of his head. She leans over him and kisses his closed eyelids. A piece of shale falls and cracks open revealing the imprint of a palm tree. Distant days come alive and distant climes come close.

The Peeping Tom don Eduardo, hidden now behind the waterfall, leans against the cold, black cliff and goes reeling back to the soft beach at San Juan del Sur, to the palms waving in the wind. He looks up and sees the trees growing more agitated, waving harder and more wildly. He is afraid for them, as if they might pull themselves out of the ground and fall. The wind pushes them over, the wind from the south pushing them north so they fall ahead into the arms of the Muries.

The fossil palm frond rolls toward don Eduardo, but he does not bend to pick it up, afraid that he will be seen. Olaus and Mardy lie side by side, arms around each others' bodies. Their kiss is long and deep, and their sigh fills the ground on which they rest, fills it like a cup. Don Eduardo feels a shudder as if the world's speech were an electric caress.

Olaus sits up and, looking straight ahead into the rock wall where don Eduardo hides, speaks of love. He remembers how once he feared being consumed by this love, as if passion could somehow destroy a person. "But you won't be destroyed by passion," he says out loud.

"It is everything, Mardy—all the living, breathing, sleeping, dying, reborn, all the rocks and twigs, the dust and sand, the water washing off the slope. . ."

"And the biologist, too," Mardy says. "Olaus, my sweet man holding a heavy black notebook in his hands, the motions he makes recording the number of parasites he finds in so many centimeters of elk intestines, other motions when he renders on paper the image of a hawk in flight."

Don Eduardo believes Mardy is speaking to him and so answers. "It was on a hot, windy beach in southern Nicaragua. Once. I made love this way, the way you do. It's true that was long ago, but, long ago or not, I made love this way, and I know what love is."

Mardy understands that it is for this that the Uruguayan wanders and is lonely and records the piercing wail of pain to which he is witness.

Olaus lies back, and Mardy wraps him in her arms again. They take off their clothes, one piece at a time, unhurriedly, showing off a little for each other and for the sky, and maybe for don Eduardo in hiding. A shoe, a sock, their shirts and pants. The Muries lie naked in love with each other and with everything around them. They rise and fly down the mountain out onto the great expanse of sage desert. They lie in their sleeping bags near a water hole. Eyes closed, they stare at the sunset through a curtain of stillness. Then arrives the gray dawn. Fifteen pronghorn come to drink, stepping quietly around the lovers as they embrace. A covey of sage grouse come, and they too drink, then melt away into the desert, unalarmed by the depth of love.

Olaus and Mardy Murie fly around the world, night after night and day after day. They believe one person can offer to another infinity, and so they do.

They are not fools. They know sorrow, and they know the cruel flex of the human mind. But that has no place here, and so they smile and with the quaking leaves they sing. Like the Muries and like the leaves, don Eduardo watches and sings, and no longer speaks.

PART III

# 1989

## SHERIDAN
## BEAUTY AND THE SACRED

The four musicians of the Kronos String Quartet do not look like they belong here. Their hairdos are foreign and spiky. Their clothes are baggy and rumpled in colors that are muted and dark. There is a watery look in their eyes, and their skin is soft and smooth. People say the music they play is modern. They mean it is music they can't bear to hear.

Kronos is perfect for this isolated, harsh land in which pleasure and pain so often amount to the same thing. The music is spare and sharp. It jabs at the listener like a cactus or like the thousand needles of an icestorm pocking the exposed skin of the listener's face. In exactly the moment when it is clear the only wise option would be to leave the recital hall, the sound turns about face and glides sweetly off in another direction. It is so gentle a man could almost sleep through it.

The *Cadenza on the Night Plain* fills the room. The house lights are already down, but it seems the air is growing still darker. And the night plain is a dim battleground of rubbish and loss. Careful where you put your foot down, there are unidentifiable bits and pieces everywhere. A fragment of "Where Was Wisdom When We Went West?" lies in the shape of a garden rake tossed aside teeth up. A listener steps on those teeth, and the handle of the rake comes slicing up through darkness to slam into the listener's face.

When the "Night Cry of Black Buffalo Woman" rises, a woman rises from her seat. She has been crying since the music began, at first a soft catch in her throat, then a sob, almost a wail. The people around her have pretended she didn't exist as, previously, they had pretended the music didn't exist, or was only some sounds that would be gone when they ended. Screaming so that hers is the only audible music, the woman runs from the room.

Two Lakota men are out hunting. The air is filled with sound, sometimes choppy and short, rapid fire like the barks of a dog, sometimes long and sustained like wailing when women wail loss when a child has for no reason died in her bed, when an old man has given up, his teeth ground to stubs in his gums, and all is wailing.

The hunting is not so good, and the men stand waiting. In the distance, there is the sound and feel of beauty—a river otter paddling on its back, a coyote who stops to stare then turns as if no one is here and trots over a ridgeline, an eagle plummeting from the sky and rising on outstretched wings in a long glide over the world.

Beauty walks, surrounded by tears. After a time, the beautiful thing coming toward the two hunters shows itself as a young woman clothed in the softest whitest deerskin, her blackest of black hair falling behind her.

One of the hunters feels himself enveloped in desire. He wants the woman. The second hunter looks closely. It's a beautiful woman alright, but also it's a cottonwood tree, it's a crow, it's a salty tear fallen from an eye. It is beauty, and so it's nothing in particular.

"Do not think of her this way," the second hunter tells the first.

Close enough that their tongues could touch, the woman calls the first man to her. His desire is pressing against him. They come together and disappear. A cloud boils. When the cloud disappears, the woman stands alone, and at her feet lies the hunter, now a pile of crumbling bones, steaming torn intestines, transparent skin. All over the mess squirm snakes, opalescent blue snakes, eating what remains of the man.

To the second hunter, the woman calls. She has brought a great gift for the people, and the hunter takes her to them. The woman bathed in beauty brings the sacred. She displays it for the people and tells them how to care for it. When she leaves, everyone is surprised to see her become a young red and brown buffalo calf.

The hall is now completely in darkness, and yet the sound is as if bathed in light streaming through rain. Every drop of water a perfect prism, the light trembles and lets itself fly apart in a thousand pieces.

The members of the Kronos String Quartet rise and throw their instruments into the air. The two violins, the viola, the cello hover like hawks about to dive. When they tumble back to the audience, four people are knocked unconscious and awaken with no memory of where they are.

The horsehair bows make the violin strings sing a song never before heard here, a song without a melody, a song that when sung comes out different in every human mouth. It is beautiful but not exactly a song.

The Kronos String Quartet and the Lakota hunters find themselves on the same expanse of prairie focusing on a fuzzy cloud. With White Buffalo Cow Woman they are one. But there are evil thoughts. One man receives as a gift what is sacred and beautiful while another, for wanting these things so badly, is destroyed.

The sun falls far below the surface of the world into a pool of black water. Kronos sings its cadenza on the night plain. The players sleep as they play, alive sleep. Those bits of music it seemed like they played? They played none of them; they played other unrecognizable bits.

The Kronos String Quartet weeps for a world gone, playing as though it were possible to replace the lost world with sound alone. Isn't longing at the boundary of desire? Who among us doesn't feel desire for music? Who would be destroyed by it? If a beautiful young woman can become a brown and red buffalo, can she not also become a cottonwood tree?

Two children stand in a puddle after rain. Far away they can see something is coming, and they want to know what it is. It's a dog, a black and white dog. And it is beautiful. And it is theirs.

# 1853
## FORT LARAMIE
### INNUMERABLE TREATIES

By Article I of the treaty of 1851, over 200,000 square miles of mountains and plains, including much of what we call Wyoming, have been acknowledged as belonging to the Indians in perpetuity. But Article I also contains a clause stating that the United States Government retains the right to build roads and forts wheresoever it will on such lands, at whatsoever time it adjudges appropriate and for howsoever many people as said government may deem necessary.

Now two years later, Indian agent Thomas Fitzpatrick is traveling alone through all his distant territories, inspecting the condition of his land and of his peoples. He is dismayed in the way of a grieving father to see the disastrous effects of the first road, the Oregon Trail, on the Indians.

"They are in abject want of food half the year," Fitzpatrick notes. "The travel on the road drives the buffalo off or else confines them to a narrow path. The different tribes are forced to contend with hostile nations in seeking support for their villages. The women are pinched with want, and their children are constantly crying with hunger. Under pressure of such hardships, the men begin to accept most immoral methods with their families to eke out an existence. . ."

Two summers past, the sun burned down on a great confluence of people—Ogallala Sioux, Brule Sioux, Cheyenne, Arapahoe, Assiniboine, Arikara, Minetaree, Crow. In July 10,000 Indians, 20,000 horses, uncounted thousands of dogs began gathering on the plain for a September 1 meeting with the representatives of the United States.

Day and night there was the babble of human languages, the neighing of horses, the barking of dogs, the pop of drums. The ubiquitous Indian traders came hauling their wagons of whiskey, and the drinking began. From the pounding of feet on the earth, the dust rose blinding and choking, coating everything. The animals consumed the grass for miles around making a great barren circle. The scarred, naked prairie collapsed in a flat sink. From hundreds of separate camps, the rancid foul smells of humans all together hung like a cloud. Though the wind blew night and day, no wind could carry away such stench and filth. The mounds of excrement grew like tailings from a mine. Garbage spread in an unbroken circle around the army's post.

To escape itself, the entire congregation moved east to Horse Creek. The talks had to begin. Food was short. The government supply wagons were late. Again, the smoke from thousands of fires rose over new ground, masking it. The deep-throated drums sang endlessly through the haze. At night, the chants and yells of the people mixed with the harmony of the coyotes and wolves. In the day, the people killed their dogs for food.

"It is the world's greatest slaughter of the canine race," a witness remarked.

Into hunger and grinding inactivity, Chief Washakie and one hundred Shoshone warriors arrive. Slipping down from the mountains onto the plains, the Shoshone come as enemies to practically everyone. Their hair is braided in bright colors, as are the tails and manes of their horses. Feathers and beads adorn their arms and legs. Unearthly fringe flies behind them, and their banners snap and whip angrily in the wind.

When the Shoshones are sighted, the bugles sound. The blue-coated cavalry wheels into line, and the thousands of Indians who are not Shoshone hurl taunts and wave hatchets in the air.

One of the white military commanders turns to his aides and asks what's happening. "What are they saying?"

But everyone is screaming at once, and it's impossible to pick one language from another. Translators John Poisal, Blackfoot John Smith, and Eduardo "Fools Self" Galeano shrug, reluctant to articulate specifically the meaning that is clear to all.

One Sioux, a young man whose father was killed by the Shoshone, spurs his horse and leaps forward. He whoops and his lone cry brings everyone else to silence. His scream hangs in the still air, the hoofbeats of the horse holding it aloft so it cannot fall. The wind drops, and everywhere but behind the racing horse, the dust settles. Washakie and his people turn to face the oncoming charge, weapons held high. The sun stops in the sky, and even the cavalry is frozen by the perfection of the moment.

Simultaneously, all three translators begin to breathe. They lean forward, and their horses run, intercepting the Sioux. Galeano leaps from his mount and slams himself into the young Indian. The two men clatter to the ground, a pile of dust and bones. The riderless horses run a little farther then stop and bend their heads down, sniff, looking for grass on the sternly cropped plain. The sun begins again to cross the sky and Washakie, and the Shoshone trot through the assembly to the camp site appointed for them.

The government wagons arrive, and food is distributed. The talks begin, and there are no surprises. All night the drums. The government wants roads. In return it is prepared to give the Indians $50,000 per year for fifty years. The U.S. Senate later decides that the fifty should be ten and that the money should be in the form of goods— food, domestic animals and farm implements. The government happily offers to the Plains Indians all these things the Indians neither need nor want but which the government hopes will hasten the Indians' demise.

Fools Self Galeano has done it again. "It would have been better to have sat upright in the saddle and watched the frozen sun refuse to move," he admits to his diary, "Better to have watched Washakie cut down that Sioux, watched the remaining Sioux rush the Shoshone, watched the U.S. troops try to avert a bloodbath, watched the bloodbath. It would have been better if they had hacked themselves to death and not been alive to see what is to come."

Fools Self knows it is a lie. Surviving is the better road. One never knows how resistance may one day finally flower and fruit, nor what sweet taste may one day fill our mouths.

## 1971
### BIGHORN MOUNTAINS
### ANOTHER CIRCLE

The Great Medicine Wheel is a circle of stones seventy-five feet in diameter. Fifteen human beings across. How long it takes the sun to push the edge of a shadow over a ridge line. A hundred dogs stand in a ring barking. And no one knows why.

"Step lightly, Edward, I want to show you the way these spokes are laid out."

Mary Back has left the Wind River behind and hiked up this mountain with don Eduardo trailing after her.

"There's something we've both left out of life, Edward. I've been thinking about it since we met. For me, it's an expansion, for you a contraction. Look, there are twenty-eight spokes radiating out from the center. Scholars at the university used to call these stone circles

180

tipi rings. They're all over these mountains."

"The scholars?"

"Well, yes, but I mean the rings. Any fool can tell they aren't tipi rings. They're all different sizes. Some of them are way too big to be covered with skins. And they'd be impossible to heat, and drafty, and the tipi poles would have to be as big as telephone poles. Others are dollhouse sized. And there's no charcoal or garbage around. These people didn't pick up after themselves. For them the world was as big as forever, and the way they lived, the plants and animals would never run out. They used things and tossed them aside. If they'd lived here, there would be garbage. And all the rings are stuck way out in incongruous spots, far from water, firewood, shelter. Who would hike way up here in these mountains to build one mansion-sized tipi and decorate the floor inside of it with strings of stone? Make for some pretty uncomfortable sleeping."

"Yes, who." don Eduardo agrees. He's sat himself down on a rock a little way from the medicine wheel, taken his black leather shoes and black men's support hosiery off, and is rubbing his swollen feet.

"Did you know there are seven basic soil types in Wyoming, Edward? One for each day of the week—shallow stony mountain, limey valley alluvial, tight gray clay and loams on salty marine shale, friable grayish brown . . ."

"María, I'm not going to remember all this."

"Oh, certainly you will, Edward, I know you, you remember everything."

"You don't mind if I call you María, do you?"

"Oh, no, it's a lovely name, and very romantic, María, summer nights and the fragrance of blossoms. You know, Edward, in ages ago untold there was a great uplifting of the earth's crust and mountains were formed. It was cataclysmic and disastrous. The land was utterly transformed; there was much death and change. Then there was slow erosion and another series of uplifts to make new mountains, and then yet another period of erosion. For a long time Wyoming was underwater; then it was subtropical. There are fossils that show this. There are fossilized palm trees and fossilized dinosaurs; all of this was a shimmering freshwater lake. Imagine, Edward, shrimp under our feet and freshwater mollusks. It's like your history—violent and transformative and utterly devoid of any moral framework. What about the vegetation zones? That'd be worth knowing, don't you think? I'm sure you can remember. What year is it?"

"I don't know, I don't even know where we are."

"Oh, you exaggerate so! We're in the Bighorn Mountains, and it's 1971."

"And when was this medicine wheel constructed, María?"

"The best guess is 1770 or '71. In your book, Edward, what do you remember from those years?"

"1771? Digamos, Madrid. Big crates arrive at the palace from the incandescent deserts of Perú."

"And the soils of the deserts? And the incandescence? What about the burning eyes of the blinded animals, what about the sun's passage across a lavender sky?"

Don Eduardo can't tell if Mary Back is sarcastic or sincere, but he goes on. "No, it's the glint of light off the barrel of a musket, a barrel oiled and polished until it's steel blue."

"Alright, go on."

"Well, hell, María, the king was amazed."

"Edward, it takes the romantic edge off María when you say it in the same sentence with 'Well, hell.' "

Going on as if he hadn't heard her, don Eduardo says, "The king has the crates opened and what does he find but the complete tomb of a Mochica king. The Mochicas lived long before the Incas, and the few descendants of the Mochicas were by 1771 bones living in rags, wretched beggars whose lands had been stolen by a pack of greedy scoundrels—the Spaniards."

"It's not as if we haven't heard this story, Edward."

"Apparently we haven't heard it enough, María. It gets told over and over, but if anyone's listening they certainly don't give that indication. Here's this South American king, over seventeen hundred years old, and he's so well-embalmed that he's got teeth, fingernails, and hair all intact. His skin is dried to paper, but it's still covering his flimsy bones. He's a book you can read. And he's covered with hammered gold and the gleaming brilliant feathers of extinct birds. He's holding a sceptre in the shape of the god of corn, and there is a series of ceramic vases around him, each filled with useful items—scented oils, spun cloth, you know. On the outside of these vases are pictured lovers embracing. May I tell you this?"

"Go on, Edward."

"The lovers are joined together in a myriad of positions. They enter each other in a thousand devious and imaginative ways. The dead king is buried in a vat of pleasure, sent from and to a world without original sin, a world for the knowledge of which we've been condemned to live in this other sad and angry world."

"Edward, how can you know any of this? How can you know anything after it is gone? Even if there are records, how easy it is to tamper with those. How easy it is to lie and contend."

"Yes, yes, María, that's it, how easy to lie and contend, how easy to manufacture history. And who does the manufacturing?"

"Yes, but what is one to do? Manufacture an alternative story? Listen, on the timbered mountain slopes there are mule deer, elk, moose, bear, mountain lion, snowshoe hare, beaver, marmot and porcupine. On the plains are the pronghorn. Have you seen the pronghorn run? We'll walk down and watch them."

Historian Eduardo Galeano limps back down the mountain, and naturalist Mary Back walks, troubled again by some confusion Edward seems to bring her. Is it impossible to join these two souls?

Long ago, scientists said the world was flat, and a boat sailing far into the distance must ultimately come to the edge and fall precipitously downward into the fullness of the universe. Later, scientists said the world was a globe, and a boat sailing would go round and round forever, never falling, never escaping the surface of the planet, forever retracing the path it had trod so many times before.

It is clear the world is neither flat nor round. The world is of no shape at all. It is a pulse. It is inside and outside of itself. Rocks are inside trees and trees are inside droplets of water. The pulse expands and contracts. It throbs. The mysterious Medicine Wheel throbs. The dead Mochica king throbs. Wyoming underwater throbs. And María and Edward throb along with.

# 1856

## BELGIUM

### IN PERFECT SUBMISSION TO THE ORDERS OF HIS SUPERIORS

Pierre-Jean De Smet, Jesuit priest and missionary to the red savages of the far West, has been ordered to leave the United States and return home to Europe. Before he leaves, Father De Smet's friend Black Hawk tells him two things: "The very contact of the whites has poisoned us." and "We are sad to see you go."

Against his wishes, he goes. Before leaving, he travels among the people he knows, joking with them that he will wear an amulet to ward off evil spirits or that he will continue his regular ritual sweats. Perhaps in Bruxelles he will build a sweat lodge of stone and willow branches in the middle of the crowded street, amidst the merchants and gentlemen. Pierre-Jean, called Black Robe by his friends, has lived so long among the savages that he both fears and hopes he has half become one.

Waving goodbye, he remembers another day, a mission of peace to the Sioux. What was the pretext that time for the white war against the red men? He cannot remember. He rode out alone toward hundreds of painted, screaming warriors. He wore his cross and held his banner, the image of Our Lord Jesus Christ on one side and of our Mother Mary on the other, a garland of stars shining brilliant in the night sky around them. Everyone had said he was a fool. All the enemies of the Sioux, white and red, had lined up awaiting the attack.

"You will be swallowed whole and spit out in pieces, like broken teeth in a mouth struck by a hammer. You will be trampled like a screaming child by a herd of buffalo."

It was the same vote of confidence Father De Smet had always received concerning his mission to the Indians.

The Sioux had watched him approach. When they recognized him as Black Robe, their screaming stopped and was replaced by wild whoops of friendship. Several hundred men thundered toward the lone man who climbed down from his horse and dropped his banner. The Sioux dismounted with him, and there in a great circle every man shook his hand, one after another, every man grasping his arm and embracing him.

It had been so long since they had seen each other and so many nightmares had passed onto the earth—smallpox, cholera, starvation, war, so much death.

Pierre-Jean remembers that, "Shaking their hands and speaking softly, I cried. Of course, they cried, too. The savages cry easily. They cry for joy, for loss, for pain, not masking their feelings as we do. That day I cried along with them. I felt as if God had lifted me from this earth and handed me gently down to Heaven, and Heaven was a circle of Sioux who embraced me and whose eyes were filled with tears."

In his last days in this land, Father De Smet continues his work of conversion. In Wyoming alone, he baptizes thousands of souls, granting them entry into the perfect peace of heavenly immortality.

"Who knows, what I have always believed could be true." Black Robe says to the sky.

Then he prepares to leave, accepting humbly the necessity of obedience. But it is not enough.

"I can't baptize them as fast as they are dying," Father De Smet admits in a letter to a European brother. "I am a medicine man whose medicine is very weak indeed."

He counsels the poor of Europe to stay at home, to avoid forever the rotten, rat-infested slums of the New World's eastern cities. He advises America's midwestern farmers to keep their farms, to abandon their dreams of the golden Rockies where wealth lies atop the earth only waiting to be picked up by the first passerby.

Father De Smet knows that more white people can only mean the extermination of the red people. Once in Montana, he discovered a source of wealth untold—a river running pure gold, a mountain of copper, rich metals everywhere at his feet, their sparkle and shine covering his boots. There were gold nuggets the size of hens' eggs. He had only to put a few in the pockets of his robes and return to the cities where the money they brought would finance his missionary work forever. He would build schools and churchs for all the Indian people.

It was a pleasant dream, but not to be. He carefully dusted the glowing shards from his clothes and shoes and returned empty-handed to civilization, keeping secret his knowledge of wealth lying naked on Indian land. He went begging through every diocese for a little cash to continue his missionary efforts.

Keeping the secret, though, wouldn't change what was to come. Father De Smet knew that. He knew that nothing would stop the whites from coming. He didn't care. Even a temporary halt was worth some hope.

There is a financial panic in St. Louis—three banks have failed—and yet plans go forward to build a transcontinental railroad across the Indian Country. Soon the steam engine will roll smoking and rumbling over the buffalo and the bear, over the quivering earth, over the silent hunters. Oregon will be a state, and when that happens, Oregon's Indians will be turned out and pushed away into sterile regions where they will find misery and death.

Kansas, Nebraska, Colorado. And one day Wyoming.

"In the newspapers from home, I read that President Pierce has ordered that the whole vast region of the Rocky mountains be organized into two territories, and these shall be incorporated into the Union and open to any white settlers who wish to move there. The Indians are surrounded, and their lands are islands whose shores are being eroded by the rising waters of an endless flood. Only Divine Providence can prevent a catastrophe."

In his private correspondence, Father De Smet becomes more bold. "Divine Providence won't do a thing. It is the never-ending fable of the lamb and the wolf, and the moral is that the wicked and the strong always find plenty of pretexts to oppress the innocent and weak; and when they lack good reasons, they have recourse to lies and calumnies.

"Do you know the story of the Grattan Massacre? A Mormon wagon train was crossing Indian Country. Near Fort Laramie one of the emigrant's cows—a lame one—wandered away. A young Brulé Sioux found the cow and killed it to feed himself, his family and friends. The Indians were starving, awaiting the, as usual, late government annuity to arrive. The emigrant found out about the cow's death and demanded restitution. Chief Conquering Bear offered the man $10 for the cow. The man demanded $25. The cow was not worth $5. The wagon train had hundreds of miles yet to go over mountain, plain, desert, alkali flat. The lame cow wouldn't have successfully crossed even a tenth part of the journey. It has been said that the emigrant abandoned the cow knowing the nearby starving Indians would kill it. In this way he planned to make a profit for himself.

"Conquering Bear said $25 was far too much and left. The Army sent out a party of men with a drunk interpreter and two cannon loaded with grape shot. These confronted the Indians and demanded the killer of the cow be turned over for arrest. The Indians offered to pay three horses for the cow, a generous offer indeed. The soldiers refused, and the Indians refused to turn the man over. The soldiers fired, killing several Indians who retaliated by wiping out the contingent of soldiers. The 'affair of the cow' has begun a new round in the war of extermination.

"I know the Indians have sinned, but I have been witness to the greater sins committed first by white men against these Indians. In Washington they say the Indian problem will be solved when the Indian has vanished from the face of the earth."

In his despair, Father De Smet had reverted to his early days and begun to lecture. He stops.

In Heaven, in a shining circle of Sioux, Father De Smet's arms fall to his sides. The last of the hundreds of friends has shaken his hand, and he stands unsure what to say. A lecture will do no good here. One last young man approaches.

"I'm sorry, I do not know you," Black Robe says. "What are you called?"

"Eduardo Galeano is my given name, but here I am Fools Self, the one who can cause himself not to know who he is. I did not come to convert nor am I converted."

Why does he say that about conversion? Are we not all called to conversion? Is not our life one long sea of change within which we must swim?

Fools Self speaks again. "Only what enters the heart can change a man. A man's heart must be open. Excuse me for speaking in platitudes."

Pierre-Jean understands that only what enters the heart can change a man. But change is dangerous. His own heart pounds—fear, exhilaration.

"Today I stand in Heaven. This is the Heaven of which I have spoken to you for many years. Tomorrow I leave for Bruxelles. I pray that there will be peace here. I will write to you. I will sign my letters 'Sincerely yours' and seal them with glue and tears. One day I hope to come here again and open my heart to yours."

# 1985

## ETHETE

### THE PAINT CEREMONY

Spur the horse and it will run. Cut the rope and the trap door will drop. Kick the barrel out from under the feet and the barrel will roll. Kick the chair, the box, the suitcase, the stool. Any of these will do and the body will swing. Just kick.

One, two, three, four, five, six, seven, eight, nine. Nine young men—eight Arapahoe and one Shoshone—have taken their lives. That's an odd expression—taken their lives. Taken them to whom? As a gift? Or for sale? And taken them where? It makes it sound as if the young men are still among us after having hidden their lives safely in some draw or under a rock at the base of a hill.

"Only the best," Scott Swistowicz, a teacher at St. Stephens Indian School, says. "Only the best are taking their lives—the artistic ones, the good athletes, the good students, the ones you want to be around, . . ."

The ones you like and you hope they like you, and my dear God whether you are Indian or White, woman or man, wolf or sheep, my dear lonely God in Heaven, nothing is more beautiful than the now and the here of the Wind River Reservation. Mother and Father, sing to us in the original tongue, pull the masks you have given us off and let us see the face we wore before this ill-fitting one.

Nine young men, the youngest fourteen and the oldest twenty-five. That oldest—his sister found him in a closet hanging above the dark cluttered floor and held to it by only the drawstring from a sweatshirt. The drawstring becomes the rope from the church bell and the rope is pulled slowly, and silently the bell rings for each funeral and every person hears. The Arapahoe drums sing their anxious song of membranes stretched tight.

Found by his sister, found by his mother, found by his grandmother, found by his girl cousin or classmate, found by his sweetheart, found by his lover, found by the mother earth that suckles us all, dead or alive.

"I think the futility of what they saw in their futures became overwhelming," the teacher, Mr. Swistowicz, says.

"When we were children," Pius Moss recalls, "The priests shaved the hair off our heads if we were caught speaking Arapahoe. If we were caught five times, we weren't allowed to see our parents after Mass on Sunday."

The Arapahoe are a silent people. The hunt requires silence, which becomes simply another good habit. When the whites and the distant god they called The Government put the Arapahoe on a reservation in Oklahoma, the people greeted the soil with silence. And the soil was silent in return. When a piece of the Arapahoe was torn away from the rest and marched in winter to Wind River, even the children and dogs, those members of the family most likely to speak, bit their tongues. Swallowing their cries, they felt the blood fall into their stomachs and, mixed with saliva, splash and sparkle like burning butterflies. The butterflies drank the blood and grew fierce, battering against the bars of the ribcage.

Accepting silence as acquiescence, the still-distant government said to the Shoshone homedwellers at Wind River, "Here are some more of your people. Give them half of your reservation."

Pius Moss goes on and so proves himself a fanatic of speech. "Every year fewer and fewer of the young ones came to learn Arapahoe. 'Who are you?' I would ask them, 'Who are you?' and they would be too embarrassed to say. In English, they could not say."

Now the Arapahoe Elders call the people to Ethete, to the Sun Dance grounds. It is October. The day is silent and still—strange for this part of Wyoming in fall when the wind should be picking up every fencing nail in its way and making noise like a barbed wire whip.

Call the people. This day will be for the Paint Ceremony. And the people come for the first time since 1918 when the Paint Ceremony cleansed them during the great flu epidemic. Now there is a suicide epidemic.

Five-thousand people come. Pick-ups litter the earth. The school children arrive on yellow buses. It is sixty-seven years since all the people have come. One by one the 5000 enter the tipi with the elders. Prayer. Smoke. Faces painted in protection. One by one in silence. Nothing need be said. The language is still, and the word is breath.

In November, ten more young men attempt suicide, but all fail; all find themselves awakening on this same piece of dry ground. They may be in pain, but they are here.

When the Jesuits came to Wind River, they brought Christianity and Basketball. If the first of these worked to destroy the Arapahoe people, it was left to the second to save them.

In 1983-84 and 1984-85, the Wyoming Indian High School Chiefs were State AA basketball champions. Now they have won 44 games in a row. The state record—46 straight victories—is held by the St. Stephen's Mission School Indian teams of the 60s. Those boys of the 60s are now the fathers and uncles of the young men who, in the 80s, must play basketball while running carefully around the bodies of their dead brothers.

"This is what the people call Rez Ball," Pius Moss explains, "Rez Ball—it means pressure, pressure all the time, when you've got the ball, when you don't, full speed, never stop, never grow tired, never cry out from the ache, never, never stop."

The Wyoming Indian High Chiefs overwhelm the white teams they play. When the Chiefs win their 47th game in a row, there is a piercing scream of joy from the ever silent Arapahoe.

Even Pius Moss is happy. "But summer will come again," he reminds us. "Off the court the white team advances like an avalanche, and the chiefs are dead. There is more to healing a sick people than winning a basketball game. To be healed, I must know the cause of my sickness. If I speak my true language, it is a daily reminder of who I am. 'Who am I?' I ask myself, and to the young people I ask, 'Who are you?' "

In the silence after cheering comes the question, "Who are you?" Some say it is time the people of the Wind River Reservation decided for themselves where the river will flow. Some say it is only the river that decides where it will flow. And some say that when those two things are one, the people will be healed.

# 1959
## PAST FARSON
## THE EMPTINESS

The land was all water and green grass along an endless shore. Very beautiful, but when the Shoshone people's grandparents—the People of the Moon—came to hunt and fish, the animals refused to die and the fish swam away. After the people prayed, the water began to drop. The water fell so low that the fish were piled on top of one another. The People of the Moon ate all they wanted and kept some for later. Of the water only a winding river remained, lined with trees and brush where hunters waited for animals who came to drink.

Now there is no water. The People of the Moon are gone, displaced by travelers who had no wish to stay here. The emptiness is the loneliness. The wild chokecherry still lives and the willow, but both live a long way from here in another land.

In that distant land of forest and falling water, another people both creates and assuages its loss and sadness. Below the forest canopy, the people sit under a leaf roof inside reed walls. The smoke from fires drifts up to the green roof; the smoke burns the people's eyes. They rise and dance. To their waists are tied rattles that lift like plumed tails behind them. They sing, telling the stories of every person who has gone, of all the souls who have become birds and fly in and out of the trees, calling to their human siblings.

They sing of the empty land past Farson, a land of which they have never heard and which they will never see, a land stripped of trees and water so that the cold stars stare down onto only another cold star.

Driven by the sorrow of the lonely, don Eduardo lurches forward with a burning stick in his hands. He stumbles and strikes out, setting on fire the shoulder of the nearest dancer. The dancer cries out in pain and keeps singing in the voice of the dead. Don Eduardo strikes again, touching fire to the dancer's chest.

The seated people wail and weep and praise the dancer for eliciting such feeling, praise don Eduardo for feeling deeply, praise the burns as they rise red and blistering.

Don Eduardo lashes out again, and the people are gone. The trees and water and leaves and smoke are gone. The stick in his hand is gone. He is surrounded by the emptiness past Farson. On the treeless plain, only the sun burns. His red fist comes down raw against the red dirt. He drives his arm down, twisting, forcing his knuckles to enter the earth. He is into it up to his elbow.

Terrified, he pulls his arm back, stands. He is Latin American and comfortable in crowds, in tumult, in animation. He tries to remember that distant home. Alone, he begins to dance, the first tentative steps of the guaguanco, hugging his arms to himself, letting his hips slide, keeping time with the blinking of his eyes.

The sun enters through his closed eyelids making everything visible. Through closed eyes, he can make out the outlines of the long sweep of land, the distant mountains, the silhouette of a passing cloud. It is almost familiar. He opens his eyes and is blinded, making out in the shadows, fragmentary images of friends long gone, of apartments whose leases are up, of tables at which he's sat, and meals he's happily eaten.

Ahead of him the rabble dances. Barefoot, hairy, drenched in sweat and perfume, the illiterate pioneers, who will never read what he's written, dance, sweeping across this northern plain in search of nothing. They dance in gratitude for nothing, dance for dancing. It's the guaguanco or schottische, the mazurka or polka, the waltz as a woman washes clothes, as a man cuts wood, as everyone runs to hide when another army passes.

They dance, lifting themselves from their former homes and driving themselves into the empty, red dirt of Wyoming. Here and there a foot disappears then the lower half of a leg. A torso fades below the dust and only a head waves slightly in time to the music. Ten-thousand heads like a field of tropical flowers. One-hundred-thousand heads. Finally the heads, too, drop below as the eyes give one last blink.

Inside there is a home wherever we are. There is no exile, and no one is a foreigner. Past Farson is a great room filled with emptiness. The souls of the planet wait there, patiently, until a dancer lurches forward and strikes out, making a fire that will burn south—downward and into the heart.

## 1985
### GUATEMALA
### BEHIND THE MIRROR

The child reaches, and the kitten and pup stare, seeking to find whose is the image that is returned to them. What was our original face? So many answers to even the simplest question. So many images drifting across a sky whose blue depth is roadless as the jungle.

Here there are no kittens and no pups. Childhood is gone before it has a chance to be. There is a girl of nearly ten years of age. She is dead by the side of the road, and her body bloats, the skin of her belly stretched tight as if pregnant, and momentarily she will give birth to a grown woman whose memory refuses to fail. That soldier carrying an automatic rifle over his right shoulder—the rifle is nearly as large as he. Boy-child become man-child, and no one lives long in the promised land. The Indians work on silently, and rare Spanish syllables hang heavy in the thick air.

Stopped at a roadblock in another Guatemalan village whose unpronounceable name suggests chaos and grace, Eduardo Galeano makes an acquaintance who will bring him a little of each. Mouth set perfectly flat, no trace of smile or frown, the lines in his face devoid of emotion, cheap mirrored sunglasses masking his eyes, the North American poet, science fiction writer, firefighter and emergency medical technician Bill Ransom awaits the return of his passport. Though he denies any political motive, something about him smells wrong to the police, soldiers, and government agents who check him so carefully. But it can't be pinned down, and they wave him along.

"Pase," they tell him in the same even tone he uses, the same expressionless eyes with which he looks, the same meaningless lines around the mouth that never opens unnecessarily. The lips may part, but the word compañero is never heard between traveler and officer. When the agent looks at Ransom, he sees nothing. It is as if the North American were Guatemalan himself, so practiced is he in the art of absence.

After a not altogether pleasant crossing of his own, don Eduardo catches up to the rapidly-receding stranger whose walk is that of one long on the road.

"You are a North American," he ventures, "I myself have only recently returned from that realm, from the sovereign state of Wyoming."

Ransom doesn't speak, as if words in any language—English, Spanish or Maya—were all the indecipherable, agglutinated songs of some wounded bird, blood bubbling up its throat.

"You do not trust me," don Eduardo goes on.

"I do not trust you," Ransom agrees without speaking.

"Poor Wyoming—it has misplaced its breath, its liberty, its word. Death there is as incoherent and unpredictable as in any of our Latin villages. And life, too, is dead. She is embalmed in engine oil under a deep layer of artificial flowers, windowless steel buildings, and the bitter, viral phlegm of each citizen's frustration."

That is quite a speech for such a hot day, and in response Ransom removes his sunglasses and the light leaps from his eyes, a light fiercer and hotter than that of the semitropical sun.

"What do you want?" he asks.

"Perhaps only some understanding. The events of El Norte confuse me. There are millions of facts littering thousands of pages, but history there remains occluded and dim. I can't make out what is of significance; I can't even make out what happened. This is surprising for one such as I who is versed by life and vocation in the ruses of deception, corruption and deceit."

Ransom puts his sunglasses back on, but his mouth relaxes a little. "I know very little about Wyoming," he says.

"I see." Don Eduardo waits, but when Ransom says no more, the historian asks, "Would you agree that it's a state in which distance is expanded and time contracted? The people live far from one another, and each passing day seemed to me to be a month. It was disheartening."

"Study the weather." Ransom says. "That'll help."

The ice broken, Ransom and Galeano travel together through all the Mayan hills and lowlands. They sit close on third class busses and astride worn donkeys. The Uruguayan recorder, whose piles make it nearly impossible for him to remain mounted for long, often must stop and rest. These piles, like music and poetry and memory, originated in jails and poverty. They are like a bitter tango with oneself, a tango begun in a Buenos Aires slum when men danced with each other or with prostitutes. And there was no music, only silence and the rhythm of silence, only silence with which to dance.

"I've been here five years," Ransom finally says, "Worked all over this neighborhood. I appear and offer what I know—I've trained firefighters in Guatemala and in Nicaragua, been a medic in both countries, and in Belize. Maybe Salvador next, or Costa Rica. I see people, emergencies, I just try to put out the fires, bandage up the victims. Almost everywhere the peasants, the urban workers, the poor are being murdered. I'm no leftist. My politics are this—that government is best which kills the fewest people. Simple as that. Here in Guatemala they're killing them by the reams. They're killing the Indians fastest of all. You're an historian. You wrote that those in power 'taught us about the past so that we should resign ourselves with drained consciences to the present: not to make history, which was already made, but to accept it.' "

Don Eduardo allows himself a moment of speechlessness.

Again the migratory birds: the man of the south goes north, the man of the north goes south. Neither cares for the customs agents of the imagination, nor the police cadres of love. What the one is doing in Wyoming is as reasonable as what the other is doing in Guatemala. It is what you are doing sitting in your chair reading this page.

The donkey stumbles on a rock in the path, and don Eduardo cries out from the pain of the dilated veins in his anus. He tries to scratch, but his hand is gone, then his arm, his belly and breast, all of him. And as if in one of those science fiction epics by compañero Ransom, the Latin American fireman, the itching throbbing historian, so shortly returned from the north, finds himself there again listening to the talk of the people as they pass. And if he listens carefully, he can hear the gentle hiss and tug of a needle passing through flesh as Ransom sews up the legs of a boy cut on the glass embedded atop the walls around a rich man's house.

# 1845
## RED CREEK
### RENAMING THE NAMELESS

The United States grabs Texas and begins to pull. Mexican Texas, a land that had extended from the Caribbean's warm shores to Red Creek in Wyoming's frozen Medicine Bow and Rattlesnake Ranges, no longer exists. What remains of Mexico slides on torn feet down precarious rocky trails.

Plodding south, the Mexicans smile darkly and cheer—"Viva México, hijos de la chingada! Long Live Mexico, child of rape! Child of violence and violation, of treachery and hatred swollen behind the thin mask of love, of suffering and corrosion, of the toxic milky residue of the maguey cactus, of failure, foolishness and passivity." And the last bitter shout—"Long live the children of fiesta nights washed by mezcal and rain."

Everywhere, these undigested vivas rise and pass into the world over chapped bleeding lips.

On Red Creek, a brother and sister, along with their mother and father, work on. The four have built a cabin of logs chinked with manure—no windows, one heavy door, the smell of cows. Both the people and the cabin think they remain citizens of Mexico, that young republic whose pungent soil stretches far away into nations unnamed and whose people speak languages not recorded in dictionaries or studied by savants. Mexico leaks across an invisible boundary north into one more country that refuses to speak.

In Mexico City, President Dictator Gambler Santa Anna shrugs off the loss of land from Texas to Wyoming and mourns the death of his favorite fighting cock. He rubs the air where his missing thigh would be, the thigh of the leg blown away by a salvo from French guns in an earlier of Mexico's interminable well-named wars—the War of the Mangos, the War of the Clay Dolls, the War of the Agave, the War of the Children. Santa Anna, that slippery specialist in patriotism and retreat, smiles when miserable and frowns when in ecstacy, all the better to confuse both his enemies and himself. All emotions are buried in his shrug.

Today Santa Anna's mouth is twisted into every shape skin will hold. Today is the day when, with one bite, older brother United States has swallowed whole sibling Mexico's disobedient province of Texas including Red Creek in the soon-to-be-named American state of Wyoming. With knifing incisors and granite grinding molars, the northern brother chews it all up—skin and muscle, gristle and bone, fat and marrow. And when older brother defecates, he picks up the steaming mass and presents it to Mexico—not as a gift but as an item for sale. And points out that there in the pile all Mexico sparkles before one's curious eyes.

While Santa Anna ponders the day's dinner menu, the cabin on Red Creek burns. Lightning struck it, or gunpowder, or fiery arrows, or the sky itself, capable today of bursting spontaneously into flame. And father, and mother, and sister and brother burn. The four become char and cinders, and no one sees. No one enters the cabin, and no one leaves.

If God had been on Red Creek, he would have cursed himself. If God could have, he would have strangled himself with his bare hands. If it were possible for God to deny himself, he would have.

God screams, "I am, and so I am just." And his powerful breath puts out the fire. But too late. The four are dead.

From the smoldering cabin comes the sound of a guitar, the strains of a tumbas. No man can worship an unjust God, but a guitar can. The music arches out and worships everything, worships itself. It is better than God, who is mercurial and besotted. When the guitar sings, the corn grows. Even at this high altitude with its short summer and long devious winter, the corn grows. And the squash. And the fruit of the earth is created by the guitar, not by God.

Santa Anna carries himself south on one leg. Ancient walls crumble, and stones make avalanches descending mountains. In Mexico City, Santa Anna's severed leg runs from corner to corner, peering in alleys for a crap game or cockfight, for anything left on which to place a bet.

The stars glitter in the sky. Dividing the highways, the center stripes flash as they pass. The stars and stripes undulate north, swinging as they go. And the stars are diamonds the size of grenades. And the stripes are rivers of blood and ice.

All this on Red Creek, where the guitar plays alone in a cabin built by hand and which, now, never was.

# 1890

## ABSAROKA
## HOME OF THE HUNT

There is every possible kind of hunt. Not until the world itself is comatose or invisible will the hunting end. Red Road climbs to the topmost branch of the tallest tree and there trembles in the slightest breeze. He is scared. Well, the truth be known, he is the most terrified Indian in all Absaroka.

But others have seen the sturdy muscles of their chests ripped out in the Sun Dance. The twines are sewn under the skin and looped tight, and the young men's bodies are lifted and pulled, dragged by other men, by horses, by memory. The young men never cry out; they never call for mercy. They neither smile nor frown, and the muscles tear, a long screaming rip of flesh wrenched free of the body.

Red Road hangs on with one hand. With the other, he carries

a soft square of white deerskin, holding it far out from his body, careful not to let it touch his skin or the bark of the tree. He begins to wipe the sky as if wiping up a puddle of water. He wipes harder, rubbing and rubbing. He is scouring the sky, sanding it, scraping at the skin of the sky until there is no skin left.

The animals of the hunt are gone, but the hunt remains. Behind the sky must be another sky, and under it, another world of mountains and rivers unending. In the fields must graze large animals, in the rivers swim silvery fish, in the sky fly night birds and rain. Red Road rubs frantically. The tree rocks lightly in the breeze then more wildly as Red Road's rubbing grows more spasmodic, more hysterical.

When, finally, Red Road releases the deerskin and leaps upward, the sky opens. But before the flying man can escape, the magnetism of the earth calls him back. He strikes like a fist, and from the hole in the sky comes nothing, the sparkling stars firmly in place.

Red Road need not worry. The elk stands firmly in place, too. Its stare is rigid yet relaxed, as if the animal were charmed by the whistle of Red Road's fall. Above the elk is the mountain sheep and among the trees the black tail and white tail deer. Protected by a blind, behind which they also watch Red Road's fall, wait the beaver, the wolf, the hare and rabbit, the sage hen and prairie chicken, the grizzly and cinnamon bear, the antelope.

Red Road has fallen on wild plum, raspberry, strawberry, gooseberry, cherry, red currant and rock grape. His body is buoyed by wild wheat and oats and hops. Over him leap grasshoppers, rising in clouds like the smoke of a great fire sweeping the earth. The grasshoppers are ruthless. The trees bend under their weight. They pass with a rush, like water spilling over a cataract, like the roaring of the sun as it sets, like the thundering endless numberless sweep of the buffalo blotting out the horizon from eye to eye. Tens of hundreds of thousands of buffalo that sweep back and forth, filling the valleys as if nothing preceded them and nothing came behind.

## 1836
### WIND RIVERS
### "A BEAUTIFUL NEW SPECIES OF MOCKINGBIRD"

It is raining in Utopia, Ohio on the freedom side of the Ohio river. Upstream in Trinity, Kentucky, a harder, hotter rain is falling. Six black men toil wet through the morning. In the afternoon, they are given permission to carry a dead brother to his final rest in the damp steaming earth. The six men bear the slippery coffin in silence, the rain dripping off the box's lid and walls.

There is no wailing, no staggering. No one has been drinking, and no one drops the coffin, neither in despair nor carelessness. No one watches as the men pass in perfect stillness, their feet sliding over the water slickened dirt.

In an anonymous spot, far from cemeteries and ministering pastors, the six men set down their fraternal burden. Among shingle oak, bitternut hickory and white ash they begin to dig. The wet clay soil clumps and sticks to their shovels. They scrape it off with their hands and keep digging. When the hole is deep and wide, they let the box down and begin again to shovel, replacing what they so recently removed. None of them speaks.

This is no sweet home. These are not beautiful trees. The men, dressed in ragged trousers and ill fitting gray shirts, turn and begin the walk back. It is still raining. They grow ever wetter. They look far west to unowned lands without rain or coffins. With nothing protecting them from the water anyway, they decide to turn their heads fully into it and swim.

Where are the men's mothers and daughters and wives beating their breasts and tearing their hair? Where are the small optimistic children, running rudely and noisily through the cortege, begging sweets and mother's milk? Surely someone is stricken by voices and visions and pulls his pathetic clothing off, 'rolls madly in the mud, screams through his frenzy and finally ends in collapse, hair tangled and filled with twigs and leaves.

There is a spot in the Wind River Range where don Eduardo sat once before and now returns—the twin crests of Doubletop Mountain and the matching shores of the No Name Lakes. From between any two points, he overlooks a glacier and listens to it grinding boulders, first to stones then to sand.

The European adventurers, who recently passed this way across a Wyoming they had not yet named, say that from here you can see all the way to the Continental Divide. It's true. Don Eduardo's sad, half-closed eyes look out and see across Absaroka all the way to Ohio and Kentucky, see east and south, north and west, see the points of the compass spinning in a magnetic storm.

For the Americas, there are numberless sacred books. One of them is the *Bible*. Another is the Mayan cosmological text, the *Popol Vuh,* that precise, orderly, harmonious tale of the world's principal tongue. That is the text that comes to Eduardo Galeano's mind as he sits trying to breathe the thin air of the Wind River Mountains, the *Popol Vuh*.

It is the story of Kukulcan, Quetzalcoatl, the Toltec God who remained faithful to the Mayan people through torrential rains drowning the world. It is the witness of the priests who embraced destruction. It is the record of the collective life of America's most oppressed people, composed in utter secrecy.

It is a coffin whose bearers begin from deepest sorrow to dance. The box spins faster and faster, dizzyingly around in ever larger circles until it flies from the hands of the living and careens across the wet earth down the embankment and against the great rocks at the river's edge. The lid breaks open, and out tumbles the dead man, face first into the water with enough speed to make it seem as if he swims halfway across the river before he begins to sink.

Like the old song says,

> "Many rivers to cross
> but I can't seem to find
> my way over. . .
>
> Many rivers to cross
> and it's only my will
> that keeps me alive. . ."

Don Eduardo never heard that song, but he knows its lyrics and cheers the dead swimmer on. He pulls his tattered copy of the *Popol Vuh* from the pocket of his worn overcoat and begins to read aloud, to share with the swimmer the will of those who've been in even worse straits.

In the middle of his cheering, a stream of pebbles slides down from above him and clatters against his head. He looks up and there scrambling down the slope is a young white man carrying a notebook and a string of glass bottles tied across his back.

John Kirk Townsend—naturalist, explorer, child of a Philadelphia Quaker family—is on his way across the Rocky Mountains. He will cross rivers and streams uncounted and unnamed. Into his jars will go snakes and lizards heretofore unseen. Today he has discovered a new bird, and in his journal writes, "a beautiful new species of mockingbird." And later, "How many novelties there are in this world." He is a long way from the Ohio.

Though it is not a mockingbird, Townsend's discovery will be named for him—*Myadestes townsendi*—Townsend's solitaire. Like Wyoming, the bird does not know it was previously undiscovered and will not answer to its name. It remains free even as it is being entered into a catalogue.

They say the solitaire's song is a flute obbligato to the wind in the pines. But this mistakes Nature's voice, for here nothing is obligatory. Here Townsend's Solitaire resides far from those lands upon which don Eduardo broods, those lands he cannot leave behind no matter how far he travels, those lands where everything is obligatory and where novelties is a word best used ironically or in a whisper.

"You are a Quaker?" don Eduardo asks.

"Yes."

"And you are trained as a physician?"

"Yes."

"Your calling is to heal."

"Yes, to heal. But I cannot and so, like the beautiful dead swimmers you see far to the east, I have fled."

And also like the swimmers he cannot help, Townsend is drawn to flight, to birds, to their songs pouring across the countryside, oblivious of boundaries or the demands of silence. Townsend, with the swimmers, flies toward a world beyond discovery, beyond names, beyond metaphor, beyond language itself.

There is a story in the *Popol Vuh* of a man who lies motionless on the ground, his face stretched toward the sky. Around his head like a wheel lie countless sleeping lizards, and radiating from his head to the lizards, like the spokes of the wheel, are countless sleeping snakes.

The story is fragmentary, though, and out of character, as if something was excised by the early Catholic priests in Guatemala, and something else was added, or as if the Mayans dreamt of happiness and hid the story's point to protect it from the government that would disappear it the same way a person is disappeared, never again to be seen.

John Kirk Townsend, the fleeing slaves, the dead man, the Mayans who get along without smiles or tears, they are all spinning down out of these Wind River Mountains carrying Eduardo Galeano along with them. They are a landslide don Eduardo is inside. And being inside, he cannot see what the slide looks like, or how fast it moves, or what makes it start and stop, or where its edges blur into the settled calm of growing trees and singing birds.

When he arrives at the bottom of Doubletop Mountain, don Eduardo lies gasping for breath. He is bleeding and bruised, but no bones are broken. After lying still for some time, he stands and walks to one of the No Name Lakes to bathe, to pick the bits of earth and rock out of the cuts covering his body. John Kirk Townsend is gone. The slaves keep swimming. The pages of the *Popol Vuh* have been battered and torn and are inseparable from bits of dried leaves. Don Eduardo splashes in the water then begins to pull at it. He pushes the water away on both sides of his body as if it would stay away and he could see to the bottom. He is looking for swimmers— fish, turtles, slaves—but he finds none.

Solitaire means hermit. Hermits must be self-sufficient. They must disdain both company and companionship. They neither seek to give nor receive assistance. The solitaire can live through the winter eating frozen juniper berries. Around the solitaire's eye is a thin, white ring making the eye seem bigger than it is, reflecting more light, giving the bird a vision more acute than would otherwise be.

1986
WASHINGTON, D.C.
TANTOS VIGORES DISPERSOS

"The transcendent beauty of the night." But transcending what—
the past? Poverty? Bad food and impure water? Don Eduardo has recently returned north from Jalapa, Nueva Segovia, Nicaragua, where
the night sky whispers rumors and the hills rattle with gunfire.
    Who is the contra? "The morally bankrupt, nearly penniless
mercenary army of the North American dictatorship." Don Eduardo
whispers, surprised to hear himself utter that unequivocal word—
dictatorship. Returning from Nicaragua, it strikes him that he has been
in Wyoming a long time now and is accustomed to its people, its
mountains and plains. Wyoming is no longer a part of North
America—it is that aspen under which don Eduardo sat, that beaver
pond beside a road in the Bighorns, that moose don Eduardo stum-

bled into in a willow thicket. He smiles remembering the way the two of them looked up surprised and fled. "How large the moose was!" he says, then, "I love it here." The word dictatorship rolls like a pebble down the side of a cliff face.

Between Green River and Rock Springs, the tired gentleman with a fairly severe case of diarrhea and a tendency to speak in Spanish without thinking stood hitchhiking under an unforgiving sun and in the midst of a wind measuring itself against the standards of the ocean's sternest breeze. A young woman in a Ford Bronco stopped.

"I could not step into your car compañera, excuse me, señorita, excuse me, Miss. . . . It is so clean and I am so dirty." Don Eduardo brushed at his pants to demonstrate. Granite dust fell.

"It's all right. It's my father's car, and it's usually not so spic and span anyway. Climb in." And the two spoke of Nicaragua and Wyoming. "I've never been anywhere," the young woman said. She sighed, smiled and went on. "I was born here and I've lived here all my life. I'm nineteen. How old are you?"

But being young and enthusiastic, she didn't wait for the answer don Eduardo would have had to make up. The Señor no longer knew his age with any certainty. He'd grown increasingly confused about not only his age but also his familial status and place of habitation. He was a traveler all right, but formerly he'd experienced the necessity to make plans concerning his arrivals and departures. He bought plane tickets, hitched rides with international aid workers, slipped under tarps on long haul trucks and into railroad boxcars whose doors had been left ajar, walked alone into villages high in mountains rarely seen.

All that had come to an end. Now Eduardo Galeano, historian and man, merely waited and things happened. A blink and he'd find unknown scenery before his eyes. Like as not, he'd be standing on some blustery frozen piece of ground in the North American state of Wyoming.

"So you've been here all your life." he said.

"Yeah, all my life," the young woman answered. "I've lived here so long I think I like it, don't even see any more what a pit it is. Listen, I was just going over to Rock Springs, but I've got nothing better to do. I can take you to Rawlins. You going east?"

"Yes, east." And when he turned to look out the window, there was another don Eduardo standing in the crosswalk outside the United States House Office Building, looking up wondering which window belonged to the Honorable Dick Cheney, congressman from the sovereign state of Wyoming.

"What can I tell him?" the emaciated historian thinks. "What can I say that he would understand?"

Here is a small girl child. Her name is Jacqueline. She is three. She is wearing don Eduardo's shoes. She puts them on with her two hands, which perfectly and miraculously are possessed of ten fingers. She loves to wear the grown man's shoes and, in them, walks clumsily, laughing and calling his name, "Eduardo, Eduardo, Eduardo."

Her parents scold her—"Be polite to Señor Galeano, Jacqueline. He is a very great man who has told the story of both our dignity and our deceit." They say this to a three-year-old, and she grins and calls out, "Eduardo, ya está, Eduardo, Eduardo."

In the day, don Eduardo works, all day, every day, building a park and playground for the children of the town. In the hottest moments, some chavalito or chavalita comes to the workers holding a tiny pink popsicle. The chavalita has spent her few cordobas to buy this sweet. And even though don Eduardo is Uruguayan, a brother in language, history and parasites, his intestines have lived too long in libraries and embassies, and he suffers great debilitating bouts of diarrhea from the bad milk and tainted machines in which the popsicles are made. Still he eats them and hurries to the crumbling outhouse across the field.

The mayor comes almost daily to see how the park is coming along. He smiles, his stomach happily escaping the bounds of his bright red doubleknit shirt. He speaks of the importance of this project—a safe, sane place for children, something that tells them the world is more than war and blood, a place secure from the nightmare of the Contra.

Who is the contra? Where does he hide at night when he sleeps? Who buys for him his clothes, and bullets and automatic rifles and rocket launchers, and mortars? What does the Contra feel when a randomly placed bomb goes off and the dead is anyone, the dead is everyone? The Devil or the Lord, it is all the same. Where is this Jalapa Valley so far from the capitals—from Managua, from Washington, from Cheyenne?

Don Eduardo helps to build a merry-go-round, and on the day it is christened, the children are everywhere, running, shrieking, craning their necks to watch the brightly painted tigers and horses spin by, wooden creatures with names like Chumba and Cielito, and with spirits. The children push and shove, and their parents ineffectually attempt to get them to wait patiently in line. But the children will not be patient. And a man, turning to no one says, "I have great hope for a people incapable of lining up."

Once don Eduardo left Jalapa for a meeting in Ocotal. He had a few spare moments and walked into a bookstore, thinking of the poets of Nicaragua and the jokes about the government. Whenever there was a problem, when it was impossible to get nails, or boards were cut the wrong length, or the price of cement had gone up tenfold in a month because of the devaluation, or there were no beans in Matagalpa and no rice in León, whenever any of this, someone would smile and say, "What do you expect of a government run by poets."

Don Eduardo stood in the half empty shop running his eyes along the dusty shelves. It was true that everyone in the country seemed to be a poet. In Managua, the historian was sitting on a bus noodling on a scrap of paper when he noticed that the driver, too, had a notebook. Each time the bus stopped, the driver scratched down a few words. Don Eduardo rode to the end of the line and spoke to this driver. Without affectation, simply as one man of the word to another, the driver spoke back.

He said he'd learned to write in a literacy workshop, that he wrote poems for his love, a woman named Beatriz. It was unclear if this love of his, this Beatriz, was real or imagined. The poems were thick and romantic, filled with flowers and the lips of the night, perfume entangling the speaker and listener alike. The driver explained that he knew what he was doing, that his was not the only kind of poem, that perhaps his was a poetry of too much sentimentality, but that was of no importance. He wrote for his love, and he repeated the word.

In the bookstore, don Eduardo continued to look, running his hands along the dusty metal shelves. There was a man sitting near the door reading a newspaper. He never moved—probably a local catching up on the news. After a long time don Eduardo went to the clerk. "How is it," he asked, "that you have no books by your great poet Ernesto Cardenal?"

"I'm sorry," the clerk said, "but we do have this anthology that includes Cardenal's poems."

At this, the man who had been reading the newspaper appeared at the counter. "Are you interested in poetry?" he asked.

"Yes, I write myself." the historian confessed. "I have tried to write poetry, but I am not so very good."

"Do you know our great national poet Rubén Darío?"

"Yes, I have read his poems."

"Have you seen this book?" And, as if plucked from the folds of a priest's vestments, he produced a small gold paperback book— *Tantos Vigores Dispersos*. One could say in English something like *So Much Scattered Strength*. It is a title that would well serve both the people of Nicaragua and Wyoming, don Eduardo thought, having come to know a little of both places.

"What?"

"Have you seen this book?"

He was insistent, making his guest uncomfortable. His behavior seemed that of a man hustling to elicit a sale.

"I have not seen this book," don Eduardo admitted.

"Look at it, go ahead, look."

Don Eduardo held the book and cautiously turned the pages:

Miserable Gold

Oh, Lord. The world goes badly. Society tugs at its seams. The new century will witness the greatest of the bloody revolutions that bloody the earth. Does the big fish eat the little? Maybe, but suddenly it won't be so. Poverty rules, and the worker carries on his shoulders, like the weight of a mountain, a curse. Nowadays nothing has value but miserable gold.

"It is a beautiful book," don Eduardo said, handing it back.

But the man wouldn't take it. "It is yours," he said, "Please, it is yours." He insisted. "Accept it as a gift from my country."

Already the dust was beginning to gather on the shelf where the book had formerly rested. Don Eduardo thanked the man and together the two approached the clerk so that the man could explain not to charge anything for the book.

"Thank you. Thank you very much." don Eduardo said.

"Please, there is no need. I want to give it to you. I wish you good stay in our country." The man smiled.

Don Eduardo has read Nicaragua's book so many times—the daughters of the poor, the hearts of the poor, the stomachs of the poor—the curse these stomachs are for women, stomachs that instead of filling with food, fill with babies, again and again, babies with open mouths begging bread, tattered babies becoming worn children dressed in the torn shirts of their own filth. This old book by this dead man Rubén Darío, whose anger was as boundless as the flow of weapons from Washington, D.C.

Here don Eduardo loses his way. In all the years chronicling the wars and struggles of Latin America, he has not been so lost as now, riding in a Ford Bronco across Wyoming, standing below the window of Congressman Dick Cheney, being given a gift in Ocotal, Nicaragua.

What can the historian tell the congressman? What can he say that has not been said ten thousand times ten thousand times. The congressman has turned from all these words and stood by a theory. He has said to send money to the Contra, to send food to the Contra, to send advisors to the Contra, to send the Wyoming National Guard to the Contra, to send bullets and bombs to the Contra.

Who is the Contra that one can come to love it more than one loves the tiny, dirty hands of a smiling child?

"Jacqueline is my child," Galeano realizes. "As I am Señor Cheney's child. Together we hold the human heart in our hands, and the heart is our own." The heart pumps blood, and only a secure hold will keep the ground from being soaked, will keep the stain from spreading beneath our feet. Once the blood is on the earth it is also on our carpets and linoleum floors.

Here is don Eduardo working on a park in Jalapa. Here he is accepting the gift of a tainted popsicle from a child. Here he is on the road from Rock Springs to Rawlins listening to the talk of a nineteen year old girl in a $15,000 car. Here he is under the window of an American Congressman, suddenly aware that one more country he thought was not his, naturally and irrevocably, is.

# 1941
## CHEYENNE
### FROM THE *WYOMING LABOR JOURNAL*

"Do you crave adventure? If you do you will be interested in this call for skilled workers on behalf of the Pacific Naval Air Base Contractors. Room, board, laundry, and medical care furnished without charge on outlying islands. Bonus for continuous service. Salary while traveling. This appears to be an opportunity for skilled young men to do a lot of sightseeing and at the same time earn for themselves a nice stake. . ."

All want ads exaggerate a little or put a clean shine on what may have a dirty dull finish, and the ad for the Morrison-Knudsen Construction Company's $20 million air base project at Wake Island, at Midway Island, at Guam Island was no different.

Thirty-four workers from Cheyenne and thirty from Cody answered the call to adventure and spent the next several years in Japanese prisoner of war camps. It's true that room and board were provided. And it's true that though the medical care was not the best, it too was free. The salary was the same whether a man was eating, sleeping, dreaming, or working. As the war went on and the Japanese began to move prisoners from one place to another more and more often, the men got a taste of the sightseeing Morrison-Knudsen had promised.

There was even, exactly as had been stated in their contracts, a bonus for continuous service. If a man lost all his teeth, his bonus was more space in his mouth to fill with thin soup. If a man's hair fell out, his bonus was the money he could save not having to buy combs, brushes and haircuts. If a man's arms and legs grew thin, and his cheeks sank, his bonus was that much less weight to drag through the days.

The most common bonus was bitterness. Men of a gentler sort welcomed the happier bonus of sorrow. One man's bonus was a hatred he would stockpile the rest of his life. Several men who kept their teeth, hair and soft fat received a special bonus—a sly opportunism that would be useful in business after the war. What of those who died? Theirs was the bonus of freedom—a fine bonus. But the best of all was the bonus of wisdom, that though conferred on only a very few, came equally to both prison keepers and imprisoned.

# 1876
## CHEYENNE
### "A PARDONABLE MISTAKE"

M. Notu, commanding general of the Japanese Imperial Army, is touring the West with General Phil Sheridan. General Notu is inspecting the rolling plains and rising mountains of Wyoming.

In Cheyenne, Mr. Notu's staff visits the city's sites. Two young captains are out for an evening stroll through the neighborhoods. The foreign gentlemen are surprised by many large, wood frame houses and by the brilliance of Cheyenne's street lights and by the warm glow emanating from so many of the houses as if the people inside were bathed in enlightenment and peace.

Often the locals leave their curtains open, and the two captains peer in the windows as they pass. Here is a man smoking a pipe—he looks so comfortable with his feet up on a Turkish cushion. There is a woman seated on a divan doing some kind of work with threads and cloth. Here are children reading books and playing on the floor with wooden models and ragged dolls. The Japanese military men are ashamed that they look in, but their eyes are drawn inexorably to these naked lives in the windows.

Coming upon the even brighter lights of the business district, the two men see two other men—occidental cowboys—walking toward them. Made shy by their inability to speak the language, the Japanese officers drop their eyes to the ground. In that moment, the two cowboys uncoil their ropes and toss them lightly into the lamp bright night.

In the morning, the two officers are reported missing. Unable to wait, Generals Sheridan and Notu regretfully leave behind the lost captains. The generals' train steams north and east toward the new mining towns of the Black Hills and the sacred land of the last remaining hostile Indians—the renegade bands of many tribes come together, tentatively, as one. General Notu will observe the American Indians, and perhaps some of them will observe him and will wonder what new creature has come West, and if, like the whites, there will now be numberless hordes of these new men with their waxy skin and thin, shining eyes.

"All of Japan would fit inside that mountain range to the West!" Notu exclaims. "All of Japan. My two officers will be swallowed up like two minnows in the great vast seas."

"Yes," Sheridan agrees, "This America is a big land."

The train rumbles past a herd of several thousand cattle walking slowly north. The steers bawl and low. The plain is an ocean of dust swirling up and away, covering the train, and causing the passengers to close their windows and curtains and look inward.

Behind the cattle, two Japanese Captains, their hands and feet still tied, sit in the cook's wagon amidst the fifty pound sacks of beans and flour. The captains listen to the clanging symphony of blackened pans, enameled plates, and greasy tin cups. The dust billows around them leaking into their lungs through the bandanas that cover their mouths and noses.

At midday the herd stops, and the two newest members of the drive are untied and led, by the cowboys who recruited them, to the trail boss.

"We got everything fixed about the cook dying," they announce,

"Couple of chink cooks we found in town."

Don Eduardo now having worked his way up from cowboy at $35 per month to trail boss for considerably better pay, is rubbing his aching knees and picking bits of beef out of his teeth with a willow twig.

"How do you know they can cook?" he asks.

"Well, they're chinks, ain't they?"

"I don't know. They look Jewish to me."

"Jewish? What are you talking about?"

"It's a joke. How do you know they're Chinese?"

"Well, what else would they be, Mister All-Full-Up-With Questions, naked dance hall girls? Maybe you could ask 'em to give us a dance or sing us a song, huh? Hey, you two girls, lift up your skirts and sing us a song."

The second cowboy goes on. "Say, Mr. Boss, You're a Mex, ain't ya? Maybe these two here's from yer neck a the woods. Coupla bad hombres from down Mexico. Maybe we'll be eating nothing but hot tamales and chiles. If they can't cook, they can always give us the weather report—chile today hot tamale!"

"Yeah, that's right. Hey, Señors, you habla Spanish? Come from Texas?"

The other cowboy turns, "You have to be polite, shitface. Uh, cómo estás, amigos? Señor? Comprende?"

But the two Japanese soldiers don't answer. Don Eduardo watches and can see that while they seem wary and distant, they don't show fear. In their silence, they seem to be studying the scene, as if they could learn their way out of this spot.

"Ok, that'll do." the trail boss says to his cowboys. "Dinner'll be along soon. Why don't you sit down somewhere and wait."

When the cowboys leave, don Eduardo hands each of the Japanese men a tin cup of cool water. He sits on the ground and motions for them to do the same. With a stick he draws a map in the dust—a wobbly coast line of the United States extending down the peninsula of lower Mexico and on along the Central American Republics to Peru and Chile. Then the line turns and comes back north up and around the rio de la plata to Buenos Aires and Montevideo. Don Eduardo carves a line deeply into the ground.

"This is Uruguay," he says, pointing to the map. He presses his hand to the spot, lifts his hand and presses it to his chest, leaving a dusty print on his shirt. "This is where I come from, far from here." He draws a line out to sea and shows it coming up the coast to San Francisco and Portland then east to Wyoming. He punches the ground where Wyoming is then waves both his arms in the air around them.

"Right here, that's where we are, in Wyoming. See that expanse of space, that's this. Where do you come from?" And he takes each man's hands and presses them to that man's chest. Then he pulls the hands away from the chest and touches them to the ground. He presses a hand down about where London would be. And Paris. He presses a hand to Mexico, Brazil, the dark continent of Africa. Showing some discretion he doesn't press their hands to the Orient. Better to let them say whatever they will. He lifts the men's hands from the ground and thrusts them into the air, waving them around.

"Maybe you come from another planet? I know this is not our true home. Everyone is looking for his true home." One more time don Eduardo presses the men's hands to their chests. One more time he presses his hand to his own chest then to the ground where the picture of Uruguay is beginning to disappear as the wind blows the dust away.

One of the two Japanese men picks up a stick and begins to draw. He extends don Eduardo's line north to the top of the world. He fills that in with some hazy squiggly lines then continues down the east coast of Canada and the United States. From there he lifts the stick and begins drawing lines into the interior. He indicates the mountains and the railroads. He draws a large X north and east of where they all sit. He jabs his finger at the X then jabs the same finger at himself and his companion. He throws the stick down.

"That's where you come from?" Don Eduardo scoots himself around to look from the other man's perspective. "That's the Black Hills. You're from the Black Hills? What do you mean?" Abandoning discretion, he takes the stick again and begins drawing the boundaries of the countries across the Pacific. He points at China and then touches the men. They don't move, and their eyes are still as glass. He points at Japan, Korea, Malay, all over southern Asia. The men look as if he were pointing at a blank page in an imaginary book.

The second Japanese man takes the stick. He etches over the X again, carving deeply into the earth, pushing so hard the stick snaps, and he falls forward on his arms.

"Ok, you're from the Black Hills. It's mighty peculiar that you don't talk. You two deaf mute twin brothers?"

Don Eduardo smiles at the men and helps them up. He points at the cook wagon and walks away leaving them there alone. They're not from the Black Hills, that's for sure.

After a few days in which the Japanese officers show clearly they know nothing of biscuits, coffee, beans or beef, don Eduardo is able to fire his foreign cooks. The two disappear on foot toward the Black Hills. And coming from that region is a crippled miner looking for work.

The cowboys spoke neither Japanese nor Chinese. The Japanese officers spoke neither English nor Spanish. No one was able to ask questions nor give answers and thus it was, according to a Wyoming historian, that in this case "the mistake was pardonable."

Some historian, don Eduardo thinks, and turns back to the trail, to the indecipherable bawling and lowing of the cows as they amble north.

1942

CASPER

ALOHA

"America has been attacked! The most peace loving, the most forbearing, the most generous and charitable, the most magnanimous nation of this world has been treacherously assaulted, without an instant's warning, by the yellow scum of the Pacific. . ."

So reports the *Wyoming State Tribune*. In Laramie, editor Ernie Linford writes that it isn't difficult for an American to hate a Japanese. The Japanese represent everything that is "vicious, snaky and underhanded."

It is the dark, cool night of the year. The wind blows across the plain and through the sage making it rustle. The frozen boards of the Burlington Station creak as the hours pass. For neither the sage nor the boards is sound speech. Don Eduardo stands in the dark waiting.

He holds a burning cigarette in his mouth, and though no words leave his lips, the silent smoke of the cigarette speaks pages of his feelings. Editor Linford is a racist opportunist. Even so, it's off to war. For almost everyone. A member of the Church of Jehovah's Witnesses chooses peace over war and for his refusal to fight is sentenced to two years in the penitentiary. After he has served his time, he returns home to Albany County and is again called by his draft board and again states that he cannot go off to kill and is again sent to prison for two years. From this man's painful stubbornness, the courts learn a lesson. Henceforth Jehovah's Witnesses who refuse the draft are given prison terms of not two but four years.

The Wyoming Constitution expressly forbids the hiring of women workers in the mines, but these are grave times. The women descend into the earth. The president of United Mine Workers District 22 local signs a contract of agreement with the Union Pacific coal company stating that as soon as men are again available the women will be released. In the meantime, women must join the union in order to work.

The smoke drifts upward and away. "Yes, I know it's crazy. No, I'm not an American citizen." Don Eduardo's thoughts hang solid in the frozen air.

It took some doing to land in the United States Army. The Casper recruiter had to find a translator when the gaunt gentleman first came to call. Then there were the physical defects to ignore: "Mr. Galeano's blood workup shows the presence of malaria, his kidney function is weak, he's got an arhythmic heartbeat and a hiatal hernia, the knuckles of his right hand have all been broken and are so badly twisted he could not accurately fire a rifle, the tendons in his ankles are both loose and inflexible such that he could run only slowly over smooth terrain and not at all over rough ground, and he has hemorrhoids."

"Yes, all this is true," don Eduardo admitted, the smoke rising jetlike in the cold air. "Still, I feel I can be of service. I speak Italian, Portuguese and Rumanian as well as my native Spanish. I know enough history to be helpful in understanding the psychology of many peoples, and I believe the racist theories of National Socialism may mean the extermination of several ethnic minorities."

The recruiter shifted in his seat and smiled. "I'm sorry, buddy, maybe another time."

"But . . ."

"Really, I'm sorry. Remember, true patriotism lies in doing what will best serve the war effort, not in rushing to be a hero. The shape you're in you'd probably wind up dead in a week."

On the platform, don Eduardo took another puff and smiled. "Dead. If only it could be true." The feeble recruit has been through more trouble in more lifetimes than the Casper recruiting officer will ever know. Ah, well.

A week later, don Eduardo had gone ahead—he'd died and been reborn. Sporting a moustache and with hair dyed light brown, he walked vigorously into the recruiter's office carrying the results of another series of tests that showed him to be in A-1, tip-top condition.

The February cold platform at the Burlington Rail Station. The members of the Aloha Committee of the American Legion smiling and shaking hands with the soldiers as they board. Each soldier given a gift pack that cost the Committee 84 cents to prepare—two five cent candy bars, a pack of cigarettes, a deck of playing cards and a Legion booklet of helpful advice called *Fall In*.

After the Aloha Committee finishes up, the American War Mothers give each boy five postcards and a memo book to keep track of the days. The days go by, the days are long, the days are dark.

The Casper High School band strikes up "Aloha." When the tune is finished, the brass players pull the mouthpieces from their horns and, to keep them warm, stick the small bits of silvery metal under their armpits. What a thin joke it would be if a frozen mouthpiece stuck to a trumpeter's lips and the blood began to pour forth here before the war had even begun. The players pull their mouthpieces from under their arms and strike up the National Anthem.

The warm smoke from the engine becomes a billowing beautiful cloud of steam in the frozen air. The train begins slowly to depart. Don Eduardo tosses his cigarette down and crushes it. Aboard, he hangs from his window and waves at all the men, women and children he does not know, all the people for whom this is home.

In Cheyenne, the train stops and the men must wait twenty-four hours for the next train that will carry them south and east. Don Eduardo walks to the USO.

"Excuse me, sir," a voice says as don Eduardo enters the former creamery turned social hall, "But this USO is for Negro troops only."

"Oh, I'm sorry," and the white soldier turns to leave. He walks across town to another USO.

"Hey, boy, this club is for white troops only."

"Oh, yes," don Eduardo says politely and ducks his head, dropping his eyes so they do not meet those of the doorkeeper. "Excuse me, I'll be on my way."

Eduardo Galeano, US Army recruit, on his way to training, is taken to be white by those who are black, and black by those who are white. All night such a man walks the streets of Cheyenne, puffing as the frozen air bites into his chest. In the morning, he again boards the train.

It is hard to know exactly why he goes to fight, hard to know what he is fighting for. Perhaps he will get off the train at its next stop and make his way to the church of the Jehovah's Witnesses, or to a coal mine run by women, or to the fields where when he bends down he sees only the dark earth and when he stands up and lifts his head he sees only the bright sky and the white clouds drifting away. It is hard to say when he will throw down his gun and walk forward, defenseless, into the bullets.

# 1776
## HOLE IN THE WALL
## A SCAVENGER HUNT

Don Eduardo bends over to pick a piece of paper from the red earth. It is a list:

Ree Twist Tobacco
Bark of Red Willow
Sweet Grass
Bone Knife
Stone Axe
Buffalo Tallow
Tanned Buffalo Calf Hide
Rabbit Skins
Eagle Plumes

Red Earth Paint
Blue Paint
Rawhide
Buffalo Skull
Rawhide Bag
Eagle Tail Feathers
Whistles from Wing Bones of Spotted Eagle

But a list to do what? Don Eduardo scratches his head. When he sticks his finger in his ear, he can hear the breeze, very light, and in the breeze, the voice of the cottonwood tree who is praying to the Spirit.

The breeze is warm as the season advances. These are the days of the Moon of Fattening becoming the Moon of the Blackening Cherries. The cold moon is long gone and forgotten. The moon is the sun, and the light glares off the white piece of paper.

A list to do what? Don Eduardo looks down and again begins to read:

Seed Corn
Rum
Window Glass
Sashing Gum
Whale Lamp Oil
Salt and Pepper
Barrel Staves
Sailcloth
Bridle and Bit
Flintlock and Powder
Herring Net
Wool Cap
Two Man Buck Saw
Pump Organ
Green Silk
Pinch of Sugar

A scavenger hunt in two worlds. Don Eduardo begins to have a vision—the Northern Plains and New England, both struggling to be free, both still held in the grip of nature.

Nature, it has been said, has no sense of humor. Beautiful, ugly, or neither, it is not laughing. But the person who said this was not listening, was dead on the January day when in twelve hours the temperature rose from twenty below to seventy, was asleep when the moon blotted out the sun and the bright center of day fell dark, was paying no attention when on a steaming summer day the hail began to fall and a baby girl held out her hand to catch the icy balls.

One who would have a vision must do certain things—must be as water, lower than all things and yet stronger than stone. That is not so hard. Then for three days not to eat or drink. The stomach will rumble like a roaring train. That is the train of nature, laughing as it comes. To take off all one's clothes and rub sage into one's skin. Sage, patchouli, peanut butter—it doesn't matter; just rub until the skin becomes something else.

Cry. Cry for what is lost, for what is in pain. Open your heart and see that it is pure. Cry from this pure heart. How long can you cry? One day? Two days? Three or four? You can cry up to four days or even more. You can cry for four thousand days.

"Wait," don Eduardo shouts at the piece of paper, waving it around. Somehow it has grown hotter and hotter. The sun's light has focused there as if through a magnifying glass, and a leaf has begun to smoke. The paper bursts into flame. Don Eduardo can't let go.

"What about the lists? Why is one list full of buffalo and willow and rabbit skin while the other holds wool caps and pump organs and rum? Or was it one list? What else did it say—feathers from a raven's beak? Sandstone? A wedding dress?"

One who would have a vision must have a guide and must follow the prescribed route. Then this one must go alone high in the mountains or far on the distant plains or out to sea in a boat built by hand. To go alone.

To have a pure heart, to be attentive, one must be poor in the things of the world. Our feet must be bare and our hands empty. One must go into the world, into Nature. There is no symbolic meaning to anything. There is no language but being. There is no morality. One must be an accident, be accidentally standing in a spot never before seen.

"Wait!" Don Eduardo shouts again. "The list is here, but the items are not the same."

Men die but live again in a world of spirit. Don Eduardo has died many times and been reborn. So this is the world of spirit. This is the sacred ground. This is the vision.

"You mean I can burn the list up as many times as I want? That it will return if I hold my hand out again? What about my hand? Can I burn it up, too?"

Off the Coast of Africa, a Rhode Island slave ship sinks. Uncounted souls are devoured by the current. In Pennsylvania, colonist and agitator Tom Paine says there is something ridiculous in a monarchy. Why not strike out for freedom, Paine suggests? All Men are Created Equal, the American Declaration of Independence claims. Its author, Thomas Jefferson, lover of slave women, pursues the revelations of nature and wants to embrace all aspects of human thought.

Don Eduardo looks down and sees the ground is littered with pieces of paper. They drift over the earth in the breeze. Here and there a piece of paper bursts into flame. When the wind picks up, the flames leap toward the trees, toward Don Eduardo's hands and clothes. Words rise off the paper and spin away unencumbered. But they're not words, they're mosquitos and flies, and they fill the air making it buzz.

# 1945
## ALBANY COUNTY
## WAR BUSINESS

A hundred trains per day pass through Laramie. The Union Pacific's gross income soars. In these hills made of dust where nothing grows but what is tended, World War II has brought money and good times. Four years after Pearl Harbor, the UP's cash and investment total is over $280,000,000; the working balance is over $200,000,000.

The Union Pacific is Wyoming's greatest single industrial enterprise, laying down thousands of railroad ties like narrow coffins on the parched earth and employing thousands of workers lining up each day to punch in and out.

Though they are making tons of money on tons of freight, the railroad's executives still worry over their profit and loss sheets. Revenues are down on some of the passenger lines. To compensate, fares are raised ten percent, and the company makes plans to abandon the 110 mile long Laramie, North Park and Western line.

The war ends and, in most circles, there is jubilation. All over Wyoming the bars are jumping, and there is dancing in the streets. People are kissing each other in public, and behind closed doors they are lying down together to make babies.

In the board room of the UP, though, brows are furrowed and mouths are grave.

"You see this?" a vice president asks, waving a wad of greenbacks. "You know where this comes from, you know what to do."

Lonely don Eduardo is home from war again, home from the ten thousandth war of his short life. He has been to the bars where he was jammed in with the crowd and felt the sweaty pressure of strange shoulders against his own. Men pumped his arms and slapped him on the back, and women and girls kissed him on the cheek. In a dark moment, he felt a hand reach inside his pants and stroke his penis then drop and lightly squeeze his testicles. He looked around, but there was no way to tell whose sly smile was for him alone. The drinks kept coming and the sweat kept flowing.

Don Eduardo made his way to the edge of the crowd and out the door. He walked the 110 miles of the Laramie, North Park and Western. He looked up at the sky and, in the quiet, felt happy. One more war was over, and it was like the old song said, "Who could ask for anything more? Who could ask for anything more?"

Someone could. The executives of the Union Pacific are hunched over a long table, their eyes scouring large sheets of paper, credits and debits, profits and losses, production and consumption. Everything taken into consideration, new plans are forming in their minds.

# 1890

## RAWLINS

## MONEY SINGS

"There is no song in the fields of Wyoming and therefore it is sad here."

Israel Boloten, Jew from Russia, arrives wearing a dirty brown derby and able to speak only two words in English—"Free Land."

"Farther up this dusty trail, Mr. Boloten, farther along." Don Eduardo, who remembers so well the handicap of not speaking one language or another, points toward the rimrock country. Don Eduardo is scraping at the ground with a dull piece of iron. Maybe he's planning to sow a crop. Maybe he's planning to start a mine. Maybe he thinks to level the ground and cut a road through these hills. He is humming to himself as he works, but under the fall of the iron, his hum is inaudible. Don Eduardo works, as a writer once said, without hope and without despair, and in apparent illusory silence.

There is no song about corn or wheat or seeds sewn in the black warming earth, no song about new grass going to green as it grows. The horses with their heavy feet like stones drag the plow in silence. The farmer walks behind, his silent thoughts looming in his mind. In silence a clod of earth turns and crumbles to dust. No rain falls, and so the drops do not sing their way to earth.

Without song, the little grain that has sprung up along the water courses is cut and threshed and stacked and stored. There are no peach trees, no pear trees, no plum or cherry. Only apples survive these winters. They cling to the branches of their trees as if falling meant striking the earth without a sound, as if the earth were an open mouth, ravenously hungry, prepared only to swallow and go on, as if in falling the apples would sink into a cool gelatin and drift down through the layers to the silent center of the planet. Silent men and women shake the branches and bend to the earth. They lift in silence the reluctant fruit. No one sings. As hard as the men and women, the apples silently work.

"There are no women in the fields and so it is sad." Israel notices. "The young women don't walk, carrying the hay on their backs, feeling the glances of the young men on their naked feet. Their feet do not sing. Even their shuffle is in silence. Surely some would sing."

"What about going home?" don Eduardo asks as Israel disappears down the road. But the quiet words of the quiet question bounce off Israel's back as he strides forward. And when the words clatter noisily to the ground, somehow Israel does not hear. Don Eduardo begins to put his question forward again, but his voice quavers as if what would come out should be the melody of a tune long forgotten, as if he would recognize in speech his own journey home not made.

It doesn't make any difference. Israel is prepared to fit in. He speaks less and less and sings not at all. He attends to business. At a lawyer's, he asks for a less Jewish name and becomes Isadore Bolten. Farther up in the rimrock country he files a claim and finds a mule team. He works quietly for the railroad grading roadbeds. He works on a ranch and saves his wages. He buys 1000 broken-mouth ewes. The American who sells them smiles slyly, knowing these sheep won't make it through the winter.

But it's the mildest winter on record. Isadore's sheep with no teeth survive and give birth to young. The price of lambs rises. Isadore prospers in silence. He begins spending his evenings at the Rawlins public library. A local widow notices him and buys him a Cadillac. Isadore doesn't need this woman's money, but he accepts the car and on Sundays the two go for a drive. The rubber tires hum against the hug of the road.

Though the hum is not song in the fields, it is a hum. It is a hum. Mmmmmmmm. From that beginning one might stretch sound to song.

# 1890
## CHEYENNE
## FOR STATEHOOD

Two new companies of troops are mustered into the armed forces—companies H and K. They are like every other company in the Army except that they are women—the first women troops in the United States Army—and they are from Wyoming, the Equality State. They are called the Girl Guards.

The girls wear spiked helmets and carry regulation army rifles in slings over their backs. Their uniforms include ankle length dresses which are very hard to run in, either uphill or down. The fronts of the uniforms are covered by rows of gold cord draped in graceful scoops, and the troopers wear white gloves for all occasions.

Companies H and K drill like every other company in the Army. For two months they drill, the only difference being that they are work-

---

ing exclusively on parade ground displays in preparation for their duty as guards of honor to the Wyoming state flag. Any company might be called on for parade duty. Companies H and K surround the state float in the statehood day parade. On the float sit beautiful young girls. They are dressed in red, white and blue high-collared gowns. They represent all the states. Each state is a lovely young woman. Companies H and K march below the states, their footprints left on the earth, just as the footprints of all the soldiers who have marched since the beginning of time, are scattered throughout the west. There are so many footprints. It is unclear who has passed and whether she has been a man, woman, child, white, Indian, runaway slave, hungry freedman, or even some large animal whose paw print approximates the flat of a human foot, the delicate toes that give us all our balance.

The girls on the float wave and smile. The girl members of companies H and K, like other troopers, look straight ahead and seem neither happy nor sad, their faces masks and their feelings indecipherable to those who do not know them.

When the celebration is over, the Girl Guards are disbanded. They are like all soldiers, happy to go home, weary with the business of war.

# 1914

## CHIHUAHUA, MEXICO
## A LONG WAY TO GO

The North Americans pour south across the good, oiled highways of the United States onto the dusty roads of Mexico. Just last year, seventy-one year old Ohioan Ambrose Bierce, that eccentric teller of tales, took a morning off from his literary duties and murdered himself. "It's not the first crime I've committed." Bierce admitted. After refusing to distinguish his stories from his life, Bierce fled into the arms of Pancho Villa, that ragged revolutionary whose spit covered the ground around him in blood and tobacco.

"I could have poisoned myself. I could have cinched tight a rope around my neck and let my malignant old body hang from the noose. I could have inserted a shining silver pistol into my mouth and down my throat and pulled the trigger. I could have done any number of things. But instead, in my old age, I joined the troops and sat waiting for a stray bullet, for a magical bullet erratically wandering over the surface of the earth, jolting in and out of the clouds of dust and reflecting the sunlight so as to be first invisible then seen from every direction. Some say such bullets are playing with human misery and pain, but I know it is I who am playing with the bullets. My dignity is more important than my life."

As Ambrose Bierce dies, his fellow North American John Reed is coming to life. Bouncing across Chihuahua on the back of a mule, Reed's eyes open wider and wider. He talks to everyone; he writes down every word he hears, every sound from the tortured throats of birds. He notes the colors of people's eyes, the look of their hands and feet, the smell of the foods they cook and of the bodies they inhabit. Reed carries only a pen and paper. He sleeps where the day ends. He eats what strangers offer him.

"¿Juanito?" the people ask him, "Where have you come from and why have you come here and how is it you are so different from other North Americans?" And many more questions.

To all of which Reed can only mumble and smile and keep listening to the voices around him. The voices tell him again and again all men are one, all women are one, all children dream of growing to adulthood, and all adults dream of living happily into their old age and dying without pain.

"But I am like the other North Americans. I am." John Reed promises.

Working his way slowly south, Eduardo Galeano begins with his eyes. He stands on a shallow rise and stares. In Wyoming, there are spots where you can look farther and see less than in any other place on earth. You can see to Chihuahua. Galeano jerks back when he realizes it's Mexico in the distance. He'd meant to leave for home, but now seeing something like it wobbling there like a mirage in the heat, he realizes he is home and may as well stay. He can see the scowl of a smile on Pancho Villa's face as the emotional general pulls out his pistol and aims it at a messenger galloping in from the north with good news. Villa fires and the bullet wraps itself around the messenger's intestines as they fall out like a dropped rope onto the ground. Other bullets fly north like mites under the wings of migrating birds.

All this don Eduardo can see. No need to get closer than here. John Reed is right—Wyoming is Mexico; Mexico is Wyoming. John

Reed has traveled from Portland, Oregon to New York to Chihuahua, from shock to shock and marvel to marvel. "It is the same with me," don Eduardo says to the south. "From shock to shock and marvel to marvel. I awoke in this land and was fed an unidentifiable stew and a pie of gray color. The people who fed me kept blinking and rubbing their faces, a gluey film oozing around their eyes. There were weapons everywhere and people willing to use them. Here, as there, blood darkened the summer sunlight, blood darkened the wind, the flowers, the grasses, the sweeping cottonwood trees. The difference is that Bierce and Reed traveled south while I came north."

Galeano admires Reed—"He is a man who rejoices with those who rejoice and weeps with those who weep."

What more can one do? Rejoice and weep. Chihuahua and Wyoming—two states familiar with war, both possessed of fields and forests. The mice swarm, gnawing and devouring what they can. There are huge, beautiful butterflies and moths almost a foot long. The creatures come upon us everywhere and give us no rest. Men like Reed and Galeano learn to move quickly, to swat the insects around their faces, to change homes as easily as gentlemen change their frock coats. Men like Galeano and Reed learn to listen and, without belief, to pray.

# 1988
## Yellowstone Park
### Fire

The long line of men and women in yellow fireproof jackets. The matching yellow hardhats bobbing up and down as the line undulates through the smoking woods. The portable shovels hinged midway up the handle and carried on each firefighter's back. The radios and chronometers, the fanny packs and water jugs, the axes, the eyes tired and soot encrusted, the rings of black.

In ten thousand years and all over the world, there have been only three hundred fires as large as this one now burning one million acres. Two thousand years ago, the fire burned in the Middle East. Four men rose changed by the flames. John was the eagle flying above the earth. Luke was the ox offering himself as a sacrifice to his God. Mark was the lion, his voice crying out in the desert. Matthew was man, troubling himself over love.

Matthew said, "Do not be anxious about tomorrow; tomorrow will look after itself. Each day has troubles of its own." Matthew believed what he said, but still he worried. After all, the flames burned on, outside him, without him.

It has been a summer of drought, of day after day hot and dry, of hot winds blowing across dry grasses and blistering pine needles, seventy mile per hour winds burning the faces of 10,000 firefighters in a line, of 4400 soldiers and marines now drafted as firefighters, too.

The smoke and ash fill the sky blotting out the sun, which has become a pure red orb. You can look directly at it. The smoke drifts across the sun's face. In and out of the hot gray fly seventy-seven helicopters trailing room sized buckets of water. They dump them then return to the river for more. Five C-130 air tankers drop clay slurry, drop chemical fire retardants, drop a blanket over fire.

Bulldozers plow down trees and, with the fire, transform dense woodlands into meadow. The firetrucks roll across plants so dry it is like rolling across millions of tiny mollusks left behind when the seas departed.

Lightning reaches down and a spark rises, flames hundreds of feet high, then the column of a firestorm 50,000 feet up. Before a firestorm hits, there is a lull. The trees sway gently and ash drifts down, slowly, like spring snow. Each piece of ash grows larger and, ultimately, bursts into flame raining fire on the forest. Up through the column of fire flashes the flame. The unburned gases ignite, and at the top of the column, miraculously though uselessly, ice crystals form.

Two-hundred souls of the Church Universal and Triumphant stand in a line facing the flames. Elizabeth Clare Prophet, Guru Ma, arises from the Heart of the Inner Retreat. With her people she chants, "Reverse the tide. Roll them back. Set all Free." Over and over they call, "Roll them back. Set all free."

The Storm Creek fire to the North. The Hellroaring fire to the Southwest. The Clover Mist fire to the South. Fire in every direction.

Exhausted, don Eduardo prepares for his first evening out under the flames. The fire comes at him like a locomotive. Full black night, and the wind still rises. With others, Galeano has helped to build 850 miles of firelines, trenches across which fire is reluctant to pass. But the fires have leaped almost every ditch and come on. Here is a fireline, next to it a backfire line, there a back-backfire line. Still the fire comes on. With his compañeros, don Eduardo shakes out a tiny silver foil tent, previously neatly folded in its yellow packet. This tent has never been used, and Galeano is not terribly confident as to its efficacy in the inferno. Still, with nothing else to do, he climbs inside the shining cocoon and hunkers down.

Now there is only the waiting, listening as the roar reaches out to him, and the fire passes over him, the fire burning across his back below a tiny protective sheen. Inside it is hotter than he has ever been, and he gasps, sucking for the little air the fire leaves as it passes, the fire gulping up all the oxygen in its path.

Fire. And why not? The helicopters have jettisoned their heavy cargo of water laden buckets and now carry "Ping-pong balls." These ping-pong balls are tiny incendiary devices. They fall in the thousands from the sky and explode on contact with the earth, starting mini-fires meant to turn the main fires.

On the ground, risen from their tents and amidst the falling grenades walk the torchers. In his arms, don Eduardo carries a can of fire. From the can's snout drips flame—more backfires to turn the main fires. With the torchers, don Eduardo has lived through a passing curtain of fire. Now he walks with them. His boots smoke and the soles periodically burst into flame. He steps down, and the fire is extinguished. His foot rises and again bursts into flame. Back and forth as he walks. And back and forth the fires and the backfires. The hair on his hands and on his neck has been burned off.

Now there is no distinction in the fires—main fire, back fire, lightning fire, firestorm, dripping fire, rising fire. Everything is fire and burns.

# 1963
## JACKSON
## AGAIN

The fences undulate across the ground like torn veins and arteries nailed onto the surface of the skin. Meant to block one thing out while blocking another thing in, the fences cling to the friction between surfaces. Every fence, notwithstanding its resigned and desperate grab for the ground, is inevitably breached. And sometimes the fences wave like moving lines, like string leaping off a spinner to follow a kite rising into the sky.

The sky is the home of flight. Lie back and the sky will hold you. The hawk and the eagle rest above the clouds, wings spread and still. The little birds jump and flap, and the sky holds them aloft, too.

The solitary mare looks up then back down, eyeing a particularly delicious parcel of earth, the dust offering to billow in the absence of wind, on a day of calm, rising. The mare lands on her back and twists left and right, rolls side to side, flips her head and pushes her face into the dirt. Her legs straight up, her feet want to lie back and fly.

It is 1963 and Olaus Murie is dead. "Long live Olaus Murie," whispers Mardy Murie, "Long live love." The whisper rises from her mouth and lies back, and the sky holds it as between parted lips. The fence is a string the eye can follow up and away. It lies back. The horse and the hawk, the eagle. Mardy Murie lets herself recline. Long live love. Olaus Murie lies back and smiles.

# 1990
## CORA
### THESE NAMES

Forever here in this moment at this point. We can love a place so deeply that the place is for us a person. The person's name makes us swoon—Cora. Cora. Cora. Not only the native but the immigrant can feel this deeply.

In Wyoming, Don Eduardo hates the cold. He hates the politics. He hates this place where streets and towns and schools and hospitals and mountains and lakes are named for the criminals of the past. Why do we hate those who delude and oppress us today but admire and honor those who did so yesterday?

Don Eduardo hates the capricious rain, the way it sits quietly in a corner for months withholding itself while the grass burns under a sun that never holds back, the capricious rain, the way when it comes it comes in a rush and tears the infrequent tree from the earth. Don Eduardo hates the coal mines, uranium mines, gold mines, the oil wells, methane wells, natural gas wells. He hates all these things that skin the earth, drain the earth, beat the earth, leave the earth behind. There is plenty to hate.

But don Eduardo has been here too long. When he enters a house and scrapes the bentonite clay from the heels of his boots, he smiles. The earth is pulling at him. It wants him. He runs its names across his tongue, tasting the corners of a land he came to ignorantly and accidentally. He closes his eyes, and all the bitter feelings and memories fly, leaving behind only the land and the wind pulling at his hair. The wind is begging him to come with it, to let his body fall apart in a million pieces and disappear into the everywhere.

He has come to live in the names—Sand Creek, Dry Creek, Owl Creek, Poison Spider Creek, Crazy Woman Creek, Fish Creek, Buffalo Creek, Wild Horse Creek, Wild Cow Creek, Antelope Creek, Muddy Creek, Big Muddy Creek, Little Muddy Creek, Sulphur Creek, Alkali Creek, Fivemile Creek, Tenmile Creek, Fifteenmile Creek, No Water Creek, Nowood Creek, Cottonwood Creek, Lodgepole Creek, Boxelder Creek, Du Noir Creek, Richeau Creek, La Prele Creek.

In the names where don Eduardo lives are Chain Lakes Flat, Alkali Flat, Greasewood Flat, Red Desert Flat, Boar's Tusk, Black Rock Butte, Sand Butte, Pine Butte, Cloud Peak, Sierra Madre, Medicine Bow Peak, Snowy Range, Wind River Range, Washakie Needles, Appolinaris Spring, Thunder Basin, Lightning Flat, Rattlesnake Range, Ten Sleep Canyon.

In don Eduardo's heart is the name—Heart Lake. And Heart Mountain, Heart Point, Heart beat. Don Eduardo places his hand over his chest and feels the beating of his heart. The thumping of his heart. His heart pounding. The constant slam and wham of his heart. His heart in every spot of Wyoming on which he has stood.

There is so much to hate. There is so much to love. One day the hating seems pointless and stupid. All that matters is what one loves. Don Eduardo falls on his face and stretches his arms and legs out in the dust, in the mud, on the ice, in a puddle soon to disappear. He is trying to embrace the entire world, and one day soon he is going to succeed.

## 1965
### LANDER
### A LITTLE SPEECH

What's in a name and a rose by any other name, but it isn't true. For everybody his name matters, and for every place its name says what it is. Each act of naming sends some to eternity and some to oblivion.

Fifteen-year-old Eddie Galeano gets up to give a speech in speech class and begins to make his arguments as to why the Wind River Reservation should be expanded to include all of Wyoming, and why at least one-third of the Western United States should be given back to the Indians who could form their own country and make their own laws and live in a way that would once again put them in contact with the sources of all life in the water and land and how there could be a picture of Cochise or Sitting Bull or Chief Joseph or somebody on the Indian Nation passport and how maybe some white people could apply for citizenship and stay on in the new land and all.

That's about how coherent the speech is and Eddie's classmates, especially his Indian ones, give him a low ranking. His teacher is sympathetic and suggests the young man try again with a more modest suggestion and a tighter argument.

"Where do we live?" Eddie asks in his next speech. "We live in Lander, Wyoming. Lander is on the Wind River Reservation, but mostly white people live in town. The town is named after General F. W. Lander who was sent by the government in 1857 to survey along the Oregon Trail and improve roads. Improve roads—I think that means make it so pioneers could just go across Indian land any time they wanted." Eddie can't help adding as an aside.

"The people who lived here called this the Valley of Warm Winds. Why don't we rename our town? Let's give it back to the people who belonged to it. Let's give it back to the wind."

The speech teacher lifts his head. That phrase—"Let's give it back to the wind." That's pretty eloquent. The teacher makes a note to check and see if the boy plagiarized that.

Eddie is going on: "Lander—named for a general. And what are our other places named for? Sheridan—for a general. Rawlins—for a general. Augur Hill—for a general. Crook County—for a general. Grenville—for a general. Barlow Peak—for a Captain. Bates Hole—for a Captain. Casper—for a lieutenant. Depot McKinney—for a lieutenant. Custard's Hill—for a sergeant."

"These are the places named for those who came here to exterminate the Indians. General Connor gave the order to his men—'Accept no overtures of peace or submission from Indians. Attack and kill every male Indian over twelve years of age.' Connor surrounded a camp of Paiutes on Bear Creek and murdered 278 Indians—all the males over twelve years of age, plus all the males under twelve years of age plus all the females of all ages. The others were free to go in peace. . ."

"Excuse me, Eddie," the teacher interrupted. "The parallel structure you've set up is good—name, general, name, general, and so forth. But don't let yourself be carried away by emotion. Sarcasm often puts people off. And remember Bear Creek didn't happen in Wyoming, so it really has no bearing on your argument in this speech. Go on."

Eddie tried to pick up the thread.

". . . there are the places named to honor those who came to ex-

terminate the animals—Laramie—for a trapper. Sublette County—
for a trapper. Colter—for a trapper. Jackson—for a trapper. And
Cody—for a psychopathic buffalo murderer turned sideshow huckster."
"Whoa, Eddie, hold it. You can't call William Cody a psychopath.
You're letting your feelings blur what can be verified historically. And
remember you don't want to alienate your listeners, you want to con-
vince them to accept your position in this matter. Don't call Buffalo
Bill a murderer, call him a hunter. And it would be better to say he
was an innovative entrepreneur not a 'sideshow huckster.' Go ahead.
Keep trying."

Feeling a little lost, or else having decided to follow his own way
no matter what, Eddie tries to begin again.

"Well," he starts up, "I was just thinking that it would be fair and nice,
too, and everything if a few places could be named for people of other
beliefs, other ideas, you know, and other races. I know there are a few
names like that—Coon Hollow for a black man who lived there and Nigger Baby Springs for a black child who was found dead in the water."

"Eddie! What did I say about sarcasm? I told you not to alienate
your audience."

But Eddie Galeano, moralizer and student, has worked himself
into a frenzy. "Oh, fuck it," he shouts.

"There will be no obscenity in my classroom, young man. You
may step down, your speech is finished."

"Fuck it, I said, fuck it and rename everything. Call the towns
Dull Knife and Red Cloud and Spotted Tail and Two Moons and Hump
and Gall and Young-Man-Afraid-of-His-Horses. Or call them Badger,
Coyote, Wolf, Bear, Pronghorn, Elk, Moose, Cougar, Fox, Deer, Porcupine, Skunk, Hawk, Magpie, Mountain Lion, Owl, Hummingbird. Or
call them Wind, Rain, Sun, Thunder, Lightning, Hail, Snow. Call them
anything, only don't call them by the names of soldiers and trappers
and bureaucrats who came to destroy everything and everyone and
almost did. Do you hear me? Call them anything else, Goddam it."
Eddie is screaming at the top of his lungs.

"You don't have to shout, young man." The teacher looks angry
and stern but, it's with a certain sympathy that he says, "We can hear
you perfectly well. Besides, you know we can't rewrite history. It's not
ours to modify the past. Please sit down, Eddie."

"Oh, anything, just anything," Eddie says again slowly and softly,
slumping into his desk.

250

1958

MOUNTAIN VIEW

THE BIOLOGY LESSON

As usual, the racked and torn body screams its agony, but does not die. This is its final defeat and only triumph. The delicate butchers slip their knives in and out of the pulsing flesh, careful to make only the prescribed cuts, the grade A approved cuts, the cuts that will exaggerate the body's beauty while rendering it unrecognizable. Those holding the knives are made delirious by the delicious taste of meat cut from living muscle.

But who are the butchers? We need not invent devils and demons for these sleep sweetly inside us. And with angels and lords it is the same. These latter thunder and sing inside our veins, and the heavy pounding bass of their music in our heads makes us first giddy then deaf.

In mid-April, the sun shines down through clouds of jostling spirit butchers. In the night, it has snowed. Under the sun's multiple eyes, the snow begins to retreat into the earth. On a fencepost making tracks in the white, shaking itself and fluttering to rise, is a meadowlark. Its watery warbling song bounces among the spirits and off the infrequent trees. It flies ahead across a field in the middle of which lies a pronghorn, dead for some time, a little skin left dried and tight over crumbling bones, or loose at the corners and flapping in the wind. Colder than the earth, the pronghorn lies covered in snow when all around the ground is bare. There, as if painted, lies the perfect white outline of the animal in flight.

The biology teacher rings the neck of a chicken. "Whyntcha just cut off its head?" some voice asks.

"Too messy," the teacher thinks, "The blood would spurt around the room. It'd be a nightmare for the janitor to clean up."

The biology teacher has asked one of his thirteen-year-old students to bring in a chicken for an experiment, and the girl has brought the most beautiful chicken the teacher has ever seen. Crimson wattle and comb, angry black eyes, shining blue feathers, rock-hard, sharp spurs. It seemed a shame not to use some more battered chicken— one reeking of mites and whose face and head are torn and scarred after narrow escapes from hawks and swinging doors, whose useless claws are puffy and oozing from bumblefoot.

Landing on the fence around the school, the meadowlark stands wearing the snowy cloak of pronghorn skin, and sings.

"Yes, yes," the biology teacher says to his students. He's dissected about everything for them and now in spring he has to move fast. Ring the neck with a quick spin, then cut the bird open along the center of the ventral side of its body. Carefully, gently, the way a first-time mother bathes a newborn baby, massage the feathers and skin away, and lift the still beating heart out of the body. It's better if a student does this as the small fingers inflict less damage on the small body. But the students don't yet have the skill.

"What I want them to see," the teacher says to the window, "is the transparency of the body's process. If I work fast enough, the heart doesn't know it's dead and will go on beating. The students can see the pumping, how the blood goes out one way and comes in another. The chicken's system is actually very close to ours and very different from those of the worm or frog."

The meadowlark lifts slightly then lets itself fall to the ground. The sun is still shining and the spring snow rapidly disappearing. The patches of bare earth, steaming, grow larger. The meadowlark throws off its mantle of white pronghorn and snow and cocks its head at the brown below. It is as if the bird stared at the deep brown of old blood on a killing room floor.

But it is spring and one of those days when a person goes looking for things—anything that verifies and makes real what is already known. Look—the blue mountains rising, the worn sharp cliffs, the frost that leaps toward the lover sun, the warm snow and running water, the windflowers, the redtail hawks circling, the thick new blades of grass blotching the brown with green.

After a long winter comes that day when the earth is no longer covered by snow. The biology teacher, the students, every resident of the state of Wyoming, even the suffering houseguest Mr. Eduardo Galeano, waving his tourist visa above his head, they all plop down on the earth, unable to stand, their bodies quivering in anticipation. They take off their shoes and plant their bare feet on bare ground. After all this time, after months and years and centuries, to again touch the earth, and to hear it sing.

Grumpy don Eduardo has slipped off his black leather shoes to touch the earth. But it is not a song he feels rising into his wobbling legs. Unable to stand, he falls to his knees and leans forward, places his ear to the ground and listens. The earth is not singing; it is screaming in agony and don Eduardo pulls away, a sharp pain in his head, his ear ringing. He throws his shoes high into the air hoping to defeat gravity. He takes off his clothes and flings them too into the air.

"Oh, do not fall," he whispers, "Keep rising and disappear forever into space."

The poor man makes his small gesture to lighten the burden of the planet. He leaps up after his clothes but when, with them, he falls back, his weight is increased. His feet slam into the earth, and the screams grow louder. Jumping will not do. He stands on tiptoe and prances like a man walking on hot coals. Some of the students are giggling and pointing at the older fellow's splotchy nakedness, at the way his buttocks, wide from the years he's spent sitting in chairs in libraries, droop, and the way his pale penis waggles from side to side.

The biology teacher has gone to place a telephone call to the police. But before the cops arrive, a few of the students have sunk to the ground and with the stranger are tentatively pressing their ears into the dirt. They jerk their heads away then push themselves down to listen again, doing their best to decipher the sounds.

The biology lesson began so long ago, but now it seems the bell announcing the end of class will never ring. In the distant school room, the chicken of the still beating heart spins on its cracked neck, and the feathers, loosening themselves with each turn, cease fluttering and begin to rise.

1927

LOWER WILD HORSE CREEK

A PHOTOGRAPH OF EDUCATION

Eight young children stand facing the camera. All look slightly
disheveled and already whipped by Wyoming's dry air and wind, all
the moisture lifted from their skin, lifted even from their internal organs. They stand desicated at the age of six and eight and ten.

On the far right is their teacher Darlene Bennick. Next to Miss
Bennick are the seven Clabaugh children, cousins in one set of four
and one of three, the sons and daughters of fathers Frank and Coy.
George and Leslie are brothers to Ida and Edith. Their cousins are
three sisters—Grace, Alice and Mildred.

To the left of these seven, several feet apart from them, and with
his head tilted as if somehow he could look both at the camera and
away from it, is George Bradford, a Negro boy. George attended the

school on Lower Wild Horse Creek for only a short time. How short a time? George is the child of someone. Whom? How did he and his unnamed parents come to be here where the sun bleaches all things white, where, after an animal's death, the darkest bones shine silvery and light?

Where should George Bradford put his hands? If, in his pockets, it will appear he is hiding something, or fooling with himself. If above his head, as if to wave, it will appear he is a troublemaker. Hanging limply at his side? Big, dumb Negro boy, taller and bulkier than the slender, toe-headed Clabaugh children.

And the Clabaugh cousins who stand apart. They are not bad children, only white children. The brilliant sun strikes hard on their pale skin so that they must squint into the camera, giving them all a sly, careful look.

A sly, careful look. A big, dumb negro boy. Seated on the hard wooden chair in the one room library at Clearmont on Clear Creek, don Eduardo has been turning the pages of the *Wheel of Time,* the history of the nearby little community of Arvada. Page after page. Now he stops and squints at the class photo. Sometimes by narrowing the eyes one gains an enlarged view of a distant object.

One child will be a banker. Another a doctor. Lawyer, rancher, captain of industry, government minister, ranking officer in the armed forces, research physicist in the Defense Industry. Mostly men, with here and there a woman, these will have dominion over the land and its inhabitants. These alone.

Still squinting, don Eduardo peers down at the grainy image. If he looks just so, he sees how strikingly he resembles one of the Clabaugh girls. Alice? No, it's Grace. How lovely that he should seem to look something like a girl named Grace.

But he can see himself too in the frumpy image of the lady teacher. There he is, Mr. Eduardo Galeano, minister to the young. He is dressed in a baggy floral print dress, faded, ill-fitting, and long out of fashion. His sensible black shoes with the chunky heels need to be polished, and the toe of one shoe rests on that of the other.

"It's always the same," Galeano whispers, "Somehow I'm always the geek and the goon." His eyes pass again to George, standing off to the side and, one would guess, lonely. The skin is wrong, but those are don Eduardo's eyes open to the sky. "Of course I resemble the black child, too," he thinks, "How could I not?"

Ten people make up the school on Lower Wild Horse Creek—the teacher Darlene Bennick, the seven Clabaugh cousins, the negro boy George Bradford, who stands somewhat apart, and Eduardo Galeano, working up a smile for the camera from just outside the frame.

# 2075
## SHELL
### SUNSET MAN

Here lies Eduardo Galeano, historian and world traveler, in almost perfect likeness of himself. In the dry climate and buried in a shallow grave of mostly dust, even his clothing and hair are preserved.

For the archaeologists he is a rare find, a pure specimen of late twentieth century confusion. Something is wrong in his bone structure and racial morphology though. And as the scientists give names to their finds so they name this skeleton—Sunset Man, the last of some line the beginning of which they have been unable to find.

Lying there, he's twisted into some odd position as if he had died in winter and been quick frozen before being buried, or as if he had been dancing to the sounds of the cumbia when struck by lightning. He lies on his back with both arms stretched out above him. His hands are turned forward at the wrists as if making a gesture, but the meaning of the gesture is unclear. His knees are slightly bent.

In death, don Eduardo has taken on the position of the slain Sioux chief Big Foot, that of a man struggling to rise. Big Foot was struggling to rise when the rifles and cannons of the American Seventh Cavalry fired again, one of the last salvos in the war of extinction waged against all Indian people in every corner of the Americas. And don Eduardo was struggling to rise, too—struggling up through the layers of lies that paper over the past.

What a grim life it sometimes seems, weighed down by the burden of knowing what one man has done to another. In death somehow it seems less grim. Galeano has a smile on his lips, and his eyes are open, their shine still alive under the dust. He wears a blue corduroy jacket with the emblem of the Future Farmers of America sewn on and the words Big Piney—Wyoming. On his head is perched at a jaunty angle a black cowboy hat, sweat around the blazing red hatband. Around his neck there is a lavender silk scarf—his glad rag. On both wrists are several beaded bracelets, gifts from those who know him on the Wind River Reservation. The beaded patterns mean nothing, or mean things that are secrets between Galeano and those who made him these small gifts.

All the births and deaths of Eduardo Galeano. All the possibilities to be filled with despair, to give up ever changing anything, ever making of life for man and woman a garden, or even a momentary respite.

Galeano never surrendered though. Like each of us, he was small and weak and a blunderer. He fell down just trying to climb a hill. He always had the wrong shoes on for whatever walk he was about to take and his shoes always seemed to be filled with pebbles that drove themselves into his flesh and blisters rose between his toes and his nose was always sunburnt and peeling and his clothes worn so that it was impossible to follow his mother's dictum to change his underwear every day just in case he was in a mortal accident and how embarrassing it would be to be found dead in dirty underwear and his mother forgot that in the moment of death a man is liable to soil his pants anyway however clean they may have been that morning and likely as not don Eduardo would end up in the wrong place at the wrong time unable to speak the language of the locals and reluctant to take up the gun and unable to get elected to office what with the cockamamie beliefs he held and suffering piles that kept him off horses and shot full of amoebas and worms and bacteria and it wouldn't be a surprise to find that the man had malaria and, even so, there was that smile on his face in death. And of all the places he could die for longer than a minute, he died in Shell, Wyoming. That word shell—the encrusted layer that protects and disguises so many creatures.

Now, with one hand, the man in the dead body reaches out. Slowly, of course, as he's been lying here almost seventy-five years, but he reaches out and begins to pull his jacket aside revealing a brown and yellow t-shirt. On the front is written "University of Wyoming Cowboy Joe Booster Club" and on the back "Arapahoe All-Indian Rodeo and Wyoming Indian High School—State AA Basketball Champions."

He reaches into his pocket and pulls out a postcard, holds it up for the excavating archaeologist to see. On the card is a horse with saddlebags. In each saddlebag astride the horse is a trout, fifteen feet long, dwarfing and disguising the horse. Next to the fish-burdened horse is a grinning man. The caption reads "They sure do catch 'em big out here in the northern Rockies."

Then laughter. Galeano releases the postcard, which flutters up and away, and with his other hand moves as if to drag something out of a second pocket. The archaeologist stares at the hand waiting for it to move again.

"There it goes. No, wait, just my imagination. There it goes, it is moving, wasn't that a flick of the little finger? No, wait, I must be imagining things. There it goes. . . no, wait. . .oh, yes, there it goes. . ."

1870

BRIDGER BASIN

FIFTY MILLION YEAR OLD EOHIPPUS

The Dawn Horse stands guard at the gate to the future. Eohippus is ten inches tall and weighs nine pounds. She is a horse with the bulk of an alley cat, and with her arched flexible back and high hind end, she has a nervous rabbity look. Instead of hooves, she has four toed front feet, and her weight is carried on doglike pads. She is a horse unsure of what to be or what she may become.

Have you given the horse strength? Have you dressed her in thunder? Watch her nostrils quiver. They are surely terrible though the horse is as afraid as a grasshopper (Is a grasshopper afraid?). The horse is pawing at the valley, breaking the earth apart. Accepting strength, she goes to face the armed men. She steps forward and stares unblinking as the shining sword waves, as the quiver rattles above her, the glittering spear and shield. She is tearing at the ground, and as it flies, she swallows it. She swallows the earth and becomes it. She does not hear the trumpets, and when she does, she laughs, smelling the battle from afar, the gnashing teeth of the captains and the shouting of the dead.

Dawn Horse is small, but the gate to the future is small, too. It is a simple matter to stand guard, to make sure nothing leaks back from days not yet born.

She leans, chewing the iron-laden dirt. On the other side of the gate, she can hear similar chewing. But the chewing comes after a sound she has never heard. Don Eduardo is scraping the earth up with his hand and then delicately placing small bits in his mouth. He clamps down gingerly, careful not to break his teeth on bits of metal or chips of stone.

Dawn Horse and Sunset Man lean in toward the gate. The one merely bends her neck, the other must lie down flat on his belly.

"¿Está alguien?" don Eduardo asks, and raps at the barrier.

Dawn Horse snorts and sniffs, leaps back as a piece of paper slips through the crack between the door's edge and the frame.

> My horse has a hoof like striped agate,
> his fetlock is like a fine eagle plume;
> his legs are like quick lightning.
> My horse's body is like an eagle plumed arrow;
> my horse has a tail like a trailing black cloud.

Unable to read, Dawn Horse eats the piece of paper. She would not recognize the horse she is beginning to be.

The Eocene morning burns toward Pleistocene noon, and Dawn Horse lies down and dies. Passages back and forth through the gate—horses walk from France to England, from North Africa to Gibraltar, from Alaska to Siberia. The horse has been a wanderer, and it has been hard to remain in service at the gate.

In the Southwest corner of Wyoming, there have been so many comings and goings—the carboniferous rocks without coal, the glowing red beds, the rising freshwater lakes, the sandstone ridges and mesas, gumbo plains and slopes, the chalk cliffs, the fossil palms.

Don Eduardo has given up writing and is pounding hard at the gate. Something on the other side doesn't smell so good. The gate won't give and he can't see through, so he is reduced to again slipping piece of paper after piece of paper into the crack and listening to it fall.

He writes messages of greeting and, generously, tells nothing about the times in which he lives. "There are more horses than there are stars in the sky," he writes, and "There have always been horses." "Did you know the Sanskrit word for horse is Asva. It means sharp and swift." "Equus is a corruption of an Icelandic word—Ekvus—which means to run." "Modern horses have self-sharpening teeth—they can eat the toughest grasses."

Dawn Horse's joints swivel in all directions, and the dead animal, spinning again into the past and her life, picks up the newly fallen bits of paper and stuffs them all into her mouth.

"I don't mean to make trouble," don Eduardo shouts at the closed gate, "I just wonder what is over there. I lie down at night, and each morning I awake hundreds of miles farther north in lands I neither know nor seek."

A chunk of dirt crumbles. Dawn Horse is extinct and only her hard fossil brother, a manhorse named Eduardo Galeano, remains, buried in the lowest horizon of the Tertiary at the base of the Wasatch Mountains. He is buried with open eyes facing a small blank wall that resembles the cover of a book.